Juniper Creek Homecoming

Amy Kristen Marshall

Copyright Notice

This is a work of fiction. Names, characters, places, and incidents are either a product of the author's imagination or are used fictitiously. Any resemblance to actual persons, living or dead, events, or locales is entirely coincidental.

Cover design by Aaron K. Alexander

ISBN 978-1-7358583-3-3 (ebook)
ISBN 978-1-7358583-4-0 (paperback)

Dedication

For my parents, who have always believed in my writing. I love you.

Table of Contents

Jenna Daly towed her carry-on behind her as she crossed the tarmac of the Pine County Municipal Airport. Heat waves rose off the asphalt, and the dry desert wind ruffled her ponytail. The air smelled of pine and juniper, a lemony, tangy scent she always associated with home.

Home. She couldn't believe her luck. After the layoff, she'd spent two months applying to teaching job after teaching job. None of the Bay Area schools she'd applied to had even extended an interview. "What about Oregon?" her roommate had said, after she found Jenna on the couch, crying into a mug of day-old coffee. "Don't you have any contacts there?"

She had one: her high school principal, Pam Rustigan.

One was all she'd needed.

She slowed down, pausing to text her dad that she was off the plane. He wrote back right away; he was already at baggage claim, waiting for her. She walked faster, speeding past other passengers toward the terminal.

Inside, a blast of cool air dried the sweat on her forehead. She strode down a short hallway, her sneakers scuffing against the faded blue carpet. Rounding a corner, she came out into the baggage claim area.

Her dad stood next to one of two claim carousels. Faded jeans, worn boots, work shirt, and cowboy hat, as always. His thick grey mustache curled up as he grinned at her.

Jenna rushed over and grabbed her dad in a bear hug. "Hi! Where's Mom?"

"Hey, Sweet Pea." His deep voice boomed. He pecked her on the cheek and stepped back. "She's at home, making enough food to feed everyone in this airport. I hope you're hungry."

Her stomach growled. "I am, but I have to save room. There's a barbecue at Pam Rustigan's place tonight."

"They're already working you, huh?" said her dad.

She grinned and shuffled a bit closer to the baggage carousel, making room for the other passengers who were starting to gather. "It's an all-staff thing. I guess she does it every year. And then in-service starts on Monday."

"Back at the old stomping grounds," he said, nodding. "How does that feel?"

"Pretty good, considering I'll have a paycheck again. Don't worry, I'll start looking at apartments next week so I can get out of your hair."

He patted her shoulder. "No rush, Sweet Pea. We're glad to have you."

The carousel rumbled to life, and the first suitcase appeared on the conveyor belt. The belt crawled sideways as more luggage tumbled onto it. Jenna spotted her bulging blue plaid suitcase and hefted it off the carousel.

"I've got it, honey." Her dad grabbed the case and grunted as he set it down. "What ya got in there? Solid steel beams?"

"Books." She had packed her textbooks from graduate school, along with other books on lesson-planning and learning theories. She'd donated some of her fiction collection to a library in San Francisco, but she'd been unable to part with the complete classroom sets of *Hamlet* and *To Kill a Mockingbird* that she'd purchased herself.

Her second suitcase slid along the belt. Her dad grabbed it and set it down with a thunk. "And this one?"

"Also books."

He shook his head. "Did you bring anything else? A coat, for example?"

"Sure." She pointed to her carry-on bag. "In here. You got the box I sent, right?"

"We did. Was that books too?" He winked.

"No, that's clothes. Well, a few books, but mostly clothes."

He clapped a hand on her shoulder. "Glad to see you have your priorities straight." He righted both the suitcases onto their wheels and popped up the handles. "Let's get you home."

They walked across the room and out into the parking lot. The heat seemed to suck the moisture from Jenna's skin as she followed her dad through the half-full lot, past dusty Dodge Rams, Fords jacked up on huge wheels, the occasional Subaru or mini-SUV. At the edge of the lot, they stopped next to a rusty, dented blue Chevy pickup.

Her dad's eyes lit up as he pulled a set of keys from his pocket. "Surprise."

"Lucy's still running, huh?" She patted the truck's side. Her dad had taught her to drive Lucy when she was fourteen, though he only let her drive it around the farm to check fences. Her permit test at fifteen had been a breeze and she'd driven the truck all through high school.

"Still running and just got new tires. I figured you'd need them." He shook the keys at her.

"Dad! You can't give me the truck."

"Why? I just got a brand-new Ford, and your mom has the van. No one's driving Lucy. You need a set of wheels to get around here. You can't just hop the bus like you did in San Francisco."

He had a point. How else was she going to get to school? Ride a horse three miles down the highway? Jenna chewed on her lip, then reached for the keys. "Thanks, Dad. I really appreciate it, and I'll pay you back."

He waved a hand. "Pfft. She needs some work, so I should probably be paying you."

She laughed. She unlocked the truck, and she and her dad stowed her suitcases and carry-on in the back. They got inside and Jenna shifted the seat forward, testing her short legs' reach to the pedals. The leather seat felt hot and dry under her bare legs and the steering wheel almost seared her hands. She cranked down the window. "Hope I remember how to drive this thing."

"Like riding a bike."

"We'll see." She buckled up, then turned on the car. It sputtered to life, the way she remembered. As she pulled out of the parking lot, she shifted gears. The engine hummed. She patted the dashboard, smiling as she accelerated. She pulled onto the highway and shifted again as she sailed down the straight empty road, pine trees flashing past on either side. Land stretched in all directions, peppered with brown grass, dark green sagebrush, and olive green greasewood. In the distance rose the rumpled foothills of the Cascade Mountain Range, and beyond them Mount Jefferson, its peaks charcoal and bare of snow. The August sky was bright blue, dusted with wisps of pure white clouds.

Her dad cleared his throat. "I suppose you know Reid teaches at the high school."

Her stomach dropped, but she nodded. Pam had warned her when she extended the job offer. "It's a small department. Four people including me. I'm sure I'll see him every day." Actually, she would probably see him tonight at the barbecue. Had he changed in the last ten years? Or did he still have the same shaggy blonde hair, the same crinkles around his blue eyes when he smiled?

"You're fine with that?"

"Sure." She sat up a bit straighter. "Speaking of school, I bet I'll have Andy Caniff in my class. Isn't he a sophomore this year? How are the boys?" In high school, she'd babysat Andy and his older brother Stephen. It seemed impossible that they could be so grown up.

Her dad drummed his fingers on the dashboard. "They're two of the best farmhands we've had, but we couldn't keep them on for the fall. Last I heard, Andy was working on the Garcia farm. Stephen was at the Dairy Queen and taking a few classes at the community college."

Her stomach twisted into knots. "Why?" She glanced at him. "Did something happen?"

"No, no, things are just a little tight."

"Dad." She slowed a bit as she took a curve in the highway. "What's going on? How come you didn't say anything?"

"Nothing to tell, really. We've had less snowpack than usual the last few years. This winter was extra warm, too, so we've got some water restrictions. We'll be fine. Nothing for you to worry about."

She passed the last mile marker before the turnoff to her parents' small farm. The yellow farmhouse was visible in the distance, but now her chest ached at the sight. How bad were things, exactly? Her dad would never admit it if he was worried, but if he'd laid off his only farmhands, then things couldn't be great.

She remembered several years of water restrictions growing up. Her parents deciding which fields to irrigate, and which ones to let dry up. Coming home to an empty house because her mom was teaching an art class and her dad was out back repairing an engine for a neighbor for extra cash.

Maybe she shouldn't look for an apartment just yet.

A minute later, she turned onto the long gravel drive that led to the farm. To her left, two dairy cows wandered the pasture. A hawk circled overhead. The truck bounced over a rut, and she shifted to a lower gear. She pulled to a stop in front of the farmhouse, two stories high, pale yellow with white shutters. A swing dangled from heavy chains, swaying over the wide porch.

She shut off the truck and hopped out. A dove cooed in the distance, and as if in answer, one of the cows let out a lazy moo.

"You go on in," said her dad, waving her towards the front door. "Your mother's anxious to see you. I'll get your bags of bricks up to your room."

"Thanks." She started up the steps, then turned around. "Hey, Dad? Do you guys mind if I stay here for awhile? Maybe I could help out on the weekends."

He smiled. "We're happy to have you as long as you like, as long that's what you want to do. Don't worry about anything else." He lifted a shaggy eyebrow.

She squared her shoulders. "I do want to stick around here. I've missed this place."

"That's fine. Go on, then, your mom's anxious to see you."

She grinned and hurried up the porch steps. Pushing open the storm door, she called, "Mom! I'm home."

Reid Walsh ran a hand over the dark blonde scruff across the jaw. He frowned at his reflection, but there was no time to shave now. Margot would be here in five minutes.

He smoothed down his blue polo shirt, the pocket embroidered with the Juniper Creek High School eagle in gold. He ran a hand down his crisp khakis. Grabbing his wallet, he hurried into the small living room.

He sat down on the faded brown couch and looked through his phone, scrolling past headlines on a news app. At least he and Margot weren't staying long at the barbecue. Half an hour, maybe, and then they'd head off to Francesca's. Date night sounded a lot better than making small talk with his ex.

He still couldn't believe they'd hired her.

His jaw twinged. He forced himself to let it fall slack. His dentist had told Reid he would need a night guard if he didn't stop clenching.

Two sharp raps sounded on the front door.

Reid hopped up and hurried to answer it. He slid his feet into his loafers and pulled open the door.

"Hi, handsome." Margot stood up on tiptoe to kiss him. "Whoa, you turned into Bigfoot." She laughed and ran a manicured hand across his scruff. "You haven't shaved yet? We'll be late."

"I'll shave later."

"But it's date night." Her smile faltered.

"No problem." He winked. "It'll only take me half an hour to get cleaned up." He half-turned toward the door.

She tugged on his arm, laughing. "Okay, okay. You're right. Let's just go. You can shave tomorrow."

"It's fortunate I'm so incredibly good-looking." He turned to lock the door behind him.

"Humble, too."

He slipped an arm around her slim shoulders and kissed her temple. "Let's go do the social thing."

As they drove toward Pam Rustigan's dairy farm, Reid glanced over at Margot. Sunlight caught in her hair and glinted off the delicate gold chain with the letter M charm that he'd gotten her this last Valentine's Day. Her short denim cutoffs showed off her tanned, muscular legs. He put his eyes on the road again. Someday, she would be his wife. Next year? *We need to set a date.*

Her hand squeezed his knee. "How was hiking? By the way, you're not allowed to be gone for two weeks ever again."

He chuckled. "It was fun, but I missed you. How's competition prep going?" Margot was a competitive dressage rider and had been showing horses since high school. In fact, when Reid had run into her their freshman year at a house party at the University of Oregon, and she'd introduced herself, he'd blurted, "You're the horse girl." She'd given him a funny look, but then started laughing.

"I still have some work to do." Her voice tightened. "Bailey's going to have to take a few of my students until the competition. John's built a pretty complicated routine and there's a quarter pirouette I just can't get right."

"Yet. You can't get it right yet. Honey, I've seen you. You're always flawless." Reid covered her hand with his own and patted it.

"We'll see." She reached for the radio and flipped it on. Soft rock music drifted from the speakers. Cranking the volume, she said, "Did they ever hire another English teacher?"

"About that." His chest tightened. "They did a couple last-minute video interviews while I was out. The applicant pool was pretty slim, you know, and the person they hired, they just really liked her . . ."

Her hand tightened on his knee. "What? There's something you aren't saying."

Oh, boy. Blowing out a breath, he cranked down the window. "It's Jenna."

There was a long silence. He peeled his gaze from the road long enough to take in Margot's wide blue eyes and parted lips. "I'm sorry," she said. "Jenna, as in Jenna Daly?"

He nodded.

"Wow. I . . . didn't expect that." She gave a short laugh. "I thought she was in California or something."

"I thought so too, but I guess she's back."

"Obviously." Margot pulled her hand away from his leg.

"It's not a big deal." He reached for her hand again and squeezed it. "That was ten years ago."

"And you wanted to marry her." Margot leaned away from him and stared out the window.

"We were kids then. I'm marrying you."

She threw him a tight-lipped smile.

Reid let the music fill the space as they drove down the highway while the land rolled past. A pinto horse, its mane whipping in the breeze, cantered through a field dotted with sagebrush. The horse looked like Fran. Jenna used to love riding her. She'd take Fran and Reid would take Stormy, and they'd barrel race around the pine that stood guard at the edge of the pasture. Her hair would stream out like a flame . . .

He winced as his jaw muscles jumped. Massaging the right side of his face, he scanned for the turnoff. It was there already, the large wooden arch that marked the entrance to the Rustigans' dairy farm. How long had he zoned out for? He veered to the right, tapping the brake as the truck rumbled onto the dirt road. Dust kicked up around the tires.

"Whoa, Turbo," said Margot. "Slow down."

"Sorry." He checked his speed and felt the truck bounce over a rut.

He drove the short distance to the small gravel lot that sat in front of Pam's farmhouse and barn. Both buildings were dark red with white trim, and cornfields and pastures rolled out like brown and yellow carpets beyond the buildings. Several cars and trucks already angled across the lot. Pulling up next to Ken Arbor's bumper sticker plastered VW Bug, he threw the truck into park.

"Are you okay?" Margot said as they walked toward the back of the farmhouse. Laughter and rock music floated toward them.

"Fine. Are you okay?"

She shrugged. "Are you going to tell Jenna?"

"About what?"

Margot lifted her left hand and wriggled her ring finger so the gold band and one-carat diamond caught the light.

"Of course." He dropped a kiss on top of her head. "I'm sure she'll be happy for us."

They came around the back into the large unfenced yard. Next to a huge pine tree, a row of tables bore platters of food. Party torches burned around the perimeter of the yard. Staff sat around at picnic tables and on the back porch, chatting with sodas in their hands. On the porch, Pam Rustigan stood next to a large grill, flipping burgers. She waved her spatula at them. "Dinner will be ready soon!"

Reid waved back, then added a wave to Steph and Elisa, the senior and freshman English teachers. They sat on the porch, drinking sodas. Reid and Margot grabbed cans from the nearby cooler and joined them.

"How was camping?" Steph said, high-fiving Reid. "You ready for the first day of school?"

His mouth quirked. "Not quite."

"Well, you better be ready for Monday," she said, nudging him. "We have curricula to review."

"Hey, I have some great ideas for new assignments this year," he said. "I just haven't written them."

Elisa rolled her eyes. "You're as much a procrastinator as your students."

"I keep telling him that." Margot made a face at Reid, then slid her phone out of her purse and tapped the screen.

Reid glanced over Margot's shoulder. Her manicured fingers scrolled through photos of a dressage routine. "Not like this one. She's working on her homework now."

"Another competition?" said Steph. "Don't know how you do that with your teaching schedule."

Margot laughed. "I don't either. My little sister's going to have to take some of my students."

As the group chatted, Reid glanced around the yard. He didn't see Jenna yet. Maybe she wasn't coming? She could still be in the process of moving home. But no, Steph's text had said, *Be sure you stop by the BBQ tonight—you can meet Jenna!*

Checking his watch, he turned to Margot. "We should get going soon."

Steph frowned. "You just got here. And you haven't even met Jenna. She should be here any minute."

"Well, our reservation is at seven . . ."

Margot flicked an eyebrow up at him. She pocketed her phone and crossed her arms. "We have time, honey. We can wait."

Oh. Good.

"Oh, there she is. Jenna!" Steph waved at someone behind him.

Reid turned around, and his heart stopped cold.

Jenna Daly walked into the yard, clutching a covered ceramic dish. She smiled at the group, white teeth, full lips. "Hi! Just a sec, I need to put this down." Her hazel gaze swept past Reid and focused somewhere in the distance. She tottered along in high-heeled sandals. A knee-length flowered skirt swished around her freckled bare legs.

"Well, she'll be back any second. You're going to love her." Steph's brown eyes sparkled.

Reid ran a hand through his hair. "Can I talk to you a second?"

She frowned. "Sure."

They retreated to the side of the yard, away from the small clumps of teachers talking as they guzzled sodas and sparkling waters.

"What's up?" said Steph.

Reid glanced toward the food table. Jenna had set her dish down, but she still stood there, talking to Saul Peters. The broad, long-haired man had taught PE at Juniper Creek since before Reid and Jenna had been students. His red cheeks crinkled in a grin and Jenna threw her head back in laughter at whatever he was saying.

Reid turned to Steph. "I know Jenna. She's my ex."

Her lips formed an O.

"We all went to high school together. Jenna, Margot, and me. I didn't know Margot well in high school, but Jenna and I . . . well, we dated for almost a year." His skin prickled with heat, and he rubbed the back of his neck. Should have worn shorts. "It's a little weird, that's all."

"Why didn't you tell me this?" Steph grabbed his arm. "You didn't say a thing when I texted you."

"I didn't feel like explaining it over text." He shrugged. "You guys like her, Pam likes her. I'm sure she'll be fine. Great. It's just not ideal that you decided this while I was out of town."

Steph put both hands on her hips. "You were in the middle of nowhere. You're the one who insisted on hiking right before we wrapped interviews. I told you we might do more, and you said it was fine. We're lucky we found her, Reid. Her former principal called Pam personally to say that she wished she had the budget to keep Jenna on, and that we should do everything in our power to hire her. You know the other candidates weren't that good."

"I know." He sighed. "Can we talk about this later? Margot will kill me if we're late for dinner."

He waited for Steph's nod, then strode across the yard. Sliding an arm around Margot's shoulders, he said, "We should get going. Nice to see you, Elisa."

Margot pursed her lips but nodded. She hugged Elisa, then slipped her hand into Reid's.

He ducked his head as they walked past the porch, where Pam was still grilling. When they rounded the house and reached the small gravel lot, he sighed. He dug the keys out of his pocket and unlocked the truck. The second he and Margot had buckled up, he threw the truck in reverse and sped out of the lot.

"We were there ten minutes," said Margot.

He tapped one hand against the side of the steering wheel, waiting for an SUV to pass on the highway so he could make the turn. "Did you want to stay longer?"

"No, but you ran off before we could even say hi to Jenna. I didn't think it would be *that* big a deal."

I didn't, either. Jenna had looked just the same as in high school: freckles like sprinkles of cinnamon over her cheeks, mounds of wavy red hair. And different too: her cheekbones more hollowed out, her face narrower, her body more muscled. Like a woman. *Well, duh, she's 28.* "It was just a little weird. I didn't feel like making small talk with my ex on our date night."

Margot's hand gently rubbed his right shoulder. "As long as that's all it was. You're not . . . embarrassed or something?"

"Of you? Are you kidding?" He reached up and pulled her hand away from his shoulder, kissing the top of it. "I love you. You know how it is, the staff is like its own small town. Steph will say something to Elisa, and Jan Davis will overhear, and then it's all over the school by Monday. I wasn't in the mood for gossip. That's all."

Margot sighed and leaned her head against his shoulder.

Her flowery perfume curled into his nostrils, and he rolled the window down a bit farther. He gulped in the thick, piney air.

All right, he'd be working with his ex. Big deal. They were teaching different grades. It's not like they'd be sharing a classroom. He would see her at department meetings and staff meetings, that's all.

And assemblies and football games and in the break room and . . .

His jaw twitched. He punched the radio power button and twisted the volume, letting the energetic guitar riffs of a Luke Bryan song drown out his thoughts.

Jenna slipped her overstuffed backpack over one shoulder, tucked a thick binder under her arm, and lifted her teal coffee thermos out of the console. She inched across the driver's seat and wriggled her way out of the truck. Shifting the backpack a bit, she turned around and used her backside to slam the door shut. She didn't bother locking it. No one was going to steal Lucy from a high school parking lot.

As she crossed the lot, she studied the grounds, gauging if the layout had changed. To the left, past the main building, stood a few boxy gray portables she remembered, followed by the woodshop. To the right, a winding path led to the football field. It was a two minute thirty second walk, she knew. She and Reid had once skipped AP History to hang out on the bleachers, and they'd had to run in order not to miss physics. Mrs. Wallace would dock you five percent of that week's grade if you were even a second late. Reid's warm hand had gripped hers, long legs striding down the sidewalk. He'd grinned at her as they dropped breathless into their seats, just as the bell rang.

She paused and shook her head. Wow, okay. No need to go down memory lane just yet.

A wide concrete terrace spread out before the two sets of double doors that led into the school. A flagpole flanked either side of the school, the American flag on the left, and the blue and gold school flag on the right, both snapping in the wind.

She crossed the terrace and tried the leftmost door. Nope. The next one wouldn't budge either. She tugged on the second set of doors and frowned. Were they all locked? Did no one else show up early?

Should she try calling Pam? No, the blinds were down in the front office window. The principal probably wasn't here yet.

Maybe one of the side doors would be open. She went around to the right side of the building and tried the first door. When it opened, she smiled. So she wasn't the only early bird.

Maybe the early bird was Reid.

Her stomach churned as she stepped into B-Hall. The polished linoleum floor reflected stripes of light from the fluorescents overhead. Banks of metal lockers lined either side of the hall. It all looked the same. It even smelled the same, that blend of fresh paint and stale French fries.

Her sneakers squeaked across the linoleum as she walked toward her classroom. She stopped in front of room B-102. A laminated sign on the door read *Miss Jenna Daly, Sophomore English.* Shifting her binder and coffee mug into a more secure grip, she twisted the handle and nudged the door open.

Inside, the white walls and empty bulletin boards waited for her personal touch. The huge whiteboard at the front gleamed. Her desk took up one corner of the front, and beyond it, rows of desks sat neatly like crayons in a box. Three wide windows looked out over the soccer field. In the distance, the Three Sisters mountains rose, their peaks bare and hazy.

She set her stuff down on the desk and flipped open her laptop. Pam had sent her the login information last week. She flipped to the inside of the binder and pulled out the printout of Pam's email.

The login worked. The Wi-Fi didn't.

Jenna frowned and scanned the email again. Nowhere had Pam included the Wi-Fi password. She tried GOEAGLES but was promptly rejected. Well, she wasn't going to sit here and just guess passwords for the next hour. Sighing, she got up and stepped out into the hallway. If the back door had been open, then at least one other person was here. She would just look in every classroom until she found someone who could tell her the password.

The first room she passed was the department head and senior English teacher, Steph Hernandez. The door was locked, the room dark. Across the hall, though, room B105 was brightly lit, the door cracked open.

She strode towards it, then slowed when she saw the laminated door sign.

Mr. Reid Walsh, Junior English.

Her stomach plunged like an elevator. She darted away from the door and pressed herself against the bank of lockers, out of sight, like she was in a spy movie. Her heart raced, and she suddenly felt cold. *Get a grip.* She would be working with Reid. She'd have to talk to him eventually, and he and Margot had escaped the barbecue before she could say anything to him. Might as well get it over with.

Blowing out a breath, she squared her shoulders. She walked up to the door and lightly rapped on the frame.

Reid sat at his desk, his head in profile as he bent over a piece of paper. Her breath caught. Long straight nose, high cheekbones, strong jaw. Wavy blonde hair that looked windblown, as if he'd just come in from a ride.

He looked up. His brows lifted, and he cleared his throat. "Welcome back."

"Hi. I don't know the Wi-Fi password. Also, um, hi." Oh, good. Instead of sounding like a grown woman, she sounded like an awkward teenager all over again. Her cheeks burned.

"It's EAGLES4LIFE, with a number 4, all one word, all caps." He spun around in his chair to face her. "How are you? You were in California or something?"

She nodded. "I did my masters down there. I was teaching at a private school in San Francisco. I loved it, but . . . I got laid off. Budget cuts." Her cheeks grew warm and she pushed her hair off her face.

"That's rough. I'm sorry." He shook his head and gestured vaguely to the room in general. "Well, at least here you aren't starting over. Not exactly. You living with your folks?"

"For now, yeah." She shifted her weight. Half her brain seemed to be watching the conversation from the outside. Here she was, talking to Reid as a colleague, like nothing had ever happened. Maybe she had expected too much. It's not like they would start unpacking the past after eight years apart. "Did you do your masters in Oregon then?" She had deliberately not kept up with him on social media. After he got together with Margot, there had been no reason.

He nodded and locked his hands behind his head. "I moved back after undergrad and went to OSU Cascades. This was my placement and Pam liked me, so she hired me. Well, she always liked me. I was one of her favorites." Half his mouth turned up in the cheeky grin she remembered.

She smiled and shook her head. "What about you? Do you live with your mom?"

"No, she retired to Florida last year. I'm renting, but we're saving for a house."

At the word "we," her heart turned over. "How's Margot doing?"

"She's good. We're, uh, we're engaged."

The words fell between them, and silence rose to fill the space. Jenna blinked a few times.

Reid's expression was neutral, his gaze steady.

"Right. I mean, that's great. Congrats. When's the wedding?" Her ears started to ring.

"It depends how fast we can save for a house. We're going into our fourth year of being engaged, so I don't know, maybe I should get a second job." He laughed.

She smiled, tried to think of a corresponding joke, and came up blank. "Uh, thanks for the password."

"Yep." Reid tipped his head, as if he was going to say something else, but then he turned around and went back to his work.

Jenna strode out of the room and hurried toward the door at the end of the corridor. She leaned heavily into the metal push bar on the door and walked outside. Sinking to the steps, she pressed her hands against the cool concrete. She took a few deep breaths, sucking in the dry, tangy desert air.

Okay. Reid was engaged. Not a surprise, really. He'd gotten together with Margot their freshman year of college. He'd gone to University of Oregon and Jenna had been at Oregon State, but she'd heard through mutual friends.

They'd already been engaged for three years, though, if they were going into year four. That was a long time. It did make sense to wait and save for a house, but what did Margot think? Jenna hadn't known her well in high school, but she was one of those girls who always seemed to want everything a certain way. She'd competed in jumping and dressage all over the state, and she'd been a valedictorian. Did Type-A Margot mind a long engagement?

Jenna shook her head, as if she could physically push away the thoughts. But memories from high school flooded back: Reid whispering in her ear, Reid bending his head to kiss her, Reid slipping a delicate silver ring on her finger. How could you love someone that much, and then get over it so fast? Two months. That was all it took for him to move on to Margot.

Whatever. It doesn't matter. Jenna stood and blinked away the moisture in her eyes. There, she had done it, she'd spoken to Reid, and now things would be easier. Next time it wouldn't be awkward at all.

She lifted her shoulders and went back inside.

That afternoon, Jenna walked next door to Reid's classroom for their department meeting. Colorful posters plastered the walls: a poster from the local library encouraging reading, an illustrated Mark Twain quotation, a one-panel comic about grammar. Hand-lettering on the whiteboard read, "Welcome to Mr. Walsh's House of Literature." The chairs and desks were arranged in small groups.

"Your room looks great," she said. "I need to get some art on my walls."

Reid glanced up, then frowned at his computer screen. "Thanks. I need to finish this."

She sighed and took a seat. She placed a small stack of handouts on an empty desk next to her and opened her laptop. Okay then, she'd just wait for Steph and Elisa.

She scanned her lesson plan one more time, comparing it to her handout. She'd practiced several times last night, and it's not like her colleagues would be grading her. According to Steph, this "curriculum huddle" was just a chance to try out new lesson plans and get some feedback. Low-key, Steph had said.

Maybe it was low-key, if you weren't presenting in front of your ex.

Steph and Elisa joined them shortly after, and the group pulled four desks together in a loose circle. "All right, kids," said Steph. "Who wants to go first?"

"I will." Jenna reached for her handouts. She passed around copies of Shakespeare's Sonnet 116, a classic and her personal favorite of his sonnets. "This lesson is designed to be part of a unit on poetry." She cleared her throat and glanced at Reid, but he was looking at her handout. "Today we're going to talk about the meaning of true love as seen through one of Shakespeare's most famous love sonnets. I'd like you to follow along as I read aloud, and then we'll discuss. 'Let me not to the marriage of true minds admit impediments. Love is not love which alters when it alteration finds, or bends with the remover to remove . . .'"

When she'd finished reading, she set down her copy of the poem. Folding her hands in front of her, she said, "What do you think it means that love doesn't alter when it finds alteration?"

Elisa threw her hand in the air. "Pick me, pick me. It means that even if circumstances change, or even if a person changes, true love remains constant."

Steph nodded. "I like the idea of constancy. Time can change a lot of things. It can even bring death, but it can't erase love."

"That's a great observation," said Jenna. "When Shakespeare writes that—"

"Wait," cut in Reid, his blue eyes snapping. "I'm not sure I agree."

Jenna's stomach twisted. *I'm right. I know my interpretation is right. What could he possibly have to say?*

"Oh, Reid, come on," said Steph. "She's new, go easy on her."

"He likes to play devil's advocate." Elisa narrowed her eyes. "Ignore him."

"That's okay." Jenna sat up straighter in her chair. Crossing her arms, she said, "What's your question?"

"Not really a question." He leaned back in his seat and locked his hands behind his head. "I just think you might be putting love on a pedestal, which a lot of people do, even Shakespeare. This sonnet talks about love never changing, but how realistic is it for love to *never* change?" He shrugged. "People might be married for fifty years or they might divorce after five. There are no guarantees just because you're 'in love' with someone."

"Obviously there aren't guarantees." Jenna frowned. "But we're talking about Shakespeare's message, which is clearly that love never changes."

"Isn't that the mistake people make, though? They say they're in love and they think that means forever. Happens all the time in high school."

A bolt of pain shot through Jenna's chest. *Oh, it happens all the time in high school? Like you and me?* "You would know, wouldn't you?" Whoops. Had she said that? That thought was supposed to stay on the inside of her brain.

He leaned forward. "What does that mean?"

"Um. Guys?" said Steph.

Jenna stared at Reid and clenched her teeth. *You told me you wanted to marry me, you even gave me a promise ring, then two months later you had a new girlfriend. Seems like that perfectly illustrates your point.*

He stared back, blue eyes flashing.

Jenna fought back a groan. Reid had always had this power over her. In high school, a mere "hello" from him could make her whole day. His smile made her heart flutter. If he seemed distant, her stomach would churn until she knew what he was thinking. One kiss and she was in love with him. Had she changed so little that she still felt his gravitational pull? Who cared if he didn't agree with her (absolutely correct) reading of Shakespeare? She exhaled through her nose, counting to three. "We have different opinions on this sonnet, Mr. Walsh, that's all."

"I apologize," he said, glancing down at his notes. "Your interpretation is . . . perfectly textbook."

Textbook? Jenna clamped her lips together again. Oh, she wanted to take that roll of masking tape on his desk and tape his mouth shut.

Steph coughed. "I think this lesson will work great, as long as none of your students are jerks." She glanced at Reid. "Let's move on. Elisa?"

The remaining peer lessons took another hour. Afterward, Elisa said, "I'm taking a coffee break. Anyone want to join?"

"I would, but I have a department head meeting." Steph sighed and tucked her laptop under her arm. "You kids have fun, though."

"I have some lessons to work on," said Reid.

Jenna sprang to her feet. "I'll come." She glanced at Reid, but his head was already down, a frown creasing his forehead as he stared at his computer.

***

"Is this new?" Jenna said as she followed Elisa into Sunrise Cafe. "I don't remember this." She paused, taking in the exposed brick walls, the polished hardwood floors, and the black and white cafe tables.

"It used to be a clothing store, but they went out of business." Elisa pointed to the hand-lettered chalkboard signs above the long white countertop. "Everything here is good, but the lavender chai is my favorite."

Jenna's mouth watered. Back in San Francisco, she'd gotten addicted to chai. She ordered a large lavender chai with almond milk and joined Elisa at a small booth in the back.

Elisa took a long drink of her iced lavender chai. "I don't want to pry . . . Well, okay, I kind of do." She leaned toward Jenna. "What's the story with Reid? He practically ran out of the barbecue on Saturday, and he gave you a super hard time today. Steph said you guys dated?"

Jenna sighed. Reid must have mentioned their history to Steph. She'd known it would come out at some point, anyway. Three of the Juniper Creek teachers had been around so long they'd been Jenna's teachers, too, and Pam was in her twentieth year as Juniper Creek's principal.

"We did."

"Sheesh. I know Reid and Margot got together in college, but he never talks about his personal life, so it's sort of blowing my mind he had a serious high school girlfriend. It's like finding out your friend is a spy."

Jenna smiled and sipped her drink. The nutty almond milk, cinnamon and cardamom of the chai, and slightly sweet lavender blended perfectly. "Well, you know how it is when you're young. Everything is . . . momentous."

"Were you in love?"

An old ache stirred, the edge of something she thought was long gone. "I was. I thought he was, too." Best to leave it at that. There was no point in explaining the promise ring, or the way Reid had made her feel, which she hadn't found since. She took another drink and searched for something to focus on besides Elisa's round, intense gaze. The wall over their booth held a framed vintage-style poster, illustrated with a woman in a 1950s dress smiling sweetly at a man in a suit. She was reaching for his coffee cup. The caption read, "Give me the coffee, Frank, and no one gets hurt."

"What do you mean, you thought he was?"

Jenna shrugged. "I thought we'd be together forever, I guess, the way you think when you're that age. We were going to different colleges and planning how we'd take weekend trips to see each other. But the summer after we graduated, his dad died. Heart attack. He was really young, too. I think maybe it was a genetic thing? Everyone was shocked."

"Oh, no."

"Reid took it really hard. Understandably. But he broke up with me a couple weeks after the funeral. He said he just couldn't be there for me the way I needed him to." She felt slightly sick to her stomach, as if she'd just posted Reid's deepest feelings on Instagram. But his dad's death wasn't a secret.

"When was this exactly?"

"Uh, early August." Friday, August 5, and he'd broken up with her on her front porch at 9:45 in the morning. She'd had to force the promise ring off; the thin silver band had molded to the shape of her finger.

Elisa frowned, ticking something off on her fingers. "He got together with Margot . . . his freshman year of college? I'm sure she said something about that once."

"October of that year." She'd immediately purged Reid from her social media and blocked his number. Not that he would have called her, anyway.

"That's only two months after you guys broke up."

"I know." Jenna shook her head. She'd thought the same thing a million times since then. "I don't know what to tell you."

"Have you dated at all since then?"

Jenna paused, feeling heat creep into her cheeks. It seemed as if she should have dated a lot more by now or had a serious boyfriend, but no. In college, none of her crushes had developed into more. Once she had moved to San Francisco, her love life had remained flat, with the occasional blip here and there. A singer-songwriter who lived in her building had taken her to Ghirardelli Square, then complained the whole time about how touristy it was. There had been a banker, a friend of her roommate's, who treated her to a couple of expensive dinners while he talked about himself the whole time. She'd mostly kept company with books. "Not really," she said, shaking her head.

"*Girl.*" Elisa's eyes widened. "We need to find you someone, stat. Or get you out on the town, at least."

She laughed at the idea of getting out on the town in a place where Main Street was actually the main street, and downtown boasted only a handful of restaurants. "Like where?"

"Like the Angry Pigeon. Have you been?"

The Angry Pigeon sat several blocks off Main, near a small used bookstore. Its wooden sign featured a cartoon of a frowning pigeon. It was the sort of place with beat-up siding and darkened windows that she'd always imagined held one video lottery machine and an aging trucker drinking in the corner. She shook her head, wrinkling her nose.

"Okay, then you have to come with us sometime." Elisa grinned. "Steph and I do karaoke there, like, twice a month. I know it looks skeevy from the outside, but it's really fun. A lot of the teachers go. And other guys *our age* go. Some of them are pretty cute."

Jenna smiled and held up her chai in a toast. "Then I would love to go with you."

"Excellent." Elisa tapped her cup against Jenna's. "I'll let you know the next time we go."

They finished their beverages and headed back to the school. As they walked across the parking lot, Jenna said, "Thank you for the outing. It makes this place feel more like home."

"Well, we're glad to have you." Elisa looped her arm through Jenna's. "Don't pay any attention to Grumpy Pants Walsh. He's probably just kicking himself because he should never have let you get away."

Jenna highly doubted this was the case, since "Grumpy Pants" was engaged to a beautiful, successful woman, but she laughed at the thought. By the time she got back to her classroom, her chest felt light. She hummed to herself as she dug through the cupboards, looking for posters she could hang to brighten the room. Who cared what Reid said or did? This was going to be the best year of her life. She would make sure of that.

Reid slumped forward and rested his elbows on the Brewers' antique dining room table. He hadn't gotten to Margot's until almost six. After a full day of teaching and a staff meeting, he'd spent a couple hours grading and lesson-planning. He wasn't done, either. He still had to finish a handout on Edgar Allan Poe by third period tomorrow. He also had to dig up a binder of old sophomore English lesson plans that Jenna had asked for.

He inhaled sharply at the thought of Jenna. They had barely spoken since inservice, except when passing each other in the halls. Yet he couldn't get the memory of her at the staff barbecue out of his head. That halo of red hair as she crossed the yard. Amber eyes and freckles. His stomach rolled, and he pushed away the image.

"I hope you appreciate how hard I worked on this dinner," said Margot as she walked in. She carried two steaming plates of Thai takeout. "It was really difficult to open those boxes."

"Looks like you did a gourmet job." Reid sat up straight, frowning as the antique chair dug into his shoulder blades. He unfolded a beige plaid cloth napkin, which matched the table runner. Lifting his water goblet, he said, "To no one having to cook."

"Cheers to that." Margot clinked her glass against his. "By the way, I heard from Bailey. She and Dad think the horse is perfect." Her younger sister and their father were in eastern Oregon looking at a young show horse.

"Oh yeah? That's great." Reid shoveled down a spoonful of pumpkin curry. The back of his throat burned. He'd asked Margot to order it extra spicy. "Think they'll bring the horse back tomorrow?"

"Sounds like it." Margot filled him in on some more details of her conversation, then said, "So? How was your day?"

"Oh, you know," he said around a mouthful of curry. "Just the usual. The kids were a little wound up in sixth period, but that's typical."

"How was everyone else?" Margot twisted noodles around her fork. "Is Jenna settling in?"

Reid gulped his water. Should have asked for medium instead of hot. "Fine, she's doing fine. How was your practice?"

"I nailed the quarter pirouette. Patrick was happy." Margot grinned and leaned forward. "Also, I have some good news."

"The quarter pirouette isn't good news?" He winked.

"It is, but this is better." She grabbed his hand. "This is a secret, okay? We haven't announced anything yet, but we're breaking ground in January. The lodge will be ready for guests by June."

Reid's eyes widened. The Brewers had been planning to open a resort on their property for a few years now. Margot had explained it as a high-end country-themed property, with upscale cabins, a main building in the style of an old hunting lodge that could host weddings and events, and even a spa. Construction had been delayed several times as the family searched for a contractor they liked and dealt with permits. "That's great." He made his smile as wide as possible, ignoring the slight twist in his stomach.

"There's more. I can't even believe . . . Dad's giving us the house." Tears pooled in her eyes as she gestured around the dining room. "This place. As a wedding gift."

Reid blinked. His father-in-law was just gifting them an entire house? "But . . . he can't do that. Where will he and Bailey go?" Margot, her younger sister, and their father all lived in the cavernous ranch house. They each had their own room plus an office, and that still left a guest room on the first floor.

"They'll live in rooms at the lodge so they can manage it. That was always the plan, I just didn't know it would happen this soon. Honey, you know what else this means?"

Reid's heart raced. "We're about to owe a lot in property taxes?"

Margot frowned. "No, it means we don't have to worry about saving for a house. We can have a June wedding."

"Next June?" Reid's voice cracked. They were going on their fourth year of engagement. A wedding had seemed so far away, mainly because they were saving to buy a house in cash. Now, he had the sudden sensation of being on a roller coaster about to drop down a steep slope. "Can we plan everything that fast?"

"I'll have to go dress shopping soon, but yes. Dad wants us to be the first wedding at the lodge. Bailey will coordinate everything. We'll have in-house catering. The ballroom will have a capacity of a hundred twenty, so we can have everyone we want. I mean, a live band, everything."

"That sounds like a lot of people." Reid's stomach lurched, and he set down his fork. Next summer. A crowd of people staring at him. Margot in a white dress. *I do.*

She sat back, shaking her head. "You don't look happy. Why don't you look happy?"

"No, no, no. It's not that." His throat felt scratchy. He took a huge sip of water. Was it hot in here? Or maybe that was the spices from the Thai food, the heat creeping up his neck. "We haven't set a date, and now we have one. It's just a lot. Zero to sixty, you know?"

Margot's mouth was a thin line. "Actually, by the time we get married we'll have been engaged for four years. That's more like zero to fifteen miles an hour at best."

"You're right." He got up and hurried over to her. Kneeling next to her chair, he grabbed her hand. "I didn't realize you wanted such a big wedding. I guess I thought we'd do something small."

She looked down at him, tears pooling in her eyes. "I want something big. This is once in a lifetime. I'm not eloping, or getting married at a campsite, or whatever you're about to suggest. I know you, Reid."

Both an elopement and a campground sounded like great options, but he would never convince her of that. "I just know big weddings cost a lot of money." He could already see their hard-earned savings swirling around a drain. "The house is a huge gift, an amazing gift." And also a lot of house, which would cost quite a bit to keep up. "The money we'll save could set us way ahead for retirement. Could we think about something less elaborate for the wedding?"

"You've got to be kidding. A hundred and twenty people isn't even that big of a wedding. It's not like we're getting married at a mansion." She grabbed her half-empty plate, shoved back her chair, and marched toward the kitchen.

Great, now he'd ruined their dinner. He grabbed his plate and ran after her. "Wait."

"I'm just confused." She set her plate down in the sink and flipped the water on. As she rinsed, she said, "We've had a long engagement because we wanted to have the money for a house first, and now that problem is solved, and you still don't seem excited about getting married."

"Honey, no." He placed his plate on the counter and touched her shoulders. "It's not that I'm not happy."

She flinched and swished water over the now-clean plate.

Reid grimaced. He needed to do damage control. "It's just happening a little fast. You know how I am. I'm always looking at the numbers."

She nodded, chin down.

Reid gently took the plate from her and shut off the water. He opened the dishwasher and popped the plate in. It clattered against the bottom rack. "I'm sorry. I didn't mean to upset you. I just was surprised. I was processing, and I really want us to be smart about our finances. You're right, we've been engaged a long time . . ." He paused, breathless. Why couldn't he put the right words together? Nothing he said was erasing the frown from his fiancée's face.

Margot shoved her hair back and slid a thick elastic from her wrist over her blonde locks, tying them back in a ponytail. "You know, I think I'm going to go practice."

"Now?" He glanced at the clock. "I thought we were watching a movie. Don't you have students early tomorrow?"

"Yes, but so do you." She pursed her lips and touched his arm. "I just need to get some energy out."

Reid nodded, his heart sinking. While Margot went to change, he finished cleaning up the kitchen, putting away the leftovers and wiping down the counter. It seemed like the least he could do.

She came down a few minutes later, carrying her boots. He walked outside with her and paused in the driveway, fiddling with his keys.

"All right, I'll call you tomorrow." She gave him a quick hug, then pulled away.

"Hey, wait." He drew her back into his arms and rubbed her stiff shoulders. "I'm sorry. I really am. Your dad's gift is amazing. I'm just overwhelmed. I'm sure the lodge will be perfect for our wedding. Okay?" He pulled back and touched her cheek. "Honey?"

She blew out a breath. "Have a good night." She pecked him on the cheek, then strode off.

Reid's chest felt heavy as he got into his truck. As he backed out of the driveway, the motion sensor lights at the barn entrance flashed on. He paused at the end of the driveway, watching as the barn doors slid open, spilling light into the night. Margot, now a mere silhouette, walked inside. The doors slid shut.

Reid sighed and peeled onto the dirt road. As he drove into town, he thought of a hundred things he should have said to Margot, a hundred ways he should have reacted that would have been better than his actual reaction. Excitement, for example. Enthusiasm. Commenting about how beautiful she would look in her dress or how he couldn't wait to marry her. Paused at a red light, he slammed his hand against the dash. What the heck was wrong with him? He had a beautiful, accomplished fiancée and now, apparently, they had a free house. He had a steady job that he loved in one of the most beautiful places in Oregon. Why couldn't he just let go and stop worrying about everything?

By the time he got home, the pumpkin curry was a lump in his stomach. Inside, Reid settled on the couch with a glass of water and breathed slowly and steadily. In. Out. He had no reason to worry. Everything was fine. No, it was great.

The water settled his stomach, so Reid went to his office and dug through his files until he found the binder that he'd promised Jenna. He flipped through it and flagged a few especially good lessons, then set the binder in the entry way by his backpack.

He settled back on the couch and glanced at his phone. Margot hadn't called, but knowing her, she was probably still practicing her dressage routines. He would talk to her tomorrow.

His fingers skimmed over his phone screen, scrolling through his contacts.

They landed on Jenna's number and slowed, then stopped.

Steph had insisted at inservice that they all program Jenna's number into their phones, and that she take their numbers, in case anyone needed coverage once school started. He already had Steph and Elisa's numbers, and there was no reason he shouldn't have Jenna's, too. There was also no reason he couldn't call his co-worker to talk.

The refrigerator hummed in the background as Reid's thumb hovered over the call button.

No. He couldn't call her. First, it was almost nine. She might be busy prepping, or grading, or just reading. She might even be asleep. Second, he couldn't call her. And third, he really couldn't call her.

He sighed and scrolled through the rest of his contacts. None of them jumped out at him. He had a couple friends he talked to now and then, but no one he could call at nine at night and talk about the weight on his shoulders when he imagined sliding a ring on someone's finger.

He went back to Jenna's number, pressed the message button, and typed.

Got a sec?

He pressed send and threw the phone on the floor like it was on fire.

Grabbing the remote, he switched on reruns of *The Office*. His phone seemed to be staring at him from the floor, its screen a single accusing eye. Five minutes into the episode, he swiped his phone and checked the screen. The message said *Read*, and three dots pulsed on the screen.

Hi. What's up?

He started typing. *Long day, just wanted* . . . He erased it and tried again. And a third time. After erasing the message for the fourth and then the fifth time, he wrote, *I just wanted to let you know I found those lessons I mentioned. I'll bring them tomorrow.*

Great. Thanks!

He stared at the phone, but she didn't say anything else. Reid groaned and flopped back on the couch.

6

Jenna scribbled a note in the margin of a student's essay, then flipped to the last page. She glanced up at her wall clock. Sixth period was almost over? The forty-two minutes of prep always flew by. She set down her pen and stood to stretch. Her seventh-period students would be here any moment.

She glanced at her phone, scrolling again to the message Reid had sent her last night. So random. Why had he bothered to text her about the lesson plans when they worked at the same school and saw each other every day? The way the little text bubbles had appeared and disappeared, it had seemed like he was editing and re-editing his response, but then his final text had simply said he had the binder. It didn't seem like a message that required editing.

"Miss Daly."

She looked up.

Reid leaned against the doorframe, running a hand through his shaggy blonde hair. He wore khakis and a black collared shirt with short sleeves that showed off his muscular arms and broad chest and—

Stop it stop it stop it.

She smoothed back her messy bun. "Mr. Walsh. What can I do for you?"

"I have those lesson plans." He waved a thick binder. He walked over and set it on her desk. "I marked the stuff that I remember working well."

"Thank you. That's great." She flipped through the binder, smiling when she spotted a few journalism handouts that would be perfect for her upcoming unit. Getting up, she grabbed her notes for seventh period. As she walked to the whiteboard, she said, "You don't mind if I write and talk at the same time?" This was the most he'd spoken to her since inservice, and she didn't want to ruin it, but she also had students coming in.

"Go ahead. I should get to class anyway."

She nodded and began to write on the board in green. The marker was still new and made a satisfying squeak as it scrawled across the clean board.

There was a pause in which footsteps did not move toward the door.

After a moment, she glanced over her shoulder. "Was there something else?"

"No, no." He shoved his hands in his pockets. "Just wondering if everything is going well so far. I mean, I haven't heard any complaints from students."

She laughed. "It's early days yet. Wait until midterm grades come out."

"You'll be fine. By the way, Margot and I set a date."

The words lingered like smoke. She turned back around and continued writing. That's what you did when you were engaged. You picked a wedding date. That was the whole point. "That's great."

"It is. Kind of weird, though."

She frowned. "Weird?"

"Surreal, I guess. One of those big life moments, you know."

Shouldn't he be more excited about it? She started to ask, but no, that was none of her business. "Well, I'm happy for you," she said. "I should . . ." She gestured to the half-completed quotation on the board.

"Yep. Have a good class, Miss Daly." He turned and walked out of the room.

Jenna turned back to the board, blinked a few times, and looked at her notes. Where was she again? She wrote the last few words of the quotation, then capped the marker and dropped it into the tray.

Seriously, what was up with that conversation? Reid had dropped the information about his wedding date out of nowhere. It almost seemed like he had cold feet or something. If he did, though, why would he talk to her about it? Did he want to be friends now, after insisting they couldn't be?

She let out a soft groan.

"Miss Daly? Are you okay?"

Jenna jumped and turned around.

Tessa Morgan, one of her students, hovered in the doorway. Blue and gold ribbons streamed from her long black ponytail.

"I'm fine." Jenna laughed. "Come on in."

"Rough day?" Tessa sprang rather than walked into the room, despite her oversized turtle shell of a backpack. She unloaded it with a thunk in front of the first desk and hopped up onto the desk's Formica writing surface, swinging her legs. She wore her volleyball uniform, long-sleeved blue shirt emblazoned with the Juniper Creek logo in gold, blue shorts and knee-high-socks.

"Do you have a game today?" said Jenna.

"Yep, at four. We're playing Mountain Crest, and they're a lot better than us." Tessa's smile didn't even falter at this declaration. "Hey, do you want to be on the Homecoming committee? I'm co-chair, and we need another teacher advisor. Rustigan says there have to be two teachers on every committee and we only have one."

"Well . . ." She paused to set her notes down on the desk. She needed space in her schedule to help her parents around the farm. Between grading and lesson-planning, she didn't have a lot of spare time to begin with. Then again, she was new, and it was good to get involved with the community. "What would I do, exactly?"

"We plan all the activities for Homecoming week, pick the theme, and decorate for the dance. But we, I mean the students, pretty much plan everything. So, like, mostly you just have to show up to the meetings. They're every Wednesday for half an hour after school." Tessa's brown eyes sparkled.

The universe had a weird sense of humor. Homecoming was supposed to be her first dance with Reid her senior year, and because his truck had broken down on the way, they'd never made it to the dance. She'd been to other high school dances, but never to a Homecoming. "I could do that."

"That's great!" Tessa grinned. "It's in the cafeteria, okay Miss Daly? Right after school."

"You've got it." Jenna made a note on her large desk calendar. "Who's the other advisor? You said you have one already?" She glanced up.

"It's Mr. Walsh." Tessa hopped off her desk and made an imaginary volleyball spike in the air. "He's coming to the game today. You should come."

"Oh, um, maybe." Jenna let her pen drop to the desk. More together time with Mr. Walsh, just what she needed.

Laughter bubbled over as several of her students drifted into the room.

She pasted on a smile.

Margot pressed two paint swatches to the dining room wall. "What do you think about these?"

Standing back about three feet from the wall, Reid tipped his head and frowned. One swatch showed three tiles in successive shades of green, and the other swatch showed three tiles in . . . successive shades of green. He shook his head. "They look the same to me."

His fiancée sighed and waved the swatch she held with her right hand. "This is more of a blue green." She held up the other one. "This one's a yellower green. You really can't see a difference?"

"Maybe if there was actual paint on the wall."

"Bailey!" she hollered.

Her twenty-one-year-old sister jogged in from the kitchen. She held a huge bowl of ice cream. "What's up? Ooh, paint colors?"

"Reid says he can't tell a difference between these. Can you?"

Bailey shoveled a spoonful of ice cream in her mouth and wandered over to the wall. She tapped her spoon against the side of the bowl as she considered the swatches. "Yeah, that one's more yellow. I like it better than the other one."

"See?" Margot looked at Reid, triumphant.

He offered a half-smile. "Sorry, I'm not great with colors."

"Good thing you aren't planning our wedding, then." She chuckled and tossed the swatches onto the dining room table.

"Are you still going with turquoise for the bridesmaid dresses?" said Bailey.

"I was, but everyone does turquoise. I'm thinking hunter green with gold accents. More of a western, hunting lodge vibe to match the resort's branding."

"I like it." Bailey waved her spoon and started toward the kitchen. "Have fun, kids."

Reid rubbed his temples. Hunter green? What the heck was hunter green? Why did the wedding have to coordinate with the future Lucky Brewer Resort? *Is it too late to convince her to elope?*

Margot dropped into the chair across from him. "Speaking of the wedding, we need to talk about the bridal party. I'm thinking five bridesmaids, plus Bailey who's obviously my maid of honor. Can you get six guys?"

"Six?" His eyes widened. "Isn't twelve people a bit . . . much?" As her lips parted to say something, he added, "But I'm sure I can figure something out."

She nodded and picked up her phone. Scrolling through something, she smiled. "I had an idea for the honeymoon."

Reid perked up. The honeymoon sounded like the fun part. A nice, relaxing vacation after the craziness of a wedding. Maybe they could rent a cabin in the mountains. Hiking during the day, a cozy fire at night, watching the sunset from a small porch, his arm around Margot. Now that sounded like paradise.

"There's this resort in Turks and Caicos I've always wanted to go to." She flipped her phone around to show him a photograph of an azure infinity pool looking out over a white beach and an aquamarine sky. "It's all inclusive, adults only, and you can take day trips like scuba diving and snorkeling."

"That does look beautiful." He cleared his throat. The photograph practically popped with dollar signs. "Uh, how much does something like that cost?"

She shrugged. "If we went for a week and a half, probably around four thousand. That's not that bad."

"Four thousand dollars?" And he knew airfare would cost more. "Honey, that's a lot. I was thinking we could do something a little closer to home."

She frowned. "Like what?"

"A mountain getaway. We've never been to Coeur D'Alene and that's supposed to be beautiful. They have all kinds of hikes and a huge lake."

"I want tropical water, not lake water. Reid, this is our honeymoon. Once in a lifetime." She took her phone and tapped the screen. "You seriously don't want to do this?" She showed him another picture, this one of a smiling couple scuba diving among a school of fish.

"It's not that I don't want to. It's that I don't want to blow all of our savings on our wedding and have nothing left for our life together. What about maintenance on the house? What if we have a medical emergency?"

Margot blew out a long breath. "We're already saving a ton on this wedding. We won't be charged a facility fee for using the lodge. All we have to pay for is catering and the band. And my dad just gave us a house, remember? How much do we have saved up? We can afford to spend a little bit on ourselves for a honeymoon."

Reid's heart rate ratcheted up at the thought of depleting their savings. He and Margot hadn't actually merged bank accounts yet, but he'd socked away almost twenty thousand dollars over the last several years and he knew she'd put away a substantial amount as well. By the time you added in airfare, he was sure this Turks and Caicos super-vacation would cost seven or eight thousand dollars. That was approaching half of his savings. He couldn't just throw away all that hard work for a vacation, not when he could invest that money in things like a college fund for their future kids, retirement savings. Or maybe even sending money to his mother, who had retired to Florida and lived on a fixed income.

Margot was staring at him. "What? What's that frown for?"

He reached for her hand. "Can we just take a little break from all the planning and do something fun?" He'd come over after dinner and had thought they were having a mini date night, but Margot had dragged him right into the dining room to talk about redecorating.

"Sure." She cleared her throat and looked away. "Why don't we go on a walk. It's nice out." She hopped up and strode towards the front door without looking back.

Reid jogged after her. In the entry way, they put their shoes on in silence. They stepped out into a crisp breeze. The sun was sliding down the sky, casting golden light over the ranch's green and yellow patchwork of pastures and hay fields. Hand in hand, they took the wide dirt path that led past the barn and wound around the horse pastures.

He looked down at Margot, whose jaw was tight. She stared straight ahead.

"You're mad at me," he said.

She glanced up. "I'm not mad, I'm frustrated. We have plenty of money saved up, and my dad just threw us the biggest save in the universe by giving us an entire house. What's the problem with an extravagant honeymoon?"

"Because we're not extravagant people. We have savings, but what about emergencies? What if I get laid off?" Every year, Reid held his breath until the annual budget was announced. Public schools were always fighting for funds, and layoffs weren't uncommon. Look what had happened to Jenna. She'd apparently taught at a fancy private school in San Francisco, one which had plenty of donor money, and she'd still been laid off.

Margot waved her hand. "You won't get laid off. That department has four teachers."

"Yeah, and last year Pine Valley, which is only a little smaller than Juniper Creek, went under and all of their students got absorbed into another district. Anything could happen. What about when we have kids? Children are expensive."

"I know they are, but sheesh. Do you have to turn everything into a doom and gloom money discussion?" Margot stopped and faced him, hands on her hips. "You barely want to spend money on takeout, Reid. We're not rich, but we don't live below the poverty level either. It's okay to enjoy what we have."

"I'm not talking about not enjoying it. I'm talking about being smart and not blowing half our savings on a vacation. What's wrong with Coeur D'Alene?"

Margot shrugged. "It's just . . . not anything we couldn't get here. Lakes and mountains. I'm sure it's pretty, but honestly, it sounds a little boring."

Boring? Wasn't the point to spend time with each other, and that should be fun no matter where they went? He ran a hand through his hair and raced through other options. "Then what about somewhere we've never been, like Arizona or New Mexico?"

"We've never been to Turks and Caicos." Her eyes flashed.

Reid threw his hands up. "There's no in-between with you, is there? It has to be a giant wedding or an elaborate vacation. What I want doesn't matter."

Margot tossed her hair and stomped down the path, and he raced after her. As he caught up to her, she said, "Really, Reid, there's no in-between with you either. You want us to get married at a courthouse and honeymoon in a yurt."

"I never said that." He had totally thought it.

"Well, you might as well. I'm shocked you even spent money on an engagement ring. Do you regret that?" She strode faster.

"Sweetheart, no." He reached for her hand. "I just want us to compromise and be smart about how we spend our money."

She pulled away and walked toward the nearby fenced pasture. Reid followed. A high wooden fence looped around a field of long green grass. Three of the Brewers' show horses stood in the field. Two munched grass and one, a stately bay Morgan horse, lifted his head to the breeze and whickered.

Margot leaned against the fence and watched the horses. Reid joined her, standing close, but he didn't try to put his arm around her. Instead, he watched her profile. What was going through her head? He'd always thought he and Margot were so similar, but they really did see money differently. His stomach churned again, and he wondered if he was developing an ulcer.

After several minutes, she turned to look at him. "Do you even still want to do this?"

"Do what?"

"Get married."

His eyes widened. "What? Of course I do."

"Do you really? You're not involved at all in the wedding planning, and you don't even want to spend money on our honeymoon." She drew in a sharp breath. "I just think we're really different people."

"We are in some ways, but that doesn't mean we can't get married." What was she saying? And yet the tiniest hint of relief crept into his mind at the thought of calling off the wedding. No, why would he even think that?

She shrugged. "I don't know Reid. Maybe . . ."

"What?"

She shook her head. "Nothing."

"Margot, what?"

"Maybe you'd be happier with someone like Jenna."

He stared at her. "Why would you say that?"

"Because she's your ex? Because she's more low-key than I am and probably would love Coeur D'Alene? I don't know."

"Do you really feel that weird about us working together?"

"I don't know." She shook her head. "I don't know what I'm feeling, Reid. I'm sorry. I'm going to go back to the house."

He stared at her for several moments, but when her expression remained stoic, he sighed. "I think I'll stay out here for a bit."

After she left, he leaned against the fence and traced the rough-cut wood with his fingers. What was going on? And how could he possibly even entertain the idea of calling off the wedding? He was supposed to marry Margot. They were engaged. They couldn't cancel the wedding. It was one fight. It didn't mean anything, did it?

But the rock in his stomach said otherwise.

Jenna strode down the hall toward the cafeteria. Clutching her notepad and pen, she took a few deep breaths. In for five, hold for three, out for five. Again.

She stepped through the open cafeteria doors and inhaled for a count of five that brought the smell of stale fries and bleach. Beams of sunlight slanted through the large windows and fell across the rows of Formica tables. A group of ten students and Reid sat tables near the empty salad buffet.

Blowing out a slow breath, Jenna wandered toward them. It was just a committee, nothing to get nervous about. So why did she feel like a sophomore in high school again, walking up to Reid's table to sit with him at lunch? Hoping he would turn that smile on her. Stomach twisting, heart racing.

This is so silly. I'm an adult.

The group had their backs to her, turned toward the easel and oversized pad of paper propped up next to the buffet. Tessa wrote across the page, adding to a long to-do list in large bubbly letters. A boy Jenna thought was named Ryan stood next to her, leaning close, saying something that made her laugh. The other students were chatting, crammed together on the long benches that ran the length of two tables they'd pulled together. A smartphone lay on the table between them, music blasting from it.

Reid sat back from the group a bit. His head nodded to the music as he doodled on a notepad.

Jenna dropped into the seat across from him. "Hi."

He looked up and tipped his head to the side. "Ms. Daly. I . . . didn't realize you were my co-chair."

"Oh. Well, surprise." Jenna smiled and shrugged. His guarded look made her stomach sink. "Tessa asked me yesterday. She just looked so excited, I couldn't say no. What a great student. Great kid, really." She shoved her hair back from her face.

"They're all pretty good kids." He checked his watch, then half-stood up. "Hey, guys? We've got the whole team. I think some of you already know Ms. Daly?"

"Hi, Ms. Daly!" Tessa waved, her ponytail swinging.

Reid sat down and faced forward, his pen and pad at the ready.

Jenna had always thought his profile made him look like a classic sculpture: straight nose, a cleft chin, high cheekbones. Ugh. She had to stop noticing things like this. It didn't matter how handsome Reid was, he was her ex. And engaged. She was just grasping onto these details because they were familiar and everything else in her life was new. She willed herself not to even look at him out of the corner of her eye as she, too, looked toward the students.

Tessa clapped. "Okay, you guys, I'm so excited for this. We have the votes and we're ready to tell you the Homecoming theme. Drumroll please."

The kids drummed their palms against the table and stomped their feet. Chuckling, Jenna joined in. After a moment, Ryan grabbed the bottom of the to-do list and flipped it up and back, revealing a page behind it that read "Forever and Always."

The small group burst into applause. "Yes! That was mine!" said one of the girls.

"Last Night of the Apocalypse was so much better!" said a boy.

"Shut up," said another boy, groaning.

As the kids bantered, Jenna glanced at Reid. "What was it our senior year? Under the Sea or something?"

"Maybe. I'm not sure." He ducked his head and scratched away on his notepad, adding to his doodle of a pack of mustangs.

Cheeks going hot, Jenna looked down at her own notepad. She scrawled across the top, testing the ink. Whoops. Way to walk down memory lane. That had been it, though - Under the Sea. That was why she'd picked out that bright blue color for her dress. She'd found matching high heels at a bridal store, and Reid had worn a matching tie. Even the ribbon on her corsage had been bright blue.

Tessa flipped the notepad back to the first page. She pointed to the checklist with her marker. "This is really serious, guys." She giggled. "But it is. This is everything we need to figure out for the dance. Let's start with the dessert table. Do we want cupcakes?"

"Chocolate fountain!" called one of the girls.

"No, you guys, we need a donut platter. That place on Main?" said Ryan.

Tessa waved her arms. "Stop, stop. I'll write them all down and we'll vote." She turned to a fresh page and scribbled down suggestions as students called them out.

Jenna looked at Reid. "Are we supposed to do anything to contribute?"

He chuckled. "Nah. These kids have it handled. We just have to make sure they don't do something too out there, like adding a water balloon fight to the dance."

The votes went to donuts and cupcakes. Two members of the chocolate fountain contingent slumped in their seats.

"What about prizes?" said Tessa. "Do we want to try to do the same stuff as last year?"

Prizes? thought Jenna. This hadn't been a feature when she was in high school. She turned to the girl next to her, who was either named Lacey or Tracey. "What prizes?"

"We raffle them off at the dance," said the girl. She leaned across the table. "Hey Mr. W.? Can the Lucky Brewer Ranch donate something again?"

"I'm sure they can," said Reid. "What do you think, same as last year? Riding lessons and a saddle blanket?"

"That's great," said Tessa, writing it down.

Lacey-slash-Tracey turned to Jenna. "Mr. W.'s fiancée helps run the Lucky Brewer Ranch. You know, that huge place off Highway 1?"

"Yep. I know it." Naturally, Margot would want to help Reid out with the raffle by donating. Juniper Creek had been her school, too. And Margot was a lovely human, and she was engaged to Reid, and the sooner Jenna could stop noticing how handsome her ex-boyfriend was, the better.

The students batted around other possible prizes, some of which would apparently be repeats from last year. They were all community-focused gifts, such as gift certificates to local restaurants or a free oil change at the local mechanic.

The students checked off a few more items, and then Tessa said, "Okay, that's it, except who wants to put the cupcake order in with the bakery?"

"I'll do it," blurted Jenna, at the same time that Reid spoke up, "I can take care of that."

She and Reid looked at each other.

"You go ahead," he said.

"No, you can. I didn't mean to . . ." Jenna's cheeks flamed again. Why did she have to blush so easily?

"Guys. It's cupcakes," said Ryan. "It's not that difficult."

Jenna burst out laughing. "I'll do it," she said. "You're using Evergreen Bakery, right?" It was the only bakery in town, and the owner, Susan, was a friend of her mother's. "I'll go in. I haven't seen Susan in years."

"Great." Tessa scribbled "Miss Daly" next to that task on the notepad. "That's it for today."

"Good work, everyone!" hollered Ryan, as chatter swept through the group. "Remember, next week, same time!"

As the students stood up and continued talking, Reid shot out of his seat and booked it out of the cafeteria.

Jenna watched him go, her skin prickling. Out of the corner of her eye she saw Tessa watching her, and she smiled and pretended to review the notes she'd taken.

"Miss Daly," said Tessa's voice, loudly and suddenly, and closer than Jenna had expected.

Jenna jumped and looked up from her notepad. "I'm sorry. What?"

Tessa gave her a weird look, then held up her phone, typing rapidly on the screen. "I'm emailing you the cupcake stuff right now. There's a purchase order you have to use that gets charged back to the school. And we need twelve dozen cupcakes." She gave her phone screen one last tap. "Okay, I sent you everything. Thanks, Miss Daly! Oh, did Mr. W. already leave? That's his easel. Could you take it back to him?"

"Sure." *I swear, I can't get away from him.* Sighing, Jenna hefted the easel and carted it out of the cafeteria.

She found Reid in his classroom, frowning at an essay like it had personally insulted him.

"Hey," she said. "Where should I put this?"

He barely glanced up. "Oh, just in the corner. Thanks."

She placed the easel into the corner he'd indicated. "That was fun, helping the kids plan. We didn't do prizes back in the day."

He nodded but kept his focus on the essay. "We only started the raffle a couple years ago. It's a good way to help the students connect with local businesses." He scrawled a comment in the margin of the page.

"It's nice that Margot can donate riding lessons," added Jenna. "I'm sure she's a great teacher. It's fun that you're both teachers."

"Mm-hmm."

Why was he being so awkward and distant? "Is . . . is everything okay?"

"Everything's fine." He sighed. "I can't really sit here and make small talk."

"You're in the middle of grading. Sorry." She started toward the door.

"That's not what I mean." He set down his pen and rubbed his forehead. "Being friends with you is just . . . it's a little weird. Because of our history, and . . . Margot. I don't know how she'd feel about it."

Jenna chewed on her lip and fought back the urge to snap at him. She wasn't trying to be friends, just friendly. They did work together, after all. "I see," she said. "I'm sorry. I'll try to keep it professional from now on. Business only."

"I don't . . ." He spread his hands wide, lips parted, but didn't finish the sentence.

"Have a good evening, Mr. Walsh." She gave him a tight smile and strode out.

Fuming, she went back to her classroom and tidied up. Who did Reid think he was? Apparently, he could do whatever he felt like. Be nice to her one day, then be borderline rude to her the next. It wasn't her fault that he apparently couldn't deal with their work situation like an adult. It didn't have to be dramatic. He was making it more awkward than it really was.

She printed out the cupcake purchase order that Tessa had emailed to her, then headed out. As she started up her truck, it coughed a couple extra times. She made a mental note to ask her dad about it later.

The bakery was only two miles from the high school, and she arrived in minutes. She found parking curbside in front of the store, something that had been a rare occurrence in San Francisco. She definitely did not miss that traffic.

A set of little bells tinkled as she pushed open the front door. She walked toward the counter, pausing to drool over the trays of colorful macarons in the front case.

"I'll be with you in a second," called a woman's voice from somewhere in the back. It sounded like Susan. Her oldest daughter Evelyn had been in choir with Jenna, so Susan had been a fixture at choir concerts, even hosting a couple end of year parties at her sprawling ranch house.

Jenna glanced around, then froze.

Margot sat at a round cafe table by the window, a photo album open in front of her. Sunlight through the window caught the bright gold highlights in her wavy blonde hair. She scribbled notes on a pink notepad as her lips moved silently.

Squaring her shoulders, Jenna walked over to the table. "Hi, Margot."

The other woman looked up and raised an eyebrow. "Hi. Buying a cake?"

"Not exactly. I'm ordering cupcakes for Homecoming." Should she mention that she was on the committee with Reid? After the way he'd just reacted to her? Probably not. He could decide what he wanted to tell his fiancée.

She glanced down at the album and pointed to one of the photos, a tiered white cake decorated with pink flowers. "That's pretty."

"Thanks. Reid and I finally have a date." Margot flipped to the next page, a glossy photograph of a light blue cake with white seashells that were probably made of chocolate. "It's next June."

Jenna hated the way her stomach plunged. "That's wonderful."

"It is." Margot gave a short laugh. "It's also a lot of work. I knew it would be, but do you know how many bands are already booked up? I'm going to have to resort to bribery pretty soon. I'm not having a deejay at my wedding." She wrinkled her nose. "Live music is so much classier."

"Definitely." Jenna had been to plenty of weddings with deejays and everyone had had just as much fun as if there'd been a live band, but it seemed like a bad idea to mention this. She wondered what other "classy" touches the wedding would have. Plated dinner instead of a buffet, probably. Not that it mattered. She certainly wouldn't be on the guest list. Or would she? That would be too weird, going to her ex-boyfriend's wedding, wouldn't it? "I'm sure it will all come together."

"Hope so." Margot bent her head and twisted her engagement ring around her finger.

"Jenna, sweetheart!" crowed Susan, the bakery's owner, as she emerged from the back. She wore a yellow apron and a matching hairnet, both accented with tiny blue flowers. "I heard you were back in town. Your mother and I need to have lunch. Tell her to call me."

"I will. I'm here to put in an order for Homecoming, actually." Jenna held up the purchase order.

"I should get going," Margot said as she clapped the photo album shut. "Susan, thanks, I'll be back."

"Bye, dear."

The door banged shut behind Margot, leaving the little bells on the handle tinkling against the glass. Susan lifted her chin in a gesture toward the door. "I heard you're working with Reid now at the high school?"

"Yes, well, there are four English teachers total." *Oh no*, thought Jenna. Juniper Creek's small-town gossip was the one thing she hadn't missed while living in California.

Susan cocked an eyebrow at her. "If my husband worked with his ex and she looked like you, I'd be worried too."

"Oh—she's not—Margot's not worried, I'm sure," said Jenna.

"Hmm." Susan pursed her lips and took the purchase order from Jenna's outstretched hand. "All right, what do those kids want this time? Are they kidding, that many? Their bloodstreams will be sugar water by the end of the night." She set the purchase order down on the countertop, smoothed it out, and made a couple of notes. "You know, those two have been together quite a long time."

"Who, Reid and Margot?"

"About ten years." Susan shook her head. "And they've been engaged for three of those. That seems like an awfully long time to wait to get married when you're in love."

"I . . . maybe . . ."

Susan circled something at the bottom of the form and turned the page around for Jenna to sign. "Twelve dozen S'mores cupcakes. Sign here."

Jenna signed, praying that Susan would say nothing more about Reid and Margot. "Thanks, Susan."

"Not a problem." She took the form. "You can pick up the cupcakes the day of the dance. They'll be ready by about two, I would say."

Jenna thanked her and headed out. On the way home, she replayed her conversation with Reid over in her head. They had dated a long time ago, over ten years ago. He clearly felt nothing for her, so why insist that he couldn't have a non-work conversation? If they were over, why couldn't he just act like a normal human? There was no reason two very old exes couldn't be friends. That's all she wanted, to be friends.

Was it, though? Some part of her still reacted to him the way she had in high school. She had long ago memorized the curve of his jaw, the breadth of his shoulders, the way the skin around his eyes crinkled when he smiled. The small cleft in his chin used to make her heart race. The way he laughed set her blood on fire. When she was a teenager. These heart-skipping feelings now were just an echo, she thought. The shadow of something that had passed. An old habit. She wasn't truly interested in Reid.

The sick feeling in her stomach eased and her shoulders relaxed. She just needed to focus on the here and now. She had her job, and work around the farm to keep her busy. She didn't need Reid to be her friend. She could make other friends, better friends. In fact, she was going to start now.

She put in her Bluetooth headpiece and dialed Elisa's number. "Hi, it's Jenna. I was wondering if you wanted to do something this weekend."

"I'd love to!" said the other woman. "Steph and I are going to the Angry Pigeon on Saturday. You should come."

Her heart lightened. A girls' night out was just what she needed. "What time?"

"We usually get there around 8:30 to get a table. Karaoke's at nine." There was a pause on the other end of the line. "Um, sometimes we invite Reid. Do you want us to?"

So much for girls' night out. "I mean, that's fine, but he doesn't seem to want to be around me very much."

"I don't know what's going on with him. He's been really grumpy lately."

Jenna burst out laughing. "He is kind of grumpy.

"You know what? Let's make it a girls' night," said Elisa. "Reid can't sing anyway. We'll see you Saturday. Well, and tomorrow at school."

"Sounds great."

After they hung up, Jenna cranked her radio, and over the static, a Shania Twain song blasted. She sang along and rolled the window down, letting the desert wind whip past her face as she drove home.

"Are you sure this is you?" Carla Fields, the school secretary, held Reid's staff badge close to her face and frowned at it. "I don't know, you look a little older than this guy in the photo." She winked, handed the badge back across the kiosk counter, and reached for her stamp pad.

Reid grinned and slipped his lanyard over his head. "That was back before this job aged me."

"Uh-huh." She inked an eagle stamp and held it out. "All right, Mr. Walsh, let me see the inside of your wrist."

Reid hiked up the sleeve of his fleece and extended his arm so Carla could stamp his wrist. The ink felt cold and clammy on his skin. He blew on it once, then tugged his sleeve down. Glancing over his shoulder, he spotted three boys from his third period standing in line. "Hey," he said loudly, catching their attention, "don't let those troublemakers into the game."

"Nevermore, Walsh, nevermore!" said one of the boys. The other two made cawing noises. Poe never failed to entertain hyper teenagers.

Reid shook his head and waved at them. He headed through the turnstile and wove around a cluster of students toward the bleachers on the left side. Stretching the entire length of the football field, they were about half full of students and parents. The opposite side, a smaller set of bleachers, was dotted with only a few supporters from the visiting Lark High team. Bright, tinny horns blasted the Juniper Creek fight song as the marching band strode across the field in various formations. Stadium lights glared down on the moving mass of blue uniforms. The scoreboard was lit up, zero to zero, awaiting kickoff.

Reid hummed the fight song to himself as he took the steps up the bleachers two at a time. He paused to scan the staff section and spotted Steph, Elisa, and Jenna huddled together. His breath hitched at the sight of Jenna's long red braid frizzing out from under a blue Juniper Creek beanie. For a moment, he was transported back in time to the Homecoming game they'd attended together. It had been cold then, too, and he'd thrown his letterman's jacket around Jenna's shoulders to keep her warm. Their breath had fogged up the night and cups of instant hot chocolate steamed in their hands. Jenna had buried her nose in the cup, saying the steam made her warmer.

He jogged up the stairs toward the little group. The only free spot was next to Jenna, and as he stepped in, he realized how crowded the bleachers really were. He couldn't keep distance from her without blocking the aisle, and he couldn't leave the aisle free without standing only an inch away from her. The scent of vanilla wafted off her, faint and homey. Her oversized work jacket—maybe her dad's?—made her petite face and frame look even smaller.

She turned up to look at him. The stadium lights cast her face into sharp angles and made her freckles look brighter. "What's up?"

"Not much. You all look festive," he said. The three women had woven blue and gold ribbons into their hair. They'd even smeared metallic gold paint under their eyes, like a glittery version of the eye black that football players used.

"I don't think you're sparkly enough," said Jenna. "I have more gold eyeshadow if you need it."

"I'm good, thanks." So that's what the gold was. A streak of it smudged her cheekbone, like maybe she'd missed or applied it in a hurry. He almost reached down to wipe it away with his thumb. Gritting his teeth, he shoved his hands into his pockets.

Jenna turned to Elisa and whispered something in her ear, but Reid couldn't hear anything over the noise of the crowd and the band.

"Where's Margot?" asked Elise, leaning toward Reid.

"Oh, she's not into football. We're meeting up at Francesca's in a bit." His stomach churned. He really should have invited Margot to the game. Not that she liked high school football. Anyway, he wasn't staying long.

"Aw, you're not staying for the whole game?" said Elisa.

He held up his hands. "It's the first home game and date night. I'm trying to juggle, okay?"

Elisa made a face at him.

"All right, everyone, we're ready to bring out our JUNIPER CREEK HIGH SCHOOL FOOTBALL TEAM!" boomed Saul over the loudspeaker.

Jenna nudged Reid and pointed down at the PE teacher, who sat at a folding table nearest their side of the bleachers. "Are those . . . dogs?"

"Chihuahuas. They're Saul's." Reid nodded toward the two small dog beds situated on the folding table. The long-haired chihuahuas in the beds each sported their own Juniper Creek sweatshirt, and tiny earmuffs.

"Since when?" She burst out laughing. "He didn't have them when we were in school?"

"No. The dogs are rescues from a few years back." He had to lean close to her to be heard, and once again a hint of vanilla wafted toward him. "They have their own special outfits for every football game."

"That is so cute!" Jenna's voice went up an octave, and she clapped her hand to her chest. She turned to Elisa and pointed at the dogs.

Reid took a step back, narrowly avoiding Jenna bumping into him with her hip.

The football team jogged out on the field, to raucous cheers and applause. Reid spotted Ryan, who was on the Homecoming committee, and cheered extra loudly for him.

The opposing team came next. There was some light clapping and a chorus of boos. The cheerleaders from each school lined up at their respective sides of the field, and Saul announced kickoff.

Reid crossed his arms and kept his eyes on the field. Red hair flashed in his peripheral vision as Jenna jumped, cheering for a successful pass. He clenched his jaw. He should have skipped the game entirely. The first home game was a big deal, yes, but plenty of other teachers had come to support. It's not like this was Homecoming.

His phone vibrated in his pocket, and he slipped it out to check. A message from Margot. *See you at 7.* No smiley faces or emojis or terms of endearment. Their text exchanges had been shorter since their argument on Monday night. In fact, they hadn't really talked since then.

The Juniper Creek team made a first down, and the crowd cheered. The cheerleaders shook blue and gold pompoms and led everyone in a cheer. "E! E-A-G! E-A-G-L-E! J-Creek is the place to be!" On this last line, they were supposed to jump to the left.

Reid took a halfhearted step, and Jenna stumbled into him. "Gosh, sorry!" She giggled as she, Elisa, and Steph righted themselves.

Sucking in a breath, Reid texted Margot back. *Actually, I can leave now. See you there.*

"Gotta run," he said to his colleagues. "Sorry."

The three women frowned at him, and Steph said, "Now?"

He waved and bounded down the bleachers. Behind him, he thought he heard Jenna tell him to have fun, but he didn't turn around. He had to get out of here; being around his ex-girlfriend made him feel off-balance, like he was getting the flu.

***

Reid pulled his truck into the small parking lot next to Francesca's. He unzipped his Juniper Creek High School fleece and yanked it off, revealing a blue and white striped dress shirt underneath. He reached for the tie he'd stowed in the glove compartment and hastily put it on. Checking his appearance in the rearview mirror, he ran his hand over his two-day stubble. *Should have shaved.*

He got out of the truck and paused with his hand on the open door. His feet felt weighted by concrete, and his stomach roiled. He tugged at the tie, suddenly too tight around his neck.

Inside the restaurant, Margot was already sitting at a small table near the back. Three small candles flickered at the table, throwing golden light onto her tan skin and blonde hair.

Reid bent down to kiss her. "How was your day?"

She shrugged. "Busy. I had a ton of students and we're starting to talk about marketing for the resort. We'll probably launch a campaign next month, get the town excited about it. How was the game? You didn't stay long."

He smiled as he sat down and flipped open the menu. "I would rather be here with you." And he would, he thought. He could breathe a little easier now, here in the warm glow of candlelight, tucked away amongst the brick walls and heavy wooden beams.

"Thanks. I . . . wasn't sure how you'd feel about that after our talk Monday." She half-smiled and reached for her water glass. Her short, manicured nails reflected the candlelight. Gold. Sparkly gold, like the paint on Jenna's face.

Reid's jaw muscles jumped. "I think we both just needed a little space, that's all."

"Hi, I'm Alice and I'll be taking care of you tonight." A short brunette with a broad smile appeared at their table, as if out of thin air. She held a pen poised, like a wand, above a notepad. "Our special tonight is a locally sourced prime rib seasoned with our house-made dry rub and accompanied by fresh steamed vegetables and risotto." The words flew out at a pace that would have rivaled anyone in the Juniper Creek debate club. "Can I interest you in any other beverages or an appetizer?"

"Just the salmon salad for me," said Margot.

Reid asked for the spaghetti and meatballs and a Coke. He usually avoided soda, but maybe the carbonation would settle his stomach.

Alice scrawled on her notepad with a flourish and whisked their menus away.

"I want to show you something." Margot's expression brightened as she pulled out her phone, tapped the screen, and passed it over. "Bailey mocked this up. What do you think?"

Reid stared at the screen. It was the image of a wedding invitation, with a dark green background. A delicate gold script read, *The Lucky Brewer Resort cordially invites you to its inaugural wedding. Miss Margot Elizabeth Brewer to Mr. Reid Franklin Walsh.* This was followed by the words *June 15, 4:00 p.m. The Grand Lodge, 1 Juniper Drive.*

"And look at this." Margot leaned across the table and flipped to the next screen for him. This one showed a prototype ad for the resort itself, a photograph of an emerald green field and mountains in the backdrop, with the words *Lucky Brewer Resort* splashed across the top. The "u" in Lucky was in the shape of a horseshoe. In the center was a smaller photograph of Reid and Margot on the day they got engaged. The copy below it read *Weddings at The Lucky Brewer Resort—The Perfect Place for Your Perfect Day*. "Imagine this is our wedding photo. We can be the models in the resort marketing materials. Wouldn't that be awesome?" She slipped her phone from his hand and smiled down at the screen. "We'll get some amazing pictures in front of the lodge. And with the mountains in the background?"

Her words landed like a rock in his stomach. "Honey." He reached across the table and pulled her hand down, waiting until she made eye contact. "I . . . I don't want our wedding to be a brand launch. We should get married because we love each other."

"I love you, Reid." She glanced down at the phone screen. "But this is a business, and it's not really just about us. It's also about what's best for the resort."

Cheerful Alice reappeared, plopping a basket of steaming sliced bread between them. "Here's some bread while you wait, along with our house garlic honey butter." She placed a small ramekin of whipped butter on the table. "Can I get you folks anything else? Refill on your water?"

"We're fine." Reid gritted his teeth and gave her a close-lipped smile.

"Wonderful. I'll grab that Coke for you." She turned and trotted off.

Margot grabbed a slice of bread and commandeered the butter. "I've been helping my dad run the ranch since I was twelve," she said, reaching for the butter knife.

Reid started to say that he knew, but he reconsidered speaking. He waited.

Margot's blue eyes flashed dark sapphire in the candlelight. Slathering butter on her bread, she went on. "Even when I was in grade school, Bailey and I did more to run that place than Mom ever did." Her gaze turned to steel. Evelyn Brewer had left her husband and two daughters when Margot was just ten years old and Bailey was only six. "When my dad retires, I'm going to be the CEO of the Lucky Brewer Resort. Bailey doesn't want that much responsibility. We've already talked about it. She'll help, but the resort will belong to me. I have to be a businesswoman first and foremost. It's like having a child. Everything I do has to be for the good of the business. If that means slapping my wedding photo on a brochure or timing our wedding day with the grand opening of the lodge, I'll do it. If that means giving up competitive dressage or not teaching riding lessons, I'll do it."

"I know," he said. "You're extremely dedicated."

"It's not me I'm worried about. It's you." She set the slice on her plate and let the butter knife fall to the table with a slight clatter. "Running a business means spending money, too. You have to spend to make money and all that. What if we want to refurbish the cabins in five years? What about paying employees of the lodge? You don't even want to pay for a honeymoon."

"That's not true." His face grew hot, and he reached for his water. Wrapping his hands around the coolly sweating glass, he said, "I want to spend a reasonable amount of money on a reasonable vacation that won't break the bank."

"A once-in-a-lifetime vacation," she said. "And what about teaching? Can you teach full-time and also help me run a resort?"

He stared at her. "I didn't realize my teaching career was in question."

"It's not right now, but at some point, I don't see how you can do both. You're so involved in the school. You can't be pulling twelve-hour days to grade papers when I might need you to manage the lodge's restaurant or check on guests."

He fell silent and took a long drink of water. The back of his throat felt scratchy. Until now, it hadn't hit him what being Margot's husband would mean for his career. Her father would retire at some point, and naturally she'd want her husband to be involved with the family business.

Cheerful Alice was back yet again, setting a glass of Coke in front of Reid, along with a small plate of lemon slices. "Here's that Coke. Can I do anything else for you folks at the moment?"

Reid glared at her. "Give us a minute," he snapped.

Alice's eyes widened, and she took a step back. "Oh, sure, I'll just, uh . . ." She backed away, then turned and darted away, her steps light as a bird's.

"Reid," said Margot. "What are you thinking?"

He shook his head. "I don't . . . I don't know."

She crammed half the buttered bread slice in her mouth and chewed with something approaching fury. Finally she said, "Are you honestly ready to commit to all this? Not just me. The resort. The business. All of it."

Her words hung in the air like acrid smoke. Reid could feel himself poised on the blade of something dangerous and irreversible, as if he had accidentally walked to the edge of a precipice with no guardrail. His heart racing, he balled up his cloth napkin in his lap.

Beyond the edge, his future with Margot spread out before him. A room full of smiling guests eating a four-star dinner while he and Margot twirled around the dance floor. That gem-like infinity pool in Turks and Caicos. Long, long days and nights, even crazier hours than he kept as a teacher. He had known people in the hospitality industry, and, unlike teaching, you didn't get summers off. Fancy guest cabins and a lodge and heaven help him, a full-service spa to keep up (according to Margot), all of which required serious cash. And what if the resort wasn't the smashing success the Brewer family hoped it would be? Juniper Creek, population 8,576, wasn't exactly the prime tourist destination in Central Oregon.

What if the money ran out?

What if he and Margot fought?

What if they didn't agree on how to raise their children?

"Reid," she said.

He forced his jaw to loosen enough to answer. "I don't know."

Margot traced one manicured nail around the stem of her water goblet. Her chest rose and fell in quick shallow breaths. "That's an answer," she said.

"No." His heart caught in his throat. He reached for her hand, but she jerked it away. "I want to have a better answer for you, I wish I did, I . . ."

She managed a small smile as her eyes filled with tears. "Wishing isn't enough for me. You're either in this a hundred percent or you're not."

He stared at her, his mind racing, tongue frozen.

She stood. "I think I need to go."

As if in a dream, he watched her slide on her jacket, slip her purse over her shoulder. He should say something, he should stop her. He was locked to his chair. Couldn't move. He watched her walk across the restaurant, head high, and then push open the front door, setting the little bells on the door tinkling as she walked outside.

Belatedly, Reid's brain told him, Go after her. He sprang to his feet and raced out to the parking lot, but Margot was slamming the door of her silver Mazda. Even as he stepped off the sidewalk, she pulled out of her spot and whizzed out of the lot.

He took out his cell and called her. It went straight to voicemail.

"Uh, sir?" said a soft, high voice behind him. "Will you be needing your food to go?"

Cheerful Alice. Right. The check.

Reid paid up and declined Alice's offer to box up the two meals. Back outside, he leaned against his truck and rubbed his eyes. He loved Margot. He could be happy with her . . . doing what they were doing. He taught English, she taught riding. He didn't want to fork over hundreds of dollars for the privilege of swimming in an infinity pool, and he didn't want to spend hours dealing with resort guests. He wanted a simple life. The life he had.

Margot was right. That was his answer.

He climbed into the truck and drove back towards town, barely aware of operating the vehicle. On autopilot, he took the familiar turns and streets until he realized he had reached the turnoff to the high school. Even from this distance, the heavy drumbeats of the marching band thrummed through his open windows. It must be halftime.

Margot and I just broke up, so I thought I'd catch the rest of the game, he imagined himself explaining to Steph, Elisa, and Jenna. The absurdity of the situation made him burst out laughing. He pulled into his usual parking spot and strode towards the football field.

Reid pushed through the turnstile and paused at the end of the field, behind a group of students. As he watched the marching band wheel around, panic sliced his chest. Everyone knew he and Margot were engaged. He would have to tell people. They would want to know why. Not that it was anyone's business, but he'd need to have an answer. What was he supposed to say?

The color guard raced onto the field to join the band. Flags flew into the air and horns blared. The scoreboard showed only four minutes left in halftime. He should get to his seat. Glancing toward the bleachers, he spotted Jenna, Steph, and Elisa, huddled together in the same spot. These were his work friends, he reminded himself. They of all people would understand about Margot. He could talk to them.

But he really only wanted to talk to one of them.

Because she'll get it, he thought, as he walked toward the bleachers. Jenna had always understood him.

Then again, his ex-girlfriend might not want to listen to his breakup woes.

If they ask about Margot, then I'll tell them, he decided as he took the steps. *If Jenna offers to talk, I'll take her up on it. Otherwise, I won't say anything.*

Three frowns swiveled toward him.

"What happened to date night?" said Steph.

"We just, Margot wasn't feeling well." Reid clenched his jaw and sidled in next to Jenna. He couldn't even get the words out to tell them what had happened. *Coward.* He zipped up his jacket and stared at the marching band, which was forming a wobbly "J" on the field.

After a moment, Jenna nudged him. "Everything okay?" she whispered. "You don't look too good."

He took a slow, deep breath. "Not exactly."

"Do you want to talk?"

Yes. "Maybe. I don't want to . . ." Don't want to what? "Take you away from the game."

"That would be great, if you don't mind," she said loudly. Turning to Steph and Elisa, she said, "Reid's going to take a look at my truck. It's been making a weird noise. We'll be back, okay?" She flicked her gaze at him, gave him a slight nod.

If Steph and Elisa thought this was an odd time to check out a truck, they didn't say anything. "See you soon," said Steph.

Reid gave Jenna a small smile and led the way down the bleachers. The two of them exited through the turnstile and walked down the sidewalk toward the school. They reached the entrance to B-Hall, where a small set of steps led up to the door. Reid gestured to the steps. "You want to sit here or go inside?"

"This is fine. The air feels nice." Jenna plopped onto the top step.

He joined her, placing a good foot of space between them. Rubbing his hands together, he blew on them a couple times. Even from here, the stadium lights threw a glow into the sky. Drumbeats thrummed like a distant thunderclap, and the horns swelled.

Jenna looked up at him. The gold makeup had faded, the glitter scattered across her cheeks. "What happened?"

He shifted, the cold from the concrete oozing through his khakis. "You sure you want to hear this? I mean . . . it's about Margot, and you and I . . ."

"It's fine. We dated a million years ago, Reid." She lightly touched his wrist. "I'm here as your friend. If you need one."

"Thank you."

"So, what happened?"

He sucked in a breath, as if by doing so he could draw in the words, could convince his mouth to form them. "Margot and I broke up."

"Oh. Oh, dear."

He grimaced and zipped his fleece all the way up. The crisp air tingled the inside of his nose with every breath. Should he tell Jenna what had happened? He wasn't supposed to spill the beans about the resort, but the marketing campaign was probably just a few weeks away. He could swear her secrecy in the meantime. "I'm not really supposed to say anything, but the Brewers are opening a resort on their property. They'll keep the horse barn and offer riding lessons, but they're building a huge lodge. Vacation condos, golf course, the works."

She frowned. "In Juniper Creek, really? Will that draw enough business to be successful?"

"They seem to think so. You can't tell anyone, not yet, because they want to announce it in a specific way. Don't say anything, okay?"

"Okay, I won't." She held her hands up. "Sorry, but how is this related to your breakup?"

"Our wedding was going to be the first wedding at the grand lodge. Everything was becoming about the business, and Margot and I have very different philosophies on money, and . . ." He shrugged. "It feels like we're more different than I ever realized. Tonight, it just all came to a head."

"That makes sense." She leaned forward and wrapped her arms around her knees. Her hair, normally a flame of red, appeared deep copper in the dim light.

He fought back the sudden impulse to reach out, smooth back the frizz escaping from her braid. Clenching his hands into fists, he said, "Margot told me, basically, I was either in or out. I wanted to be in. I did. I just . . . couldn't be. She made it clear the business would always come first, and that's understandable. But it's not for me."

"There's nothing wrong with that. Sometimes people are just different."

"Then why do I feel like such a failure?"

"Reid." Again, she placed her hand on his wrist. A light touch, fleeting, like a dragonfly. "From what you're telling me, you and Margot realized that you have different priorities, and neither of you wanted to compromise. Where's the failure in that?"

He tipped his head back and stared up at the sky. Not even the light pollution from the football stadium could dim the bright white moon that floated in a cobalt sky. Wisps of cloud drifted by, temporarily aglow as they passed the moon. A line from *Romeo and Juliet*, which he'd taught a dozen times since becoming a teacher, sprang to his mind. "'Arise, fair sun, and kill the envious moon, Who is already sick and pale with grief, That thou, her maid, art far more fair than she.'" He clamped his lips together. Maybe he shouldn't be quoting Shakespeare's iconic love story to his ex.

But Jenna just smiled. "So, you do like Shakespeare."

"I never said I disliked Shakespeare." He winked. "I didn't necessarily agree with your interpretation of that sonnet."

"That's right. You called it, what was it? Perfectly textbook." She nudged him, her amber eyes sparkling. "For the record, my students agreed with my take on it."

"True love never dies?"

"Exactly."

He hadn't mean to lean so close to her. Just inches away. He had forgotten about the freckle just above the rosebud of her mouth. Vanilla and honey drifted toward him. What was it? Shampoo? He pulled away, leaning back to look up at the sky again. Very interesting sky. Definitely not filled with stars that looked anything like her freckles. "How are your folks these days? I see your parents in town sometimes, but I haven't really talked to them much. The farm's doing okay?"

"Mmm . . ." Her shoulders slumped. "Honestly, the farm isn't great. My parents had to lay off the Caniff boys. Between droughts this past summer, and water restrictions, I'm not sure what kind of harvest we'll have. I'm trying to help out around the place where I can. But you know how it is with lesson-planning and grading. It's hard to find the time to do it all." She shook her head. "We could probably use some of my salary to hire the boys back, but the real problem is the ongoing lack of water. It doesn't matter if we have extra hands or not, if the farm isn't producing enough to be sustainable long-term." A frown rumpled her forehead. "Please don't tell them I told you. Or anyone. I don't think they want it spreading around town."

"Got it." His legs and seat complained about the hard steps. Standing, he stretched one leg and then the other. "What do you have to do this weekend around the place?"

"I don't know, but Dad said something about repainting the barn. There's always a ton of stuff to do. You know how it is."

He nodded. His parents had raised horses and sheep. There were always animals to feed, stalls to muck out, fences to repair, a never-ending cycle of chores. "What time?"

She hopped to her feet. "Oh. Reid, no. You don't need to help out."

"What if I want to?" When she started to protest, he added, "Think of it this way. If I help you, that leaves you more time and energy, which means you won't run yourself into the ground. And you have to stay healthy, because we have a long time until Christmas break."

"That's true." She frowned. "I'm starting to get very sleep-deprived, so I'm going to say yes, but you can't tell my parents that I spilled the beans about our situation."

"I swear. What time tomorrow?"

"Eight?"

"Eight?" he scoffed. "That's late for a farm. I'll be there at six."

"Okay, overachiever. Thank you. I can pay you. My parents won't like it, but . . ."

"Absolutely not." He crossed his arms. "You just gave me free relationship therapy. That's your payment."

Her lips twitched. "That's very generous of you."

"I want to help. I know I've been standoffish, but . . ." He held out his hand to shake hers. "Friends?"

"Friends." She grasped his hand.

He squeezed, his hand almost covering hers. She always had cold hands, he remembered now. In high school he was constantly using warming up her hands as an excuse to hold them. He let go and shoved his hands in his pockets. "You want to head back to the game?"

"I think I'm going to head home, actually. The halftime score was looking pretty promising, and I need to get some rest." She yawned. She adjusted her scarf, then looked up at him. "I guess I'll see you tomorrow, but if you change your mind, no worries."

"I'll be there at six. Go get some sleep, Pixie."

His high school nickname for her escaped his lips without a thought. The word burned in the air. *Whoops.* "I mean Jenna. Wow, I'm tired." He could hear how fake-loud his own laugh was.

"Sure. Me, too." Her full lips pursed together. "See you soon."

Reid leaned against the railing and watched her stride down the sidewalk, braid swinging. His gut clenched. Maybe spending Saturday morning with her wasn't the greatest idea. But he'd already offered, and he did want to help. In any case, he'd be doing chores, not hanging out. He and Jenna would barely have time to talk.

He checked his phone again, but he had zero messages from Margot. He slipped the phone back into his pocket and sighed as chants and cheers rose from the football field.

Jenna groaned when her alarm went off the next morning. Half-sliding out of bed, she stumbled to her dresser and rooted around for grubby work clothes. 5:45 was way too early to be awake on a Saturday, but on a farm, you got up before dawn. The family's two dairy cows would be hungry, and there would be a list of chores a mile long.

She followed the smell of coffee downstairs into the kitchen. Her parents stood at the kitchen island together, heads close as they bent over some kind of list. Her mom looked up and smiled. "There's our girl. How did you sleep?"

"Fine." She yawned. "Do I smell coffee somewhere?" *Please, God.*

Her dad nodded toward the coffeepot next to the stove. "I made it extra strong. Sure you don't want to go back to bed, Sweet Pea?"

"You asked me that last weekend. I want to help." She kissed him on the cheek, then walked over to pour a cup of coffee. "What's on the agenda?"

"Most of the produce is ready to harvest," said her dad. "You could start on that if you want."

"Sure." She grinned as she poured a steaming cup of coffee. "I love fresh produce. You have beets, right? Maybe I can make us a beet salad for lunch?"

Her parents traded glances. "Well, a lot of it's going to the farmers' market in Redmond tomorrow," said her mom. "It's actually a great market. The Caniffs and the Garcias go, too. You'd love it."

Jenna narrowed her eyes. In the ten years she'd been away, her parents had never once mentioned the farmers' market. Was this another way to make extra cash for the farm? She took a long sip of her coffee. "All right. I can come with you to the market tomorrow, too."

Her dad waved his hand. "You're doing plenty. You do have a full-time job."

"But I want to be useful." She crossed to the island and sat down at one of the bar stools. Another sip of coffee. Deep breath for courage.

"In fact, I wanted to talk to you about contributing part of my salary to the farm. If I—"

"Sweetheart, no." Frown lines deepened her dad's wrinkles. "That's your hard-earned money. You need to take care of yourself."

"But—"

"No. No way. We'll get by just fine."

Jenna frowned and looked to her mom. "I'm living here, and you guys aren't even charging me rent. Why can't I help?"

"Honey, no. We have a couple other sources of income. I'm applying to teach an art class at Pine Valley Community College, and your dad is repairing engines for some of the neighbors. The engine repair business is doing pretty well." Her mom smiled and squeezed her dad's shoulder. "We want you to focus on taking care of you. Let us worry about this place."

"We've always gotten by," said her dad.

Jenna sighed. *Okay, then.* "Well, you'll have some extra help this morning. Reid's coming over."

Silence fell as her parents stared at her. Her dad's thick bushy eyebrows scrunched together. "Reid Walsh?"

"No, a totally different Reid that you've never met." She laughed. Her parents didn't. Clearing her throat, she said, "I saw him at the game last night. We were talking, and . . . I just told him I was helping out around here, and he offered to help, too."

Her dad's eyebrows reached even closer together as a deep V appeared between them. "I don't suppose you mentioned money was tight."

"I didn't mean to. It just sort of came out." Her face went hot. Here she had cautioned Reid not to let on that he knew her parents' financial situation, and now she was calling attention to it herself.

"Everyone we know is struggling, Dave," said her mom. "I'm sure he's heard about the droughts and water restrictions from his students already. It's nothing that isn't obvious. And we could use the help."

"Hmm," he grunted.

Jenna's mom crossed her arms. "Are you telling me you're going up on a ladder to paint the barn by yourself? People die falling off ladders, you know."

His eyebrows relaxed a fraction. "I suppose." He snorted. "Maybe he can get Ed Brewer off my back."

Jenna set her mug down. "What do you mean?"

"Dave," said her mom.

"No, she might as well know. Ed's offered to buy the farm."

Jenna's stomach plunged as if she had just taken a roller-coaster dive. The Brewers already owned an enormous ranch—so large they were building a resort, according to Reid. What did they want with a small alfalfa farm? "When was this?"

"'Bout a week ago." Her dad shook his head. "I told him no, but the man won't take no for an answer. He offered again. Cash."

How much? she wondered. Enough for her parents to make a nice profit and retire? Enough that they would be tempted? The thought of losing the farm made her throat ache, but her parents shouldn't have to break their backs working multiple jobs for the sake of principle. "Do . . . do you think maybe . . ."

A knock on the front door cut her off. Reid was probably here. Jumping up, she ran to answer.

He smiled as she opened the door. He held up a cardboard carrier packed with to-go coffee cups and paper bags. "I brought some breakfast from Sunrise Cafe. Have you eaten?"

"No, not yet. That's so sweet. Come in." She stepped back to give him room.

As he stepped inside, she caught a whiff of citrusy soap. His curls lay tight and damp against his head, as if he had just showered. A plain white t-shirt clung to his broad chest and for a second she forgot how to breathe. Her stomach hitched remembering how he'd called her Pixie last night. *Don't be ridiculous, he just broke up with his fiancée.*

She led him toward the kitchen, taking deep breaths as she did. Her heartbeat would slow down any minute now. This breathless feeling had to do with the strong coffee she'd gulped down, and nothing to do with Reid.

***

Jenna swiped sweat off her forehead with her shirt sleeve. Standing up, she dusted her hands off on her faded, torn jeans. A few bunches of bright green leaves peeked up from the raised garden beds, but most of the beets, arugula, and sweet potatoes now rested in the wooden crates next to her.

The sound of a power saw firing up cut the quiet air. Her dad's workshop stood about twenty feet from the gardens. He must have left Reid to paint the barn on his own.

She stretched from side to side, wincing at a twinge in her lower right back. Too many years away from the farm had weakened her muscles. Keep up these chores every week and she might get buff by Christmas.

Reid's pretty buff. Her thoughts drifted to the white t-shirt he was wearing today, the one that revealed his rounded biceps and broad chest . . . *Shut up, Jenna. He's off-limits.* Maybe if she spoke sternly to herself, her thoughts would behave themselves. She bent to grab the first wooden crate which she'd packed full of sweet potatoes. Perhaps she'd overfilled it a bit. She staggered over to her truck, which she'd parked next to the gardens. With a grunt, she hefted the crate into the truck bed.

"Need some help?"

She stepped back from the truck to see Reid walking toward her. Sweat stained the front of his shirt and beaded on his forehead. A blob of dark red paint on his right cheek resembled poorly applied clown makeup. With one eyebrow arched, she said, "I thought you were painting the barn."

"I am, but I ran through the first can and I can't find where your dad put the rest."

"He's in his shop." She gestured toward the wide tin shed. "The paint's probably in there too."

"Let me help you pack these up first." Without waiting for her to agree, he strode toward the stack of crates. The tendons in his forearms popped as he lifted a crate spilling over with leafy greens.

Jenna remembered she was supposed to be working, not drooling over arm tendons, and hurried over to grab another crate. With two people, the process of loading the truck went much faster. Reid stacked the final crate, and she closed the creaky metal door on the back of the truck bed.

"You should oil that," said Reid.

"It's just Lucy's arthritis." She patted the rusted metal. "You want a ride back to the barn? We can throw some more paint in the truck."

"Good idea." He headed toward the workshop, and she watched him stride away, those broad shoulders, narrow waist, and not a bad view at all from the back. Gritting her teeth, she looked away. The paint wasn't even dry on Reid's breakup. She shouldn't be thinking about him this way. They'd agreed to be friends. Friends didn't admire each other's backsides.

Back at the barn, she and Reid had just finished unloading the crates of produce when Jenna's mom rode up on Buster, the family's horse.

"I see progress!" her mom sang out. She dismounted from the horse, landing on the ground as light as a dancer. "The barn's looking good, Reid. Thank you."

"No problem. Do you want us to brush him down?" Reid stepped toward the horse and took his reins. Buster lowered his head and started munching a stray patch of grass.

"That would be great, actually, thank you," said Jenna's mom. "I need to take care of some things around the house. Oh, and you got the produce, too. That's great. Careful, we might ask you to come back." She patted Reid's shoulder and started toward the house.

"Hey, I helped too!" Jenna called after her mom.

Her mom waved and blew her a kiss.

Jenna rolled her eyes at Reid. "I think my mom wants to adopt you."

He made a face at her. "I'm just that lovable. Come on, bud." He tugged on Buster's reins, and the horse lifted his head.

While Reid got Buster sorted, Jenna unpacked the produce onto a series of racks her parents had stationed outside the barn. She sprayed down the potatoes and beets, then turned the pressure on the hose down to a trickle and rinsed off the arugula. Leaving everything to drip-dry on the racks, she wandered into the barn.

Low, off-pitch notes filled the air. "I'm goin' down to Jackson . . ." Reid was singing? She frowned and strode down the aisle toward Buster's stall. Peeking inside, she giggled at the sight.

Reid brushed Buster's coat in rhythm to the song lyrics. "When I breeze into that city, people gonna stoop and bow . . ." He paused to drop a kiss on the horse's velvety nose. "Such a good boy," he cooed. "Such a handsome boy."

Jenna leaned against the open stall door. "Can I come in, or should I leave you two alone?"

Reid shot her a grin, his face growing pink. "I miss having horses around."

"I bet." She remembered going over to his parents' ranch in high school. They used to take horses out to the fields and barrel-race around the trees.

She slipped into the stall and stroked Buster's velvety nose. The horse lowered his head contentedly, his eyes half-closing. She leaned closer, inhaling the musty, rich smell of horse hair. Reaching into the tack box, she grabbed a hoof pick. As Reid continued brushing Buster, Jenna lifted the horse's front left leg and began cleaning dirt out of his hoof. She glanced at Reid. "How are you doing today after, you know? All of it?"

He shrugged. "A little better, I guess. Still kind of processing everything."

"You haven't heard from Margot, have you?"

"No, and I don't know if I will." He grimaced. "I wonder if her dad will still give her the house."

"Sorry?"

He groaned. "Her dad was gifting us their house for our wedding."

Her lips parted. "Wow. Most people get a blender, you get a house. I mean, got." Her face went hot. "Sorry, silly joke."

"No, it's okay." He half-smiled. "The plan was for Ed Brewer and Bailey to move into the grand lodge once the resort opened, so they could help run the place. Now, I don't know what will happen. Maybe all three of them will live in that lodge. Maybe the ranch house will be converted to more guest rooms or something."

The mention of the Brewer family brought back her dad's comment this morning. Pursing her lips, she gently released Buster's hoof. Would Reid know why Margot's dad wanted to buy her family's farm? Even if he did, should she put him in the middle by asking? He had enough on his plate dealing with a breakup. He probably didn't want to talk about the Brewers more than he had to.

What he really needed right now, she thought, was to get out of the house and have a little fun. Tonight was supposed to be girls' night out, but Steph and Elisa would understand if she invited Reid along after all. "Hey. Why don't you come with me to the Angry Pigeon tonight?"

He stopped brushing for a moment, then resumed swift strokes along Buster's caramel coat. "Karaoke? Not sure I'm in the mood."

"Steph and Elisa are going. It'll be an English department outing. The Four Musketeers." She smiled, lifting her brows. "You've already got a song, it sounds like. And I can do a passable June Carter Cash."

"That's right, you actually sing." He sighed. "I don't know. I have grading to catch up on."

The image of him sitting in a quiet apartment on his couch, bent over a stack of papers, made her heart crack. He was sporting dark undereye shadows, she saw now, and she'd bet he hadn't slept much in the last twenty-four hours. "There's *always* grading," she said. "Come on, it'll be good for you."

He chuckled. "Do I look that bad?"

No, you look good . . . She stepped to Buster's other side and reached for his right front hoof. "Just thought maybe you could use a friend."

She wanted to tell him that no, he looked far too good. "I just want to be your friend."

"They do have two-dollar baskets of cheese fries."

She glanced up. "Baskets?" Her mouth watered at the thought of salty fries. "And what are cheese fries exactly?"

"Fries piled with three kinds of melted cheese and spices. I think it might be taco seasoning."

"Sounds like a heart attack on a plate." The phrase left her mouth without a thought, and she stared at Reid, her stomach wrenching. "I didn't mean to use that analogy. It just slipped out."

"No, no, I know." He cleared his throat.

"Reid, seriously, I . . ."

He shook his head. "Hey, I know what you meant. It's okay, Pixie."

There it was again. The second time in less than a day he'd called her Pixie. What did it mean? Anything? Nothing? The nickname brought a flush to her cheeks, a warmth spreading in her chest. It looked like Reid could still stop her heart with a soft word. *Great.*

He leaned down, running the brush over the same spot on Buster's coat. "I guess grading can wait. Karaoke's at nine, so I can pick you up at what, eight-thirty?"

Pick her up? They were driving together? That made sense; why waste the gas? It was better for the environment. Maybe he planned to pick up Steph and Elisa as well. Carpooling was just smart. "That sounds great."

"You better sing with me. I can't carry a tune."

"I know." She made a face at him.

He looked startled, then burst out laughing. "What do you think, Buster?" He patted the horse's flank. "Do you like my singing?"

The horse snorted and turned his head to nudge Jenna's shoulder.

"I guess he likes you more," said Reid, placing a hand over his heart and sighing. "Probably because you're so much prettier than I am."

The skin around her collarbones flamed with heat. Reid had always been like this, teasing, complimentary. He probably didn't even realize he sounded flirtatious. Certainly, he wasn't flirting with her. His ex-girlfriend. How ridiculous. "Ha," she said.

They finished grooming Buster in silence. A couple times Jenna glanced over at Reid, but he hummed to himself, his eyes on the horse. She could still hear his deep voice in her mind. *It's okay, Pixie.*

Her insensitive joke about a heart attack might be okay. But she wasn't sure she was. Her blood ran hotter simply being near Reid. She wanted to run her hand through those curls, now a mess with sweat and dust. *Oh, heavens.* She might not be okay at all.

Reid stood on the Dalys' front porch and cleared his throat several times. He glanced down at his faded jeans and boots, wondering if he should have worn something else. But the Angry Pigeon was the kind of place where peanut shells littered the floor and the booth tables felt sticky. A dive bar, not a five-star.

His phone pinged, and with his pulse spiking, he checked the screen. Nope, not a message from Margot. Just an automated text reminder about his upcoming electric bill payment. They'd been broken up all of twenty-four hours, he reminded himself. She needed time. They would talk at some point, but right now he needed to leave her alone. He wondered what she'd do with the engagement ring. Keep it for sentimental reasons? Pawn it? He couldn't decide which option made him more depressed.

Shoving his phone in his pocket, he rapped on the front door.

"Come in," called Andrea Daly's voice. "It's open."

Reid stepped inside and a wave of nervous energy washed over him. It felt like high school all over again, when he'd come to pick up Jenna at this same house for a date. The Dalys' front door was always unlocked and sometimes wide open, but he always knocked. When Reid starting dating in high school, his dad had lectured him about polite greetings. "Never honk to get a girl to come outside. Always come to the door, and always knock. Don't barge in like you own the place." Franklin Walsh would have been proud to know that his son still remembered that lesson all these years later.

Reid's eyes watered a bit, and he wiped away the moisture.

He found Andrea in the living room, sitting on the couch. "Hey. How's the barn looking?" When he'd left at one o'clock today, he and Jenna had nearly finished the first coat on two sides of the barn, and Andrea had started on the trim.

She put down her book and stood up to greet him with a quick hug. "Oh, coming along. We'll probably finish the first coat this week.

Have a seat." She gestured to an overstuffed armchair next to the couch. "You were a huge help today, Reid. We all appreciate it."

"My pleasure. I'm happy to come back, if you need me." He settled into the seat, sinking into a slight dip in the cushion. "Where's Dave?"

"Still in the shop. He's fixing a riding mower for the Smiths." Andrea sat back down and clasped her hands together. Leaning forward, she said, "I heard you and Margot parted ways. I'm so sorry."

Jenna had either told her parents, or they had heard the news from three other people because news spread fast around here. He nodded. "Thank you. I thought about taking out a billboard ad, but I figured the Juniper Creek grapevine would do the trick."

Andrea's lips pursed in a wry expression identical to the one Jenna sometimes wore. "I know it doesn't feel good right now, but you know it's better to break off an engagement than a marriage. You don't want to marry someone unless you're sure it's right."

"That's true." Reid thought of his own parents, who had always seemed deeply in love. His mother used to say, "Your father is my first and only love." She had moved to Florida last year to be near her older sister. Reid spoke to her every week, and even now, he knew she wasn't dating anyone. She sometimes claimed that the romance chapter of her life was closed.

He turned his attention back to Andrea, who seemed to be waiting for him to say something else. "Well, at least tonight should be fun."

"You're doing karaoke, I heard."

"That's the plan. Although I can't actually sing." He winked. "Good thing Jenna can."

Andrea shifted in her seat. She pursed her lips, the same way Jenna did when she was thinking hard about something. "I know it's none of my business, but I just have to say something. Dave and I are so glad that Jenna's home, and she seems really happy working at the high school. She needs friends right now. As I'm sure you do too. I know you have a history, but I'd hate to see her get hurt again."

A fist squeezed his chest. He'd told Jenna goodbye for her own sake, to save her from his pain, because he couldn't love her when he was blind with the loss of his dad. Losing Jenna had hurt him, too. No point in explaining that to her mother, though. He was the guy who'd broken her daughter's heart, plain and simple.

Before he could form an answer, Jenna yelled, "Sorry, sorry, I'm coming!" as her footsteps thudded down the stairs. She dashed into the living room and slid the last few feet on the hardwood in her socks. "Thank you, thank you," she said, bowing. "For my next trick, I will put my boots on without falling over."

Andrea chuckled.

Reid sprang to his feet, his eyes widening. Jenna wore a black tank top that hugged her small curves, and jeans that fit like a glove at the hips before flaring out over the ankle. She'd left her long red hair loose, and it draped over her freckled shoulders in fiery waves. She looked like a country version of an Irish fairy—a pixie, just like her high school nickname. "You look nice," he said, keeping his tone neutral.

"Thanks. Mom, look." Jenna lifted the pair of cowboy boots she held in one hand. "Remember these?"

"Oh, yes! We got those in Bend, didn't we? You wore them for your senior pictures."

Jenna bent down to tug on the boots. She glanced up and through the curtain of her hair gave Reid a wry smile. "You remember these, don't you? I wore them all the time."

"Did you? Oh, that's right." Liar. He remembered the boots. He remembered what color dress she wore to Homecoming and how in the spring her hair turned a lighter copper and how her forearms tanned and freckled in the summer.

Jenna pulled on the other boot. "I forgot how comfortable these are." She straightened up and lifted one foot, admiring the boots. "Okay, let's go sing."

On the drive downtown, Reid found himself looking over at Jenna as she sang along to the radio. He remembered her voice—he had attended her choir concerts in high school, and she'd sung around him all the time—but he'd forgotten how surprising it was coming from her petite self—a husky alto, invoking dimly lit bars and warm humid nights. Some protective layer fell away and he could swear they were back in high school, driving to the lookout at Pilot Butte the night of Homecoming.

"Remember breaking down on the way to the homecoming dance?" he said.

Jenna stopped mid-lyric and burst into laughter. "I don't think I could forget that. How long did we have to wait for your dad? Two hours?"

"Something like that." He'd driven his dad's old truck, and it had broken down on the highway, halfway between Pilot Butte and Juniper Creek. Reid had a cell phone, but both sets of parents were at a barbecue and no one was answering their phones. It took an hour to get ahold of his dad, and by the time Frank Walsh arrived in his truck with the trailer hitch, the dance was half over. They'd ended up sitting in Reid's backyard in their dance clothes, wrapped in blankets drinking hot chocolate. It had been a great night, but he'd still felt guilty for making Jenna miss the dance. "Your dress was blue, wasn't it?"

"I'm surprised you remembered that."

"Oh, well." He shrugged. "Sometimes random things just stick out." He didn't add that he would never forget how she'd looked in that dress, a deep blue, her hair copper against the soft fabric. How could he forget watching the sunset with her on top of Pilot Butte, the sky turning gold and pink. Pulling her into his arms and kissing her for the first time, the way her mouth tasted like spearmint.

"You know, I've still never been to a Homecoming dance," she said. "Senior year was the only time anyone asked me."

He chuckled. "You'll get to go this year. We're on the committee, so we'll be expected to chaperone."

"Oh. That's good, then."

He couldn't read her tone, and when he looked over, he also couldn't read her expression. She looked straight ahead, focusing on something in the distance. Probably reading too much into it, he thought. Jenna wouldn't be thinking about sunsets or first kisses, not this many years later.

So why was he?

He shoved away that question and focused on the road. It was too easy to drive on autopilot around a small town. He found parking a couple blocks from The Angry Pigeon, and they walked through the doors shortly before nine p.m.

A blast of rock-influenced country music, with heavy guitars, filled the air. The place smelled like the yeastiness of beer and the tantalizing grease of burgers and fries. Rainbow-colored Christmas lights, which the owner left up all year, ran along the wood-paneled walls and over the long wooden bar, casting a cheery glow over the tables and booths. In the back, an older woman sat at one of the two video poker machines, her face aglow with the neon light.

Reid waved to Saul, who in an expansion of his announcer capabilities, also ran karaoke every Saturday night. He stood at the karaoke booth, his long silvery-grey ponytail draped over an Angry Pigeon t-shirt. There was no sign of the chihuahuas, but Steph had told Reid once that the owner let Saul keep them in the back when he ran karaoke.

Saul looked up from a tangle of microphone cords and grinned. "Hey! You two gonna sing?"

"You know it!" Jenna nudged Reid, then waved at someone in the back.

He followed her line of sight to see Steph and Elisa sitting at a cozy booth. The two women grinned and waved back. Reid felt Jenna's hand close lightly around his wrist, towing him toward the booth. It was an automatic gesture, he felt sure, something she didn't realize she was doing. His heart hitched and he gently slid his hand out of her grasp.

She glanced at him, her cheeks flushed, and clamped her hand to her side.

Steph and Elisa scooted over to make room for Jenna and Reid at the table. Jenna slid in next to Steph, and Reid squeezed himself next to her. It was really more of a half-booth, designed for four smaller people. His left hip bumped into Jenna's as he adjusted. "Sorry," he said, trying to scoot back, and finding that half his backside now dangled off the booth seat. "Do you have enough room?"

"I'm fine. Scoot in, I'm not going to bite." Jenna's eyes were amber jewels in the deep warm light. She didn't seem concerned about anything, least of all how close they sat. Turning to the other women, she reached over to hug them.

Reid slid closer, his entire left leg and hip butting up against Jenna's right leg and hip. Enjoyable, but not helpful, because he was also close enough to smell vanilla in her hair, close enough that he could easily have slid his arm around the back of the booth and let his fingers run over her shoulder. Clenching his jaw, he spotted a basket of cheese fries on the table. He reached over and snagged a handful.

"Sure, steal all of our food," said Steph.

"They're two dollars," he mumbled around the mouthful of fries.

She rolled her eyes. "Dude, I'm kidding. We've ordered like five more baskets." She glanced at Jenna. "You knew him in high school. Was he always this uptight?"

"Not always." Jenna shot him a look, her hazel eyes twinkling.

She was close enough to kiss. That freckle above her mouth taunted him. Was she wearing lipstick? *Ugh.* He shoveled more fries in his mouth and shrugged at the group. Steph rolled her eyes, and Elisa laughed. The four of them settled into an easy conversation, gabbing about their classes and how Steph wanted someone else to teach AP senior English next year.

"Check, check, check," said Saul into a microphone. "We're just about ready to start karaoke, so come on up if you haven't already and put in your request."

"I already put our names in," said Elisa, with a wicked grin. "You're welcome."

Steph glanced around, as if she thought someone might overhear, then leaned toward Reid and Jenna. "My roommate knows Bailey Brewer and saw her last night, and I heard . . . You already know what I'm going to say, don't you? Is it true?"

"Oh, boy," murmured Jenna.

Reid sighed. "Margot and I broke things off last night."

"Wait, what?" Elisa, who'd been looking at her phone, dropped it on the table and huddled in. "Oh my gosh, are you okay?"

"That's why you came back to the game," said Steph. "Ah, Reid, I'm sorry."

"What happened?" said Elisa.

"Hey, guys, maybe he doesn't want to talk about it." Jenna frowned.

"No, it's fine." He gnawed on another fry while he ran through the best way to summarize the breakup. Jenna wouldn't have told the other two about the resort, would she? No. He could trust her. "We're just really different. People change. There's not much else to say. Anyway, let's have some fun." Lifting his water in a toast, he said, "To a night out with friends."

They clinked their cups together. Jenna gulped half her water, her cheeks still pink.

"All right, everyone," Saul's voice boomed into the microphone. "We are ready to get started. Up first are Steph, Elisa, Reid, and Jenna. That's right folks, our entire Juniper Creek High School English department is here to serenade you. Come on up."

Applause filled the bar, along with shouts of "Go Eagles!" from a few of the other staff who were there. Reid followed his co-workers up to the booth and Saul handed them microphones. Reid looked up at the karaoke monitor, hoping Elisa had at least picked something he knew. The title "Friends in Low Places," by Garth Brooks, flashed on the screen. Okay, he did know this one.

Hopefully Jenna's singing would drown out his frog-like croaks.

The four of them launched into the song, Jenna's sultry voice rising to fill the small bar. Several of the patrons whooped, and Steph shot Reid a startled look. He grinned. He was in no way responsible for Jenna's voice, but he stood a bit straighter anyway.

At the chorus, the three women slung their arms around each other. Jenna draped one arm on Reid's shoulder, drawing him closer. He hesitated, then slipped an arm around her waist.

She fit.

She had always fit. In high school he used to hold her close and think they were made for each other, that her smaller frame was designed to fit against his taller broader one. Holding her to his side now felt like coming home after a long trip, like throwing on pajamas and flopping on the couch with a favorite book. It just made sense.

Some logical part of his brain suggested he take several steps away from Jenna Daly right now. He ignored it.

The four of them swayed back and forth for the rest of the song. Reid had been keeping his voice soft to let Jenna have the forefront, but by the end, Steph and Elisa were belting out the lyrics, and Jenna was laughing so hard she could barely spit out the words. Reid joined in with what his mom had always (affectionately) called his "braying mule."

Just as the song ended, the door opened and a couple people slipped into the bar. Reid's mouth dropped open as he choked out the final words.

Margot and her little sister Bailey had just walked in the door. In a sea of flannel and denim, they stuck out in their fitted jeans, high heels, and black blouses.

Margot's gaze went straight to his.

Reid stared. *What's she doing here?* Margot hated karaoke. He'd tried to convince her to join him at The Angry Pigeon a dozen times and she'd turned him down. Had she guessed he would be here? No, that didn't make sense. She wouldn't come looking for him in a dank bar.

Bailey leaned over and whispered something. Margot shook her head, said something back, and the two women walked toward the bar.

"I can take your mic," said Jenna.

He blinked and looked down.

Jenna held her mic in one hand, her free hand extended waiting to take Reid's mic. Her gaze dropped to the floor as her face turned the color of beet juice.

"Uh, thanks." He passed his mic over.

While Jenna returned the mics, Steph ushered Reid back to their booth. "I just saw Margot. Do you need to leave?"

"No. No, it's fine." His face went hot. It was bad enough running into his ex. He didn't need his colleagues treating him like a little kid and trying to protect him. He sat down, leaning back in the booth. "It's fine."

Steph and Elisa traded looks and slid into the booth.

Jenna hurried up to them. "Are we leaving?" She sounded breathless. "I saw her at the bar."

"He says no." Steph rolled her eyes.

Elisa leaned over and touched Reid's forearm. "Are you sure? We could sneak you out the back."

"Really. No big deal." He turned his head just enough that he could see Margot and Bailey at the bar. They huddled together, frowning as they talked, and his stomach sank.

"Okay, here." Jenna grabbed a half-empty basket of fries and shoved them at Reid. "Eat these and whatever you do, don't look up."

"She's not a vampire," muttered Reid. The three women's solicitous expressions, all of them leaning in, it was suddenly too much. He wanted to crawl out of his skin. He threw up his hands. "It's not a big deal, guys, I'm not dying here. Can you all give me some space? Please?"

"Methinks you doth protest too much," said Steph in a singsong tone, but she scooted back, as did Elisa.

Reid looked toward the bar again and squared his shoulders. *Just get it over with,* he thought. *She's here. Go up and say hello.* To Jenna, he said, "Can you let me out?"

"You're going to talk to her?" Her eyes narrowed. "Is that a good idea?"

"Whether or not it's a good idea, I'm going to do it. It's a small town and we're going to see each other eventually." He shrugged. "Might as well be now."

"Reid, I don't know . . . What if things get heated? You're in a public place."

"It's not your fight, Pixie," he said softly. "I'll be fine."

There it was again, the nickname, on his lips as soft and easy as a prayer. If only she hadn't noticed over the general din of the crowd, if only the elderly man now singing Elvis had drowned out his words. But the small startled rosebud of her mouth told him she'd heard loud and clear.

She slid out of the booth and stood to let him pass.

"I'll be right back," he said to his colleagues. Three sets of narrowed eyes met his declaration. He sighed and trudged across the bar as the Elvis wannabe drawled on.

As he approached the bar, Margot and Bailey swiveled toward him as one unit. "She doesn't want to talk to you," snapped Bailey.

"Bailey," said Margot softly, holding up her hand.

Her left hand.

Reid hadn't seen her ring finger bare in three years, and the sight felt like a punch to the jaw. This had been a bad idea. "I'm sorry," he mumbled. "I'll leave you alone."

"No, wait." Margot touched his arm. "It's okay. Did . . . did you want to go outside for a minute?"

"Sure." He glanced at Bailey, who narrowed her eyes at him. *I wonder what Margot told her.*

"I'll be right back," Margot said to her sister. Glancing at Reid, she hopped down from her barstool and started toward the small hallway. Her high heels crunched over scattered peanut shells.

Reid raced after her, still feeling Bailey's knife-like gaze digging into his skin. He followed her past the bathrooms and through a back door that opened onto a small loading dock and an empty parking lot.

The door slammed shut behind them, and Margot leaned against the side of the building as she adjusted her small cross-body purse. "I figured it was quieter out here."

"Good idea." He noticed goosebumps on her bare arms and had to force himself not to reach for her, to slide his arms around her. He shoved his hands in his pockets and let out a long slow sigh. "So . . ."

She shifted her weight back and forth and rubbed her arms. "Are you and Jenna here, like, together?"

"No, no, definitely not. This is a work thing. The whole department came out. They just all happen to be women." Guilt rose like bile; he had just been staring at Jenna's mouth, wondering what it would feel like to kiss her. Nothing's happened, he reminded himself. They're just meaningless thoughts.

"Okay." She crossed her arms. "I just . . . It's harder than I thought it would be, to see you out with her. Or anyone."

"I'm not *out with her*. And I didn't think I'd see you here."

"Neither did I." She managed a short laugh. "Bailey thought I should do something outside of my comfort zone. She was trying to cheer me up. I forgot about karaoke."

"It's a small town. Guess it's inevitable we'll run into each other."

She sniffed and flicked away a tear. "I know we're really different. I get that you don't want to pour your life into my family's business, and I think we're doing the right thing, but . . . this is hard. I love you. You jerk." She half-smiled, tears pooling in her eyes.

"I love you too." He pulled her into a quick hug. For a moment he was tempted to stay there. To change his mind. He could quit his teaching job, he could become the husband of Margot Brewer, CEO of the Lucky Brewer Resort. They'd have money and stability.

But would they be happy?

Stepping back, he said, "I think we both love each other, or we wouldn't have gotten this far. Maybe we're just not . . ."

"In love?" She nodded and swiped at her eyes. "I've been wondering that too. We've been together so long I've forgotten what being in love is supposed to feel like."

"I think we're supposed to feel more *sure*."

"You're probably right." She exhaled unsteadily. Looking down, she snapped open her small purse and pulled out a familiar small black box. She extended it with a shaking hand. "I was going to bring this by your place tomorrow, but since you're here . . ."

"Oh, Margot, no. Keep it." He couldn't take the ring from her on top of the breakup. "You can sell it if you want, but it's yours."

"I can't possibly keep it, and I would never sell it." She took his left hand and placed the box in his palm. Closing his fingers around the box, she said, "Please take it back."

The edges of the box dug into his palm. His throat closed, and tears turned her into a blur. He grabbed her into a fierce hug and felt her breathing hard against his chest, but she didn't make a sound. When they drew apart, her eyes were dry.

"I'll see you," she said.

"Yes. I'll see you." He cleared his throat. "It's a small town. We'll talk."

She nodded. Turning, she walked back inside. The door slammed behind her.

Reid stood there with his hand clenched around the ring box until he felt sure the wood had cut open his palm. But when he opened his hand again there was just a small red mark on his skin.

Jenna craned her neck toward the bar, but there was no sign of Reid or Margot. She had been checking every thirty seconds or so, waiting to spot them walking back down the little hall. Elisa had told her there was a back door past the bathrooms, and that they had probably gone outside. But that had been twenty minutes ago. What was taking so long? Realistically she knew it wasn't long, not for a first conversation between exes, but it felt as if each minute spanned an hour.

"Jenna, stop looking for Reid. I'm sure he's fine," said Steph. "He'll come back inside when he's ready."

She nodded. "I'm just worried about him."

"I can see that." Steph flicked her brows up.

Jenna flushed. Steph seemed to see right through her anxiety to its source. She was concerned about Reid, but not just as a friend. A small, selfish part of her feared that Reid and Margot were outside kissing and making up.

And why would that be a bad thing? she scolded herself, reaching for her diet Coke. Then he would be happy again.

Would he, though? He hadn't seemed happy at all, except today when they were taking care of Buster. The way he'd explained the breakup with Margot, it sounded like they'd grown apart. She couldn't imagine Reid giving up his teaching career to run a resort; that just didn't sound like him.

She took a sip of the Coke, which had gone flat and tasted of fake sugar. She wrinkled her nose and set down the glass. The cheese fries sat like a greasy brick in her churning stomach.

"Well, Margot's back," said Elisa. "But I don't see Reid."

Jenna's gaze snapped toward the bar, where Margot sat next to her sister. Her heart sank. Had Reid decided to cut and run?

Wouldn't be the first time.

She fought back an unreasonable tide of panic that she knew had nothing to do with this evening. She was right back in high school, standing on her front porch with Reid, tugging the silver promise ring off her finger. Watching him turn and walk away, she had thought she might break in half under the weight of physical, crushing pain.

She hadn't broken. But the scar was still there.

A movement at the front of the bar caught her eye. The front door swung open, and Reid stepped inside. The vise around her chest loosened and she realized she'd been holding her breath.

Reid's shoulders slumped as he trudged toward their booth. He stopped in front of the table and shoved his hands in his pockets. "Sorry about that. I think I'm gonna head out," he said, raising his voice over the three college-age women belting a Lady Gaga song. His gaze locked on Jenna's. "I can pick you up later, if you want."

"Don't be silly, I'll give her a ride home," said Steph.

"No." Jenna reached for her purse. "If you're leaving, then I'm coming with you." She saw pain in those blue eyes, and she couldn't let him leave alone.

"I'm fine . . ." His voice trailed off and he shrugged. "I mean, do what you want."

She flinched at the flat tone of his voice. Turning to Steph and Elisa, she gave them quick hugs across the table. "I'll see you Monday."

She followed Reid outside and they walked toward his truck in silence. The muffled din of singing from the bar faded into the sound of a crow cawing from some nearby rooftop. They passed the front window of the cafe, with its empty pastry case. From somewhere inside the building, a dim safety light cast the interior into deep shadow.

Reid unlocked the passenger-side door and held it open.

"Hey." Jenna touched his shoulder, but he flinched away. Her heart raced. This felt all too much like the summer after graduation, after his dad had died. The stiffness in his shoulders, the sadness darkening his eyes like a stormy ocean, the gaze that said he was a million miles away in his own mind. "Please talk to me."

"Not much to say. She gave me the ring back, we said goodbye." He closed his eyes and rubbed his forehead. "I don't really feel like rehashing the whole thing, okay? Let's just go."

"You're still doing it." Tears threatened to bubble up, a tightness in her throat. "You're pushing people away who care about you. I thought . . ."

"What? You thought I'd changed?" He snorted. "Come on, Pixie, people don't change, not really."

There it was again. The third time he'd called her by her nickname. Her breath caught and she wanted to ask why, or if he was even aware, but she held back. "You don't have to talk about the breakup, but you're clearly not okay. I'm not letting you go home in this state."

"I'm in a normal state for a person who just went through a breakup. And it's not your job to protect me. You always . . ." He shook his head. "Never mind."

Always what? Always looked out for him? Always tried to save him from his own grief? She pursed her lips and searched for words that wouldn't put him further on the defensive. "Could we just take a walk before we go home? Down to the park, maybe?" *If I can stay with him, I can get him to talk.*

"I guess we could take a quick walk." He slammed the door shut and locked the truck. Pocketing the keys, he started down the sidewalk.

Jenna fell into step beside him. They turned onto Main Street, which took them past City Hall, a square brick building with arched windows and a wide set of front steps bordered by iron rails. "That's where they're having Homecoming, right?"

"Yep. Funny, we only got the gym."

"Well, those were the olden days," she said. "You know, when we walked a mile to school uphill in the snow and all."

"Right." He snorted. "No, wait, senior prom was at that country club in Bend. Whose family was it that had a connection?"

"Steve Markham." Jenna shook her head, remembering the excitement that had swept the senior class upon learning their prom would be at such an upscale location as a country club. She'd imagined some kind of colonnaded mansion, and had felt a rush of disappointment as she and Reid pulled up in front of a nondescript brick building. The interior had been dark and low-ceilinged, and the dining room had smelled faintly of ketchup. "The music was super-quiet, remember? And the chocolate fountain broke."

"I forgot about the fountain." Reid laughed. "Didn't people start scooping out chocolate with punch cups?"

"Yes! Allie Wright spilled it all down the front of her white dress." Jenna grimaced.

Reid chuckled. "And then we all drove to Allie's parents' beach house and got there at some ungodly hour."

"Three a.m. You fell asleep on the floor and used your jacket for a pillow. You gave me your sleeping bag because we had only brought one." She still remembered waking up the next morning, rolling over on the couch to see Reid curled up on the rug.

Past City Hall, they took a right onto Main Street. A few minutes later they veered onto a small side path that led down to Juniper Creek and its namesake park. The park featured only native plants: bushy thinleaf alders with pale green leaves; clumps of purple sage; and wax currants. A paved path wound through the park on the south side of the riverbank. Jenna and Reid took an empty bench under the canopy of a juniper tree and sat back.

Jenna inhaled, filling her lungs with the woodsy, citrusy scent of the juniper tree. A full moon shone, tinging the sky an indigo color. She leaned her head back and felt her temple brush Reid's shoulder. Whoops. Too close. She shifted left and crossed her arms and stared up at the cold moon, struck by the vast canopy of the sky.

"You're shivering." Reid was slipping off his jacket. "Here."

"I'm fine."

"You always used to say that." He draped the jacket over her shoulders.

She wasn't sure if he pulled her towards him, or if she was the one to lean in. One second his hand was lingering on her shoulder, adjusting the fabric, and the next second she was snuggled into the crook of his arm with her head against his chest. An electric charge seemed to shoot down her spine, along with a nauseating sense that she had entered dangerous territory. She froze there, not wanting to move, not wanting to ruin anything.

After a moment, when Reid didn't seem inclined to spring away from her like she was a lump of molten iron, she relaxed into his chest. But only slightly. Arms crossed. Couldn't get too comfortable. She tipped her head up to look at the sky again and said, "Did I ever tell you I used to think about falling up?"

His chest shook slightly with a deep chuckle. "What do you mean?"

"Into the sky. When I was a kid, I'd go out on the porch at night to watch the stars, and I'd try to imagine I was floating up toward the moon, into outer space. How the air would get thinner and colder until I was above the earth. Floating through the void."

"And you were going to survive this scenario how? There's no oxygen in outer space."

"I don't know, I never thought about it." She shrugged. "I just thought it would be cool to fly into space. I was a kid. A weird one, I guess."

"No, that's cute, Pixie."

She bolted upright. "Reid, why do you keep calling me that? My nickname? From when we . . ."

He groaned. "I don't know. It just slips out. I don't know."

Why don't you know? She wanted to scream at him. Did it mean something? And if she wanted it to, why was that?

They stared at each other. His chest lifted in shallow breaths. He started to lean toward her.

"We shouldn't," she said.

He froze. "I'm sorry."

"No, I'm sorry." She shimmied out of his jacket and practically shoved it in his hands. "We have to be careful. We probably shouldn't even be out here." It was too easy to fall into old patterns. He was twenty-four hours out of an engagement, and she was, what? Stuck in the past? Afraid to let go of something they had when they were children?

Reid stood as well but kept his distance. "Maybe the problem is that we're overthinking it."

She frowned. "What? How?"

"Well, we used to date, and that's awkward. But I'm also just out of an engagement, which is also awkward. So we're trying to be careful about what we say and walking on eggshells around each other. If we just agree we're friends, we can stop worrying about everything and we can just enjoy being friends. There's nothing wrong with being friends. We just can't let anything get in the way of that."

"Okay." She narrowed her eyes. His argument didn't make a ton of sense, but maybe he had a point somewhere in that rambling speech. Maybe they were overcomplicating it.

He held out his hand to shake. "Friends and friends only?"

"Friends and friends only." She grasped his hand, warm and comforting. It took effort to pull away. *Oh, crud.* "I think I'm ready to go home."

They were silent on the walk back to his truck, and silent on the drive back to the Daly farm. Jenna pressed her cheek against the cool passenger window, trying to calm the hot flush on her face, and ran through a mantra. *Just friends just friends just friends.* This stomach-twisting sensation every time she was near him was just anxiety over navigating their adult relationship. Her nostalgia about his warm hands or the way he used to give her his jacket all the time was simply that—nostalgia. Something automatic, or the remnant of something long gone, an echo. Just like when he'd called her Pixie, it was a reflex, a meaningless habit.

As Reid pulled up in front of the farmhouse, he said, "Thanks for the fries and the karaoke, buddy of mine."

Jenna smiled and unbuckled. "No problem. I'll see you Monday."

As she walked toward the house, her heart sank. Behind her she heard the crunch of gravel as Reid backed out of the drive. Nothing had changed between them at all, and yet somehow, something had shifted. A tiny crack in plaster, water damage creeping unnoticed up a baseboard, the first stirrings of a shift in a tectonic plate. The quiet moment before the glass slips from your fingers and shatters on the floor. She was falling up, drawn by the gravitational pull of Reid into the sky. If she wasn't careful, she knew, she'd float completely away from the earth, and drift away.

Jenna let out a sigh as the last student exited her classroom. Her prep period was next, and for once she didn't prop her door open. She shut it, then sat down at her desk, relishing in the quiet. Today had been odd, even for a Monday. Her normally quiet third-period class had been chatty and distracted; her new lesson on journalism terms had resulted in several students staring at her with blank expressions; and when she'd run into Reid this morning at the copy machine, he'd said hello with head bent, avoiding eye contact.

She couldn't stop thinking about Saturday night, about the solid warmth of Reid's chest, the way he'd leaned toward her in the moonlight. For a second she'd been sure he was going to kiss her. Or that she was going to kiss him.

She had to stop. Stop thinking about him, stop wanting to talk to him all the time, stop replaying the soft intensity of his voice calling her Pixie. They had sworn to be friends. She had to stick to that.

Someone knocked on the door. Jenna flinched and looked up, half-expecting Reid. But it was Tessa Morgan who peered through the glass pane. Jenna waved her in.

Tessa opened the door and quietly shut it behind her. "Miss Daly, do you have a second?" Her voice shook, and her chin wobbled.

"What's wrong? Please sit down."

Her student let out a shaky sigh, dragged a chair over to Jenna's desk, flopped down, and burst into tears.

"Oh, oh dear," murmured Jenna. "Okay, here." She shoved an entire box of tissues at the girl, then rummaged around in her desk. She kept a steady supply of protein bars, something she'd long ago learned was necessary to making it through a long day of teaching. She pulled out three different flavors and held them all out to Tessa. "Are you hungry?"

The girl nodded, sniffling, and picked the chocolate protein bar. As she unwrapped it, she added, "I'm supposed to be in Chemistry right now. I just—I can't. I have that class with Ryan, and . . ." Her voice trailed off, and tears ran down her cheeks. She grabbed a handful of tissues and blotted her nose.

"Ryan Brandon?" said Jenna. "Your co-chair on the Homecoming committee?"

Tessa took an enormous bite of the protein bar. "Uh-huh. And you know Melissa Cantrell?"

Ah. Jenna was pretty sure she knew where this was going. "She's a senior, right? Cheerleader?"

"Yeah, well, he just asked her out. And they're going to Homecoming together." Her voice slightly garbled around her snack, Tessa went on, "Ryan and I have been hanging out a lot, you know, because of the committee. I thought we were, like, close. But Melissa's a senior and she's gorgeous, so I guess she wins."

A familiar sadness settled into Jenna's chest. Hadn't she felt the same way when Reid got together with Margot? That somehow, Margot's willowy frame and glossy blonde hair proved that she was more worthy of Reid's love. As if the new relationship demonstrated that Jenna had never been enough. Now here Tessa was, a smart and beautiful girl with a bright smile, berating herself for losing to another girl. And losing what? A guy who didn't recognize her worth? She handed Tessa another tissue and leaned forward. "Relationships are tough. But you're a wonderful girl. If Ryan can't see that, then someone better will."

"But I like Ryan so much." Tessa's eyes filled with tears again. "He's funny and sweet and cute and we like all the same things."

"I know it's hard."

"How do you know? Has this ever happened to you?" Tessa shoved the remaining protein bar in her mouth and slumped in her seat.

"Oh, yes. I had my heart thoroughly broken in high school."

"Really?" Tessa raised her eyebrows. "What happened?"

Now what? She couldn't mention Reid by name. Maybe if she just omitted some details . . . "I was in love with this guy for . . . years, really. We dated my senior year and then he broke up with me over the summer. I never heard from him again." Until this year, but if she said that, Tessa would figure out the identity of Jenna's lost love pretty quickly.

"He, like, ghosted you? That's so harsh."

"Well, he was going through some fairly serious things at the time. What's important is that I eventually got through it. I know it sounds trite, but so will you."

"Thanks, Miss Daly." Tessa folded the protein bar wrapper in half and dabbed her nose with her wad of tissues. "Do you have a boyfriend now?"

Jenna laughed. Students always inevitably wanted to know the relationship status of their teachers. "Not right now, no."

"I heard Mr. W. is single now."

She kept her face blank. "Oh?"

"Everyone's talking about it. He and Margot Brewer broke up. He's pretty cute, Miss Daly. You should go out with him."

"That's very sweet of you to think of me," said Jenna. She reached for the wad of tissues and scooped them into the garbage. "But I'm sure Mr. Walsh has other things on his mind if he just broke up with his fiancée."

"I hate boys," sighed Tessa. "I don't even have a date for the dance. *Me*. I'm on the Homecoming committee."

"You don't need a date to go to the dance," said Jenna firmly. "Why can't you go with a group of your friends from the team?"

"I probably will, it's just . . . not the same." Tessa heaved another huge sigh and wiped her eyes with the back of her sleeve. Her nose was slightly swollen, but otherwise she didn't appear to have been crying. "Thanks, Miss Daly. Can you write me a note to be late to math? Can you *please* not say why? Ryan's in that class and if he finds out I cried over him, I'll die of humiliation."

"Don't worry. We'll say you were doing a make-up test." Jenna scribbled an excuse note for her and handed it over.

"Thanks again, Miss Daly." Tessa gave her a shaky smile and hopped up. She walked toward the door, her shoulders a little higher, chin lifted.

Jenna felt tears sting her own eyes and reached for a tissue. This was why she'd become a teacher, back when she was a bright-eyed graduate student, before she'd realized just how much teaching felt like an uphill battle, before she'd encountered difficult parents and disengaged kids and mountains of grading. She had wanted to make a difference. You could go days, weeks, months, without feeling like you were having an influence on any student at all. Moments like this made the job worth it.

The rest of her prep period flew by, followed by her final seventh-period class. Tessa was in that class, and she seemed like her bright and lively self, which was a good sign.

When the last students left, Jenna looked at the two-inch-high stack of essays sitting on her desk. Ugh. She had at least a few hours of grading ahead, and she'd promised her dad she would start exercising Buster, the family's horse, every evening. *This is gonna take some serious caffeine.*

She headed to the teachers' lounge, which was located off the cafeteria. The small room boasted industrial dark orange carpet that probably came from the 1980s, a few small tables and a threadbare couch, and a fridge. When she walked in, Steph and Elisa sat at one of the small tables together. They huddled next to each other, voices low, frowns deep.

"Hi," said Jenna. "You guys okay?"

Steph glanced over her shoulder. "Oh, hey. We're commiserating. Want to join us?"

"As soon as I get some fuel." Jenna opened the cabinet and grabbed a mug from the random assortment. This one had a cracked handle and read "A+ Teacher." She filled it nearly to the brim, then plopped into the seat next to Steph and took a sip of her coffee. Tepid, but still strong. "What's going on?"

"I'm losing my star volleyball player."

Jenna winced. She knew how much Steph loved coaching. Last week Jenna and Elisa had gone to a game, and the whole time, Steph had been right there on the sidelines, calling out instructions, encouraging her players. The team had come back from a slow start to tie and then beat Pilot Butte. At the end of the game, the girls had pulled Steph into a crushing mass hug and when they backed away, Steph had been wiping tears from her eyes.

For a second Jenna thought Tessa was dropping out, but that wouldn't make sense. Tessa loved volleyball as much as Steph did. "Who's leaving?"

"Rose Morris. She's the co-captain."

"And a senior," said Elisa. "Don't forget that. She's about to lose out on her whole senior year."

The name rang a bell now. Rose was six feet tall, and she'd scored the winning point at last week's game. "Wait, isn't she the one you told me was playing for U of O next year? Why would she drop out?"

"She and her family are moving to Portland. Next week." Steph shook her head. "Rose is devastated. Three of her friends have already offered to put her up for the year, but her parents said no."

Jenna swirled the coffee around in her cup. "Why would they move now?"

Elisa shrugged. "Her parents sold their farm to Ed Brewer. I guess it wasn't doing too well, with all the water restrictions this last year."

Jenna's stomach sank. The Morris farm also abutted the Lucky Brewer Ranch. Was Ed grabbing for any land he could? "You know, he offered to buy my parents' place, too."

"It's been tough for a lot of people these last few years," said Steph. "I hear irrigation costs are way up."

"They are." Jenna's parents had told her the water district had tightly restricted irrigation water this past year, and that the price per acre had skyrocketed. They'd had to selectively irrigate only certain fields, letting others lie fallow. Profits from the sale of alfalfa, which hadn't been high to begin with, had dipped. "It's probably for the resort, don't you think?"

"What resort?" said Steph.

Oh, crud. Jenna chewed on her lip, a cold sick sensation washing over her. She'd promised Reid she wouldn't say anything, but . . . "I wasn't supposed to tell you. Ed Brewer wants to build a high-end resort on his property. Like Black Butte Ranch, I guess. With a golf course and fancy cabins and stuff."

Elisa wrinkled her nose. "How is it responsible to build a golf course in the middle of water restrictions?"

"Exactly."

Steph frowned. "I suppose the tourism could be good for the town, but . . ."

"But it would change everything." Jenna ran her finger over the handle of her mug, tracing the tiny fault line in the ceramic. Tourists would inject money into the economy, but they would also bring traffic and noise. Take the Angry Pigeon, for example. She could easily imagine it changing from a funky, fun local watering hole into a pit stop for obnoxious out-of-towners. Karaoke nights wouldn't be the same. And if Ed Brewer bought up acres of farmland, what would happen to people's livelihoods? Would they end up working for Ed, serving five-dollar lattes to retired vacationers? Would they end up leaving?

The door creaked open behind her. Jenna twisted in her seat, her stomach zinging as Reid walked in.

"Well, that was a day," he said. "Is there something in the water?"

"Something," muttered Steph. "It's gonna be a long road to Christmas break."

Reid wandered over to the coffee maker and lifted it, testing its weight. "Sweet, there's still caffeine in here?" He poured a cup and raised his eyebrows at the three women. "What? Do I have something on my face? Is my fly unzipped?"

"Rose Morris is moving to Portland with her family," said Steph. "The whole team is upset, especially Rose. She doesn't want to leave all of her friends her senior year."

Reid frowned and rubbed his jaw. "That's too bad."

"I know," said Steph.

"Is Jenna right?" said Elisa. "Did Ed Brewer buy the Morris farm for that resort he's building?"

Reid narrowed his eyes at Jenna. "You weren't supposed to say anything."

"How can I not? He offered to buy my folks' place, too. Did Margot tell you that?"

He stared at her for several moments. "No." Lifting his mug, he took a swill of his coffee.

"Well, don't you think it's a little greedy?" Jenna crossed her arms. Didn't he care that Ed was trying to take away her parents' farm? The one they'd owned since before Jenna was born, the only home she'd ever known. "Just how big is this resort going to be?"

"And who else is he trying to buy out?" said Elisa, her brown eyes flashing.

Reid set his mug down on the counter with a hard crack. "I don't know. The Brewer family doesn't tell me every detail of their plans. But Margot and her family are creating an entire marketing campaign around the resort, and they have a very specific timeline for the launch. If this gets passed around town, and she finds out I'm the one who spilled the beans, she won't be happy with me."

"I thought you were broken up." Steph's eyes snapped. "Why do you care what she thinks?"

"Because I care, okay? I promised her I wouldn't say anything. My promises mean something." He leveled a look at Jenna, which sliced straight to her gut.

"Well, this community means something too." Steph shot out of her seat. "So you should have warned *someone,* at least, when you found out the Brewers were planning this. What are they buying next, City

Hall?" She stalked out of the teachers' lounge. The door clapped shut behind her.

"Um, I'll be, uh . . ." muttered Elisa. She sprang out of her chair like a rabbit and bounded out of the room.

Reid turned to Jenna. "You understand that this puts me in an incredibly awkward position with Margot and her family. Why would you tell Steph and Elisa about this?"

"I'm sorry, but I can't sit back when Ed's trying to grab all the land he can find. It seems . . . well . . . greedy. Doesn't it?"

He crossed his arms. "I think the Morris farm has been struggling, and Ed saw an opportunity."

Jenna's jaw tightened. "Like the 'opportunity' to buy my parents' farm?"

"You said things have been tough there, too. I'm sure it's business, pure and simple."

"But farming is a way of life here." She leaned forward. "For a lot of families, their farms are all they have. You really support people losing their livelihoods to a golf course?"

"I don't know, Jenna, it's not my business. The Morrises sold willingly." He put his hands up. "I'd really rather not discuss this. The Brewers have been like family to me. I have a lot of respect for Ed, whatever you think of him. If the rumor mill keeps running, it could ruin their whole plan. Margot and her family don't deserve that." He got up and started toward the door.

Jenna ran after him. "My family's involved too. My parents are in a vulnerable situation right now, and I think Ed's taking advantage of that."

He shrugged. "I don't know what to tell you. I can't take sides here."

Oh. Once again, he was choosing Margot over her. Even when the two were no longer together. He was taking sides, even if he didn't think he was. Jenna bit down on the inside of her cheek and sucked in a breath. *Don't let him get to you*, she thought, but she stood so close she could smell his pine-scented aftershave, so close she could have reached up to brush the hair away from his tanned forehead. Her traitorous fingers twitched at her side.

"I need to go," he muttered. He turned and walked out the door.

Jenna forced her breath out through her nose with a slight vibration at the back of her throat, a technique she'd learned in yoga class. She looked around the now-empty break room. Did she hide out in here or go back to her classroom?

The stack of papers on her desk beckoned, reminding her they needed grading. The problem was, if she left now, she'd walk right by Reid's room. Also, she'd probably walk right by Reid, because he was only about ten feet down the hall.

Well, so be it. Chin in the air, maybe an inch higher than was actually necessary, Jenna strode down the hall. *Move, short legs.* She power-walked, weaving around a couple students heading the opposite direction and quickly caught up to Reid. *Don't look at him, pretend you don't see him.* She walked right by him, facing forward. His blonde hair bounced into her peripheral vision, and she sped up.

Reid passed her, jaw set, stalking down the hall. He always had such long legs.

She broke into a jog. A necessary pace when competing against someone a foot taller than you.

"Running in the halls is against the rules, Miss Daly!" Reid said.

She glanced over her shoulder, just long enough to make eye contact, then ran down the hallway, her sneakers screeching across the linoleum. She raced to the end of the hall, yanked open her classroom door and dashed inside.

Sitting back down at her desk, she flipped through the pile of papers and pulled out an essay at random. Picking up her green pen—she never graded in red because it made students nervous and had a punitive association—she started reading Cam Jordan's essay. She read the first paragraph four times before she understood what it said.

Groaning, she tossed down her pen. Reid! That man was infuriating. Here he was interfering with what should have been a nice productive grading session. How could he side with Margot's family on this? How could he be so casual about the impact this resort would have on Juniper Creek? Especially when Jenna's own family might be affected?

And especially when, just a couple days ago, he had almost kissed her?

The problem was, she shouldn't have agreed to be friends with him. They couldn't be friends; they couldn't even have a rational conversation. Reid was always putting up walls, and that didn't work for her anymore. Not even in a friend.

She picked up the pen again and felt the heavy weight of finality in her chest. From now on, she'd be nice to Reid, but that was it. No chitchat in the break room, no weekend karaoke, and he better not try to come help out at her parents' place again. She should have known that getting close to Reid Walsh only got you burned.

Jenna locked her classroom door behind her and twisted the handle to check. She hadn't meant to stay quite so late, but she'd blazed through a huge pile of grading, so it had been worth it. She'd told her parents she would be home late, but still, if she didn't leave soon, her mother would probably assume she was dead in a ditch and come looking for her.

Her stomach rumbled at her, reminding her she hadn't fed it since 11:30 a.m. She headed down the corridor, passing Reid's dark, empty classroom. She was probably the last teacher in the building, except for Pam. Steph had said she'd left once at nine p.m. and the principal's light was still on. Elisa claimed Pam had a sleeping bag in her office. Wouldn't be that surprising, really. Pam often said the Juniper Creek High School community was her family.

On the drive home, Jenna wondered what Reid was doing tonight. Grading? Ordering pizza? For some reason she pictured him in a dark living room curled up on a couch, a Perry Mason rerun flickering shadows across his face. He'd always liked Perry Mason. The image made her heart sink, but she pushed it away. Reid was more of the type to hide in his work than drown his sorrows in a pint of ice cream. Probably grading or lesson-planning.

When she pulled into her parents' driveway, her stomach flipped over. In her usual spot sat Reid's truck, attached to a small horse trailer. She pulled up beside the black Ford and got out. It quickly became obvious he wasn't in the car, and as she walked around to the back of the trailer, one of the doors fell open. Inside sat a saddle, blanket, and tack box.

What in the world? Had Reid bought a horse? What was he doing here?

The barn doors were open. As she walked inside, she caught the cadence of male voices. Reid and her dad. Curiosity growing, she hurried to the end of the aisle.

Reid and her dad stood outside the stall next to Buster's. The stall was occupied by a muscular dappled grey horse with a white mane.

"Thanks for doing this, again," said Reid to her dad.

Doing what? Had Reid actually bought a horse? Maybe her dad had advised him on the purchase? But then why was the horse looking so comfy in that stall?

Buster dropped his head over the edge of his stall and whickered at Jenna. She rubbed his velvet nose absently. "What's, uh, what's going on here?"

Reid turned toward her with the same expression a kid would wear if caught with their hand in the cookie jar. "Well . . . this is my horse, Deschutes."

"Since when do you own a horse?" She heard the sharpness in her own voice and cleared her throat. "I mean, you've never mentioned this."

"I rescued him last year, through the Humane Society. He was a neglect case. Skin and bones when I got him."

His eyes went round and sad, and Jenna's irritation melted. You couldn't be annoyed at someone who would save a neglected animal. "So he's here because . . . ?"

"Your dad offered to board him. I was keeping him at the Brewer ranch, but . . ."

Right. He couldn't very well board his horse at his ex-fiancée's. Awkward. Trying to keep her voice level, she said, "Is this just a temporary thing?"

"It's a trade," said her dad. "Reid's gonna work here three nights a week in exchange for board. He's gonna ride Buster, too."

Her dad, ever generous. He could have charged Reid for board and actually made money for the farm, but no, he was trading services. She gritted her teeth. "Dad, I'm exercising him already." Did her dad not think she was doing a good enough job? But at his raised eyebrows, she added, "But I'm sure he could use more outings."

"We're trying it out for a month, seeing how it goes." David took a step back from the stall. He turned and gave Jenna a quick hug. "I've gotta go help your mother with dinner. Reid, you're welcome to join us."

Sure, why not? Reid might as well just move into the guest room while he was at it.

"I'll help you and Mom," she said. She glanced at Reid, but he was petting Deschutes. Not even going to say goodbye to her? Okay then.

As soon as she and her dad were out of earshot of the barn, she said, "Dad, you're really letting him keep that horse here?"

"Why not? Thought you guys were friends?"

"We are, but . . . he's being . . . difficult."

"I see." Her dad rubbed his mustache. "Well, difficult or not, he's an extra pair of hands and we could really use those. The rest, you two will have to work out." He slid his arm around her shoulders and squeezed. "Why don't you go show Reid where to put all his gear? The man *is* giving me free labor. I can help your mother."

"Sure." She sighed and trudged back toward the barn. So now, three days a week, she would see Reid at home as well as at school. It might not be that hard to avoid him, though. If he came by in the mornings, she could just go to school extra-early those days. If he planned to help out in the evenings, she would stay late. She just needed to find out his schedule so she could work around it.

As she approached the stall, Reid looked up. "You're back."

"Dad wanted me to show you where to put your tack." She pointed across the aisle to a small stall that the family was using to store saddles, bridles, and miscellaneous cleaning supplies. "There should be room in there." Duty done, she wheeled around.

"Pixie."

The nickname stopped her in her tracks. She closed her eyes, bracing against the warmth that spread through her chest. She turned. "Yeah?"

"I'm sorry to spring this on you. I only talked to Margot this morning. She used to keep Deschutes for free, but now that we're broken up, she wants to charge me full price. I can't afford that. I couldn't think of anyone to call besides your dad."

Jenna grimaced, in spite of herself. Lucky Brewer Ranch definitely catered to a high-end clientele. Many of the horses the Brewers boarded were show horses whose owners lived in Bend or Redmond. Jenna herself probably couldn't afford riding lessons at the ranch, much less full room and board for a horse.

"Today was chaos, and I tried to find you after school to talk about it, but I couldn't," he said. "I know we don't see eye to eye on Ed Brewer buying the Morris farm, but that doesn't mean I want your folks to lose their farm. I offered to pay your dad to board Deschutes, and he wouldn't let me. Offering to do chores was the best I could do." He spread his hands, palms up.

The steel around her heart threatened to melt. "My dad's real stubborn." She stepped closer to the stall door and held her hand palm up to Deschutes' nose, letting him sniff her hand. He nudged his nose against her hand and made a snuffling sound. Laughing, she stroked the side of his face. His white-spotted grey coat felt like silk. "What a sweetie. He's gorgeous."

"Isn't he? It took me weeks to get him to trust me. He loves people now, though." Reid reached up and patted Deschutes' neck.

As if the horse knew they were talking about him, he lifted his head and whickered. Then he dropped his head over Reid's shoulder, almost like a horse hug. It was ridiculously cute, too cute for Jenna to be mad at Reid.

He paused and shuffled from one foot to the other. "Look, I really do want to be friends. I'm going to be here three days a week."

"I was about to ask your schedule." She smiled wryly.

"Monday, Wednesday, and Thursday evenings. Why, were you planning to stay late at school to avoid me?" His blue eyes twinkled, and she realized with a flutter that he could still read her, better than she'd realized.

"Maybe." She crossed her arms. "But I might be convinced to go riding with you. If we're going to be friends."

"I'd like that."

"Do you want to take the horses out now?" The words flew out of her mouth before she could stop them. "Deschutes needs to get used to his new home, and Buster loves going out."

He grinned. "That would be great. I just need to grab all his gear."

"I'll get changed."

Up in her room, she tried on three shirts in a row before picking one, and then fussed with her hair in the mirror over her dresser. Why did she care what she looked like? She'd just agreed to be friends with Reid. Friends. It didn't matter if he thought she looked cute in her riding shirt, or if he noticed that she was leaving her hair loose under her hat.

So why did she feel like a teenager again, competing for the attention of a boy she liked?

She took one final, critical look at her reflection and then rolled her eyes. "Get it together, girl," she muttered to herself. This was ridiculous. She didn't need to impress Reid, and loose hair was impractical when riding. She threw her hair in a braid and ran back out to the barn.

By that time, Reid had saddled up Buster for her, as well. They led the two horses outside, and let them spend a few minutes sniffing each other, getting acquainted. Satisfied that their animals would get along, Jenna and Reid mounted up.

"Where to?" said Reid.

She thought for a moment. "Towhee Canal?" The canal ran north of the Daly farm, and it was a nice, flat ride out in the open. With daylight waning soon, she didn't want to go too far.

"Sounds good to me."

Jenna nudged Buster forward, and set off through the pasture to go for a nice, friendly ride with her ex.

Reid and Jenna rode side by side through the pasture. The temperature had dropped to the mid-fifties, and the air felt clean and fresh. Scattered clouds, puffy as sheep, drifted in the sky. In the evening light, the clusters of sagebrush turned gold, and the pine trees appeared olive green. It was beautiful, thought Reid.

So was his riding companion.

He wished Jenna didn't look so distractingly lovely. Her thick red hair, woven into a braid, shone copper in the sun. Her hat shaded her smiling, freckled face, and she rode with an easy confidence. She just . . . glowed.

She always had.

Talk about something, anything. He couldn't just sit here in silence, or he would keep thinking these dangerous thoughts. He searched for something neutral to ask her about. "How were your classes today?"

"Fine," she said. "Tessa seemed to be doing better today, which was good."

"Tessa Morgan, right? Homecoming committee? What do you mean, better?"

"Yesterday she came to my room completely heartbroken because Ryan Brandon asked Melissa Cantrell to Homecoming. Poor thing. I told her I'd had my heart broken before, and funny enough, that seemed to cheer her up."

His shoulders tensed. "You tell students those kinds of personal details?"

"Not typically. She was just so upset. I mean, sobbing at my desk." Jenna shook her head. "It's rough being a teenage girl."

His stomach flipped. Ordinarily he would feel bad for Tessa too, but right now he needed to know exactly what Jenna had told her. Whatever it was, the information was probably all over school by now. "We can't have students knowing our history. It could affect how they see us in the classroom."

She shot him a narrow-eyed look. "How do you know I was talking about you?"

"Oh." He cleared his throat. "You weren't?"

"Well, no, I was." Her cheeks went red.

The blush derailed his annoyance, the way it highlighted her high cheekbones, a contrast to her creamy freckled skin. Argh. He was a lost cause.

"But I didn't tell her *details*, Reid, good heavens. I didn't even say your name. I'm not that indiscreet." She nudged Buster, moving ahead of him.

"I'm sorry. I'm a little sensitive right now." He pulled even with her and glanced at her profile. She was chewing on her lower lip. He fidgeted with his grip on the reins and added, "Was it bad for you? When we broke up?"

She didn't answer for so long that he would have thought she didn't hear him, except she was still gnawing on her lip. He waited, sucking in anxious breaths of lemon-and-cedar air.

"I was devastated. You were my first love. I mean . . ." She shrugged.

Reid's throat closed up as he thought back to that summer. He still remembered the exact moment he'd realized he had to break up with Jenna.

***

The details were as sharply embedded in his mind as a carving scratched into rock. He and Jenna had been watching a movie at her house, and she'd fallen asleep in the crook of his arm. Reid had stared down at her, taking in the slight droop of her sleepy mouth, the deep shadows under her eyes. She'd been up until three a.m. with him the night before, talking to him on the phone until he finally drifted into a restless sleep.

Most nights since his dad's heart attack, he didn't sleep at all. He would lie awake and stare up at the ceiling, missing his dad so much it physically hurt, terrified and angry at the same time. His mom was already talking about selling their ranch. She couldn't afford to keep it going on her own. What if something happened to her, too? What if the same freak heart attack that had taken his own father—two weeks ago now—was due to a genetic cause, and it took him too?

What if something happened to Jenna?

He looked down at her again. Since his dad died, she'd been with him every day. She had brought dinner. She had helped him and his mom sort boxes of his dad's belongings. She had gone to the funeral.

Reid loved her, so much.

It wasn't enough. He wasn't enough. He could feel nothing but pain now, could sense himself recoiling from the haunted, sympathetic look in his girlfriend's eyes.

He and Jenna were about to go off to different colleges, and even though Corvallis and Eugene were less than an hour away from each other, he knew it was going to be too far. He couldn't bear to be away from her, but he couldn't bear the weight of her love, either.

He was holding Jenna back. And he had to let her go.

***

"I almost didn't go through with it." His voice cracked as he looked at Jenna now. "I just knew if I didn't do it then, I wouldn't do it at all. I know how it probably looked, getting together with Margot, but that was a total surprise. I wasn't looking. I swear. I . . . I thought I'd never get over you."

"Oh." Jenna's voice was raw and scratchy. She pulled Buster to an abrupt stop, and Reid stopped Deschutes next to her.

He looked over at her. She was using her sleeve to wipe her eyes. "Sheesh. I didn't mean to start crying. Sorry."

"Hey, it's okay, Pixie." He couldn't stop the old nickname from leaving his lips once again, and on impulse he reached over and squeezed her hand. She held on tight, but after a few moments, she released his hand.

"We're doing that thing again," she said, sniffling. "The thing where we fall into old patterns."

"Right. I'm sorry." Reid dropped her hand, reflecting that he seemed to be saying the wrong things and apologizing all over the place lately.

"No, I'm sorry."

"We're just two apologetic people." He chuckled, and after a moment she did too. "Speaking of apologizing," he added. "I wanted to say I'm sorry for not being more understanding of how you felt about the resort. I know that farm has been in your family for generations. And it's sad for Rose Morris to have to move her senior year. I do get that."

"Thank you," she said, with a small but grateful smile. "I'm sorry I spilled the beans to Steph and Elisa."

"I understand. I actually had an idea." He'd thought of the idea a bit earlier, and he hoped it would show Jenna he did appreciate where she was coming from. "When are you starting the journalism unit?" All sophomore English classes surveyed several different styles of writing, from journalism to memoirs.

"Soon, actually," she said. "Why?"

"Why don't you ask the students to report on water scarcity in Juniper Creek? I'm sure that had an impact on the Morris family's decision to sell. Your students could research water rights, talk about the impact of water issues on the local community. They could write in-depth profiles about some of the local farms. I mean, half of them live on farms. Maybe make a rule that they have to interview another family besides their own."

"Huh," she said. "That's actually a really good idea."

"You could even have them submit their stories to the school paper. Or the *Gazette*." The local paper came out once a week. Reid had thought about having his own students submit to the *Gazette,* back when he taught sophomore English, but he'd been too busy to call the paper and arrange something.

"They'd love that." Her face lit up. "I wonder if I can get one of the writers for the *Gazette* to come talk to my classes."

"I'm sure you could. I just have one request."

"Don't tell the students about the resort?" Her eyes sparked fire. "Don't you think that's a perfect topic for the journalism unit? It's a prime example of how water scarcity is impacting our community. I could call Margot to ask her permission, if that would help."

The thought of Jenna calling his ex-fiancée made him regret having such a big dinner. "That might stir up too much dust, don't you think?"

"You mean it might make things awkward with Margot." Her eyes flashed. "You know it won't matter if the town hears about the resort through a shiny marketing campaign or a class project. They're not going to like it either way."

"Some of them might," he said. "What about the boost to our economy from tourism?"

"Well, maybe one of my students can write about that," she said archly. She kicked Buster into high gear, and they took off at a canter.

Reid sighed and nudged Deschutes after her. Stubborn woman.

She glanced over her shoulder at him, then pushed Buster into a gallop. Reid glared, but in spite of himself, laughter bubbled up in his chest. *All right, if that's what you want.* He urged Deschutes on.

The two horses pulled even, and they galloped side by side across the open field.

Leaving the Daly property, they turned onto a narrow road that meandered past other farms. Jenna finally drew Buster down to a walk, and Reid fell into line behind her. "Not bad for a city girl," he said.

She tossed her braid over her shoulder. "City girl? I was born and raised here, the same as you."

"Yes, but you've been away. Living it up in the big city, forgetting how to hold proper form while riding. I saw your heels go up in your stirrups. You're supposed to keep them down, you know."

"You're infuriating," said Jenna, but she was laughing.

They took the road at an easy pace. After about a quarter mile, it curved around and met up with a dirt road that ran east-west along the banks of the Towhee Canal. Ditch riders used it when inspecting the canal and its head gate. But irrigation season had ended in early September, and the head gate had been closed and locked. The canal was dry now, and it would remain so until next spring.

Reid eyed the dimming sky and wished he and Jenna had thought to bring headlamps. He started to ask her if she wanted to turn around, but a dark coil on the path ahead caught his eye, and he froze.

It was a rattlesnake.

"Snake," he said sharply, pulling Deschutes up short.

Jenna tugged on Buster's reins, but the horse snorted and sidestepped.

The snake writhed and rattled its tail.

"Come on, buddy." Jenna nudged Buster with her heels and moved the reins, but the horse wasn't turning around. He snorted and reared up on his back legs. Then he wheeled and took off at a dead gallop through an open field, with Jenna clinging to his back.

Reid's heart stopped, and the world froze, and then he took off after her.

As Buster careened through the field, Jenna pitched forward. She squeezed her thighs against the horse's sides and after a few moments managed to right herself. She could almost hear her dad's voice in her ear, teaching her to ride when she was young. *If your horse bolts, stay on him. Don't jerk on the reins. Stay calm and get him under control gradually.* She pressed her legs against his sides and let go, pressed and let go, pulling steadily back on the reins each time. "Whoa, buddy, whoa."

Buster ignored her and tore through the grass. He'd seen that snake, evaded death, and he was getting as far away from the grim reaper as possible.

"Come on, buddy, whoa." She tried again. He would get tired of running . . . eventually. She tried nudging him to the right so they could make a wide circle around the pasture, but the horse wasn't having it. He snorted and kept running flat out, straight towards the fence that separated the Dalys' land from the Brewer ranch.

The shift seemed to happen in slow motion, Buster's muscles bunching, Jenna sliding back in the saddle, the horse launching himself over the fence. Mid-launch, she tilted sideways and scrambled to grab the pommel, but her hands, slick with sweat, slipped off the saddle.

She landed hard on her left side, just on the other side of the fence. Buster bounded away, making a beeline for some unknown destination that his horse-brain deemed safe.

Jenna groaned and took stock of her body. Limbs, back, and head all seemed intact. She rolled slowly to a sitting position, wincing at the throbbing pain in her left ankle. She slid off her left boot and peeled off her sock. Her ankle, already swollen, puffed up even more as she probed it for further injury. A sprain, most likely, but she wouldn't be able to get the boot on again tonight.

Nor would she be able to walk very well. Gritting her teeth against the pain, she scanned the field. Buster stood a couple hundred feet away, his head lowered, munching grass like nothing had ever happened. She rolled her eyes.

"Jenna!"

She turned the other direction. Reid, on Deschutes, galloped toward her. She waved. At least she wouldn't have to walk far.

Reid pulled to a stop, jumped off Deschutes, and loosely tied his reins to the fence post. He vaulted over the fence and knelt next to Jenna. "Hey, are you hurt?" He touched her hair, her cheek, her shoulder. "What's broken?"

"Nothing's broken." She pointed to her ankle. "A sprain, I think."

"That looks bad. Let me see." He sat back and propped her leg up on his lap, gently touching her swollen ankle. When she sucked in a breath at the slight pressure, he frowned. "We need to get you to a doctor."

"Can you get Buster first? I don't want him to run off again." She gestured towards the horse. "There's a gate a few hundred feet down that way. We can bring him through to the other side."

He nodded. "Okay, stay here."

She had to laugh at that. "Where would I go?"

Reid walked towards Buster, baby-talking him. The horse didn't even look up from his evening snack.

Reid rode back to Jenna, and from there it was a bit like moving chess pieces around. He got down and helped Jenna mount up. After rescuing Jenna's boot and sock from the grass, he led them along the fence line down to the gate. Back on the Daly side of the fence, they walked back towards Deschutes, who whickered at them, as if to say, *What took you so long?*

Reid untied his horse and swung up into the saddle. He glanced at Jenna. "Do you think you can ride back?"

"I don't think we have a choice. We're losing daylight." In theory Reid could lead Buster home and then drive back in the truck to get her, but that would take much longer than just riding home. She didn't relish sitting in a dark field by herself with a busted ankle. The other option, going to the Brewers for help, would take just as long if not longer. The ranch was around fifteen hundred acres and the house was on the other side of the property.

They started for home at a walk. Jenna would have liked to go faster, but her ankle was useless, and she wasn't going to fall off a second time.

"How's your pain?" he asked.

"Not great." She gritted her teeth as the left stirrup clicked against her puffy ankle. "Let's just get home."

"Don't you worry. I'll get you to a doctor as soon as we get back."

"I don't need a doctor. It's a sprain. I just need to rest it."

"You need a doctor."

"I don't."

Reid smiled, his eyes flint. "But we're going anyway."

Jenna rolled her eyes. Her ankle hurt like heck, but Reid was acting as if she'd just broken her leg. She didn't need medical treatment. She needed to get home, ice her foot, and most importantly locate her pajamas.

The sun had begun to set, and across the horizon, wispy clouds lit up with fiery pink. It might have been romantic, if not for the whole sprained ankle, ex-boyfriend situation.

Jenna's ankle pulsed with pain at every step Buster took. If she thought about it too much, it seemed to hurt more. "Can you tell me a story?" she asked. "Distract me."

"What kind of story?"

"Literally any kind of story," she said between gritted teeth. "I'm trying to ignore my ankle."

"Oh. Okay. Uh, let me think." Reid cleared his throat. "Once upon a time, there was a princess with red hair. She rode her trusty steed all over the land, fighting dragons and keeping everyone in the kingdom safe. But then her trusty steed got spooked by a very tiny, flightless dragon, and the princess fell off and hurt herself. So she went to the royal doctor to make sure she hadn't broken her royal ankle."

Jenna glared. "You're impossible, you know that?"

"Says the stubborn one." His voice held a note of tenderness, and the soft look he gave her melted her insides.

Ugh, why couldn't she stop feeling things around this man? She ran through the usual laundry list of reasons not to like Reid: *He's your ex, he broke your heart once, he's fresh off an engagement, he has a fear of commitment.* She still wanted to reach out and grab his hand.

Also, she really wanted some ibuprofen.

They reached the Dalys' barn without further incident. Reid insisted on having Jenna wait with the horses while he ran inside to get her parents. He returned shortly with a worried-looking Andrea and David. Her dad helped her down from the horse, while her mom bent to inspect her ankle with a flashlight.

"It's just a sprain," said Jenna, feeling like a broken record.

"You should still get it looked at." Her mom clicked off the flashlight and stood up. "Remember when I broke my toe throwing pottery, and walked around on it for two weeks?"

"Best safe than sorry," said her dad. To Reid, he added, "You want to drive her to the clinic and we'll take care of the horses?" He didn't need to specify which clinic. Juniper Creek had only one urgent care clinic, jointly run by the town's two resident doctors. The nearest hospital was twenty minutes away, in Redmond.

Jenna opened her mouth to protest, but Reid scooped her into his arms before she could finish saying the words "I'm fine." She tipped her head back so she could aim the full force of her glare at his face. "You don't have to carry me."

"But it makes me feel so manly." He scrunched his face up in a mock-wounded expression.

"You're impossible," she muttered, but she relaxed against his chest. There was something nice about Reid holding her in his arms, but she couldn't afford to get too melt-y. This situation wasn't helping her resist him.

The urgent care clinic was empty, and they got in right away. Dr. Kerry, who'd been Jenna's pediatrician as well as Reid's, saw them. Silver strands now ran through her curly black hair, but she seemed as lively as Jenna remembered. She smiled and asked about Jenna's teaching job while she examined the injured ankle. "I agree it's a sprain," she said. "I'll wrap it for you, and you need to do the good old rest and ice routine. If the swelling doesn't subside in a couple days, though, I want you to come back."

"Yes, ma'am."

"Good to see you both." The doctor smiled again, a secretive hint in her smile that gave Jenna a stomach twinge. Did the doctor think the two of them were together?

They left the clinic with a pair of the shortest crutches the doctor had on hand, and a prescription for extra strength Tylenol. Reid offered to drive her to the pharmacy, but Jenna shook her head. "I can go in the morning. Honestly, I'm starving."

"What do you want to eat? Burgers? Tacos? Um, burgers and tacos?"

She laughed. That about covered it for fast food. The town boasted a Dairy Queen, a Burger King, and a Taco Bell. The thought of soft-serve ice cream brought her close to drooling, so they stopped at the Dairy Queen drive-through and ordered burgers and Blizzards. Reid insisted on paying. This was like the world's weirdest date, Jenna thought. She almost made the joke but stopped herself. That might be flirting, and flirting led to more feelings, and feelings were bad. Best to keep it neutral. Instead, as she clutched the warm paper bag of food, she said, "Thanks for being there. This is above and beyond the call of friendship."

A slight frown flashed across his face, or maybe she imagined it, because his face smoothed into a smile. "It's no problem." He squeezed her hand, once, quick, and pulled out of the parking lot.

Back home, Jenna's parents had readied a comfortable perch in the living room. They'd piled blankets and pillows onto the couch and brought extra pillows so she could prop up her foot. "You two eat up," said Jenna's dad. "We need to check on the other animals. Horses are bedded down already. Thanks for taking care of our girl."

"My pleasure." Reid looked at Jenna, not at her dad. She felt the slow drip of inner glacial melt.

As her parents headed out to the barn, Jenna dug into her food. She took down half her burger in a couple bites.

Reid laughed. "It's good to see your appetite hasn't been affected by your injury."

"My appetite isn't affected by anything." Not strictly true. She'd lost her appetite for a few days after he broke up with her, but he didn't need to know that.

After they finished eating, Reid tucked the blanket around Jenna. "Do you want a cup of tea? Water?"

"I'm okay, really," she said. "I think I'm just going to read, if you want to hand me that . . ." She started gesturing to the Agatha Christie book on the coffee table, but Reid was already snatching it up and handing it to her.

"Are you sure you don't need anything else?"

She hesitated, playing with the edge of the blanket. It was late, and she should send him home, but . . . "Do you want to sit with me a minute?"

"Sure. Want me to read to you?" He held out his hand for the book.

She hadn't expected that offer. No one had read to her since she was a kid. But it did sound nice, sitting back and listening to the tale of how Miss Marple used her wits to solve a crime. She settled back against the couch cushions. "Okay. I marked my place."

Reid cracked open the book and thumbed through to the folded-down page. He looked at her in horror. "You *dog-ear* your pages? No bookmark? But . . . you're an English teacher."

"I know," she said dryly. "It's sacrilege."

"I've changed my mind. We can't be friends."

"Are you one of those people whose books all have perfect spines? Because then we definitely can't be friends."

"I'm affronted," he said. "I take very good care of my books."

"Well, I love my books."

He rolled his eyes. "Clearly."

She nudged his leg with her good foot. "You're supposed to be reading to me."

"Right, right. So demanding." Reid cleared his throat and began to read. His voice, deep and gravelly, washed over her. Despite her throbbing ankle, Jenna smiled. This reminded her of their relationship in high school—the easy banter, the relaxed hangouts, the comfort in simply being together. The friendship.

Reid read to her for over an hour, well after her parents had come back inside from seeing to the animals. Jenna's mom gave her a curious look but didn't say anything as she followed her husband into the kitchen.

"All right," said Reid finally, as Jenna yawned for the fourth time. "You're crashing. Probably all that adrenaline. Or maybe all that food you put away."

"Which was delicious." She took the book from him and very deliberately dog-eared the page to mark the new spot.

He shook his head. "Why don't I just pick you up for school tomorrow? We're going to the same place, and we have Homecoming committee after."

She frowned. "But it's my left ankle that's injured. I'm totally capable of driving."

"I know, but you'll have to tote around those crutches. Anyway, I'm helping your parents out tomorrow, so I would be coming here anyway. Seems silly to waste the gas."

"Oh." She twisted a strand of hair around her fingers, picking at a non-existent tangle. "Okay, if you're sure. Thanks."

"I'm sure." The smile he gave her felt intimate. Tender. Her heart jumped.

He gathered his keys and wallet, then leaned down to hug her. Did she feel his lips brush the top of her head? No, she must be imagining things, because they had sworn to be friends, and friends didn't kiss friends on the tops of their heads.

"Good night, Pixie," he said. "Sleep tight."

"Good night." She didn't bother correcting him. She ought to remind him not to use the nickname, but her eyelids felt heavy, and it didn't seem important. Maybe it would be later. But not now . . .

Jenna winced as she propped her injured ankle up on a folding chair next to her desk. She'd decided to eat lunch in her classroom and catch up on lesson-planning, since she'd been too exhausted last night to do any work. She'd originally planned to go riding today after the Homecoming committee meeting, but now, thanks to her own klutziness in falling off of Buster, that would not be happening. Instead, she would be taking a pile of grading and curriculum-in-progress home and sitting on the couch.

Also, Reid would be driving her home, working around the farm, and then staying for dinner. Her mom had already invited him this morning when he'd picked Jenna up for school. Not that she minded. The problem was that she *didn't* mind. She liked the idea of sitting around the dinner table with her parents and Reid, just like in high school, when he'd had a standing invitation to their house for dinner. He'd eat seconds and even thirds, then insist on doing all the dishes. Her mom would break out her seemingly endless stash of cookies, and they'd sit around playing Monopoly, which Jenna's dad always won. Reid just fit right into the family. He always had.

Face it, girl, you still have feelings.

She tried rotating her ankle. Needles of pain shot up her lower leg. Gritting her teeth, she stuck two textbooks under her ankle to prop it higher. It was a poor substitute for her couch. Zero out of five stars for comfort.

Sighing, she went back to editing her handout for the journalism unit, which she planned to kick off next week. The handout was almost ready to post on her page on the school's website, but she wanted to add links to a few news articles. Just examples to get the students started in writing their own articles.

She'd already decided all her examples would be local. *The Oregonian* for state-wide news, and *Willamette Week* for a more alternative source. She would also include a sample from the local paper, the *Juniper Creek Gazette.* Opening her browser, she typed in a search for the *Gazette.*

The paper hadn't had a website when Jenna was in school, but surely in ten years, even a small-town publication had reached the twenty-first century.

She found nothing. She tried a few other searches, with no luck. Bemused, she checked the Juniper Creek city website instead. After a few tries, she found a page that listed the phone numbers of local businesses, including the *Gazette.* Bingo.

She dialed the number and waited. It rang three times, then four, then five. Did this place even have an answering service? She knew it was still in business, because her parents got a hard copy of the paper every Monday morning, delivered to their front door.

After six rings, a deep voice answered. "*Juniper Creek Gazette*, Matt O'Reilly."

"What kind of newspaper doesn't have a website?" she said.

There was a pause. "I'm sorry, can I help you with something? Are you a customer? Because Eva manages our subscriptions, and she's out right now, and I honestly have no idea what she does or how she does it."

"No. I'm sorry. I'm Jenna Daly?" Jenna realized her voice was inflected up at the end, like she wasn't sure of her own name. She cleared her throat. "I'm an English teacher at Juniper Creek High School. My class is doing a journalism unit. Could I speak to one of your writers?"

"Would you settle for the owner?"

Heat flooded her cheeks. "I take it you're the owner."

"That's what it says on the back of the paper. So far no one's found out I have no idea what I'm doing." His voice sounded jovial. "I can send you to one of my other writers, if you prefer, but I'm the only one here right now."

"No. No! I didn't mean to sound so abrupt." She blew out a breath. The combination of exhaustion and pain had made her unable to carry on a normal conversation. Oh, and Reid's presence, because this was definitely somehow his fault. Glancing at her notes, she said, "I'm running a journalism unit with my sophomores, and I want some examples of local writing." She explained the unit in more detail, and how it would culminate in her students pairing up to write news articles together.

"Sounds like a great project," said Matt. "Why don't you make it a contest? Any interested students can submit their final articles to the paper. My staff and I will pick a winner and I'll help polish the article up for publication."

"That's amazing, but I have to warn you, I have almost a hundred students. Maybe you could just come talk to my classes?"

"I can do that, too. But I'm happy to do anything that gets young people interested in journalism. We'll hold the contest. Oh, and I'll send you some press clippings to show your students. I can fax them. We do have a fax machine, just not a website."

She chuckled. "Why is that? You still haven't told me."

"Well, you see, the owner of this paper is extremely old-fashioned. He believes in things like wearing ties to work and communicating via carrier pigeon." He paused for effect, and Jenna laughed. "Actually," he added, "I'm just technologically challenged."

"My students could help you with that. They were born with smartphones in their hands."

They chatted for a few more minutes, then hung up. Jenna decided she'd made enough progress on the journalism unit to justify staring out the window. She slumped back in her chair and watched a few kids toss a frisbee around in the soccer field.

"Hey," said the deep, gravelly voice that made her pulse race.

She sat up, turned to Reid, and gestured to her closed laptop. "Hi. I'm being super-productive here, as you can see."

"Clearly." Reid grinned. He strode into the classroom, grabbed a spare folding chair, and plopped down next to her. His hair looked extra-mussed, as if he'd just wandered in from the beach. "What are you not working on?"

"Journalism unit. Do you know Matt O'Reilly?"

"Sure. Owns the *Gazette*. Good guy. Why?" His smile seemed to flatten a bit.

"We just talked, and he offered to help me put on a contest." She described their conversation and Matt's idea for the writing competition.

Reid nodded. "Sounds fun."

Something in his voice gave her pause. "What? You don't think it's a good idea? Too complicated?"

"No, no." He ran a hand through his stubble and laughed. "No, I'm just being . . . Never mind. It's a great idea."

Just being what? She wanted to push him, but he leaned over and gently touched her bandaged ankle. "How's it feeling?"

She sighed. "Pretty sore. It's a perfect day for riding, too."

"Well, I need to exercise the horses this evening. Why don't you come with me?"

"Ha, ha." She rolled her eyes at him. "And injure my other ankle, too?"

"I'm serious. Not by yourself. We can ride together. The doctor will never know." One corner of his mouth lifted, and his eyes twinkled.

Together? That would involve sitting behind Reid on a horse and holding onto his waist. Not a good idea if she intended to just be his friend.

She glanced out the window. The sky was bright blue. The soccer fields looked apple green in the sunlight.

"Sounds perfect," she said.

***

Jenna held tight to Reid's waist as they rode Deschutes around the pasture. The horse stepped over a small molehill, jostling Jenna closer to Reid. His back was warm and damp against her chest, and a woodsy cinnamon scent drifted off his skin. She closed her eyes and leaned in. No one, not even Reid, had to know that she was drinking him in, relishing the closeness, or that she wanted this ride to go on forever.

He pulled Deschutes to a gentle stop and let the reins go slack. The horse dropped his head and munched grass. Reid pointed toward the horizon and said, "Mountains are out."

She sat back and followed his line of sight. Mount Washington rose to a white-capped peak. To the southwest, the Three Sisters mountains huddled together, their slopes mostly bare and brown. The sky formed an azure umbrella overhead.

"Oregon is magical," she said, sighing.

"You don't miss San Francisco? Art and theater coming out your ears? Amazing food? Or at least I imagine it's like that."

"I miss that part of it," she said. "I don't miss living there. It's go-go-go, and the traffic is horrendous. I like being home."

"Well, Juniper Creek likes having you home. Several students have said good things about you to other teachers. Steph and Elisa adore you. And I know Pam thinks the world of you, because she's told me."

A few moments of silence passed, and Jenna realized she'd been waiting for the thought to finish, waiting for him to add, *And I like having you back too.* He wasn't going to say that. Disappointment cooled in her veins and she stumbled over her words. "That's, ah, that's really sweet."

"I'm not saying it to be sweet. It's the truth." He twisted a bit to look at her, and she leaned a little left so she could see him better. Riding double in a saddle didn't make for the most ideal conversational conditions.

And what about you? How do you feel? her mind screamed. She bit down on the inside of her cheek, tamping down the words. She could not, would not go down that mental road. "You're okay then?" she blurted.

His forehead crinkled. "Okay? You mean . . . because of the breakup with Margot? It's been tough, but I think it was for the best. Where did that come from?"

"I don't know. You're just good at hiding how you feel." She glanced down. *Ugh.* She couldn't even be normal around Reid. She had to make things awkward.

"Hey," he said softly.

She looked up.

Reid tipped his head toward hers, so their foreheads and noses touched. She could see every tiny line around his eyes, could see the freckles forming on his tanned cheeks, could feel his warm breath against her face. "I'm not always good at hiding it," he said.

He was going to kiss her. There was no other direction for their mouths to go. All the breath left her lungs and the moment lingered, suspended like a hovering hummingbird.

Reid turned to the side, his cheek brushing hers. "I don't know what to do with you," he murmured, and then faced forward again.

Kiss me. Tell me you feel this, too. Jenna wanted to shake him. Instead she wrapped her arms around his waist again, and he took up Buster's reins. They rode back toward the barn in total silence.

***

Jenna sat in front of her class with her leg propped up on a second chair. She held up her copy of the handout she'd just distributed. "Okay, let's talk about this. We're starting a journalism unit today. You'll want to review this handout tonight, because tomorrow there *might* be a pop quiz on journalistic ethics. Maybe." She winked. "As part of this unit, you're also going to draft a feature news story, so let me review—Yes?"

Roberto López, one of her more eager students, had already shot his hand in the air. "Can we pick our own topics for that?"

"Not exactly." When several groans met this answer, Jenna held her hands up. "Hold on. I'm giving you a broad subject, so you'll have a lot of leeway. I'd like you to write something about Juniper Creek. You could profile a local business, you could write about an issue that impacts the town, like water scarcity, you could write about a town tradition like the Fourth of July parade. You'll be working with a partner, so take some time to find a topic you're both interested in."

Roberto's hand popped up again. "Can we pick our own partners?"

"Yes." She'd hesitated over that decision, because students always picked their friends, and inevitably someone was left out. It was still early in the year, though, so the cliques hadn't fully solidified. She hoped she wouldn't regret it later. "Here's the fun part. Any teams who are interested can submit their articles to the *Juniper Creek Gazette*. The owner has agreed to select one for publication."

That did get a reaction: excited and surprised murmurs. Jenna smiled. "The rest of the time today is yours. Find a partner and start brainstorming. I want to see a list of your possible topics by the end of the period."

The classroom erupted into the scrape of desks on linoleum as students paired off and pulled their desks together. At first the room filled with the white noise of paper fluttering in notebooks, pens scratching, chatter, a few giggles. Slowly the noise faded to a dull hum. Jenna stood, ignoring her crutches, and limped around the room to check in with each group.

Roberto had paired off with Tessa. When Jenna reached them, Tessa was writing at a furious pace in her notebook, nodding at something Roberto was saying.

"Looks like quite the brainstorm there," said Jenna.

Tessa looked up. "Miss Daly, can we write about Rose's family selling their farm and leaving town?"

"Absolutely." A small pain pinched Jenna's chest. "You were close to her, weren't you?"

"She was one of my best friends." Tessa sighed. "The team isn't the same without her. She said she likes her new school okay, but I wish she could have stayed here."

"She was so torn up about leaving," said Roberto. "It stinks. And you know who they sold to, right? Ed Brewer."

"I heard he's auctioning off their cattle this weekend." Tessa wrinkled her nose. "I guess he wants more land for all those show horses."

Jenna gritted her teeth. *It's for the resort,* she wanted to shout. She knew she should stay out of it. Reid would be furious if she spread the news around.

On the other hand, if her students found out the information on their own, that wouldn't be her fault, would it?

"That's a good angle," she said. "See if you can find out why he bought the land."

"Because he's greedy," said Roberto. "That's gonna be a short story."

Jenna bit back a smile. "Okay, but what if he wants it for something specific? Check public records and permit applications. Maybe the Secretary of State website, or City Hall, even. See if he's filed anything recently." Reid had said the Brewers were breaking ground on the resort in January. Surely they would have filed for a business name by now, at least.

"Miss Daly?" said Tessa. "Do you, like, know something?"

"Just a hunch."

Tessa scribbled a note on her paper and underlined it. "Are we allowed to interview Ed Brewer?"

"You can try." Jenna's stomach knotted. Reid would be furious if he found out she was encouraging this topic, but so what? It was a resort, not a matter of national security. People would find out about it eventually. "Make sure to tell him it's for a class project. He might be more inclined to speak with you." She had only met the man a handful of times, when she was much younger, and he'd never struck her as warm and fuzzy. But maybe he would see the interview as a chance for free publicity for the resort and would admit to the whole plan on his own.

After class, Jenna paged through the stack of notes her students had handed her. They all had some good ideas, and it appeared that many of them planned to interview friends or family members about water issues. She paused on Tessa and Roberto's paper, which was filled with Tessa's flowery handwriting, describing their detailed plan for interviewing Ed Brewer about his purchase of the Morris farm.

"Miss Daly?"

She jumped and looked up. Reid stood in her doorway. He wore a fitted, collared shirt that showed off his muscular shoulders and arms, and her heart skipped at the sight of him.

He pushed his shaggy blonde hair back from his face. "How's your ankle?"

"It's okay." She laughed. Did she sound nervous? Could he tell? "A little painful."

"I bet. Hey, I'm going to come by the farm this evening to check on Deschutes, after I run a few errands. Will you be there?"

She raised an eyebrow at him. "I live there."

"As opposed to here, putting in grueling hours grading papers."

"I'm doing my grueling work at home, on the couch."

"Okay, then. I'll stop in and say hello." He started to say something else, but three students walked into the classroom. Reid gave Jenna a little wave and disappeared into the hallway.

She took a few deep breaths to calm herself. She wasn't sure what she was more nervous about: her students reporting on Ed Brewer, or the prospect of spending more time with Reid.

The second his last student left the classroom, Reid packed up and hurried out to the staff parking lot, his heart pounding. The sooner he did these errands, the sooner he could get on with his life, he reminded himself. He was glad he'd decided to take Deschutes riding this evening, because he would need the stress relief.

He drove downtown first. Traffic was light, and he arrived at his destination quickly. He parked in front of the store, squared his shoulders, and walked through the front doors of Three Peaks Jewelry.

Inside, Bev Saunders, the owner, stood at the front counter. She was hanging several pairs of delicate earrings on a small stand. From her guarded smile, Reid guessed that she already knew why he was here. "Reid, hi. What can I help you with?"

He dug into his pocket and took out a small black box. He set it on the counter with an apologetic smile. "I'm afraid my circumstances have changed. I need to return this."

"Ah," she murmured. "I heard about you and Margot. I'm so sorry. How are you doing?"

He shrugged. "It was for the best."

"I suppose it's better to figure that out before the wedding, rather than after."

"I suppose," he said. He liked Bev, but he didn't feel like going into an analysis of his breakup. He reached for his wallet.

"Unfortunately," she said gently, "as I would have explained when you bought the ring, I can't do returns on special orders."

Reid's face fell. He did, vaguely, recall her pointing out the return policy on the receipt. At the time—over three years ago, now—he hadn't paid that much attention. He'd been more focused on the earth-shattering realization that he was buying an engagement ring, and the sticker shock. He'd never dreamed he would need to return it.

"I do remember something about that, yes." He cleared his throat. "So . . ."

"I can give you store credit. Which never expires. I've got some lovely bracelets that would be perfect for your mother, or . . . a friend? Maybe for a Christmas present?"

"I'll keep that in mind." With how much he'd spent on this ring, he could buy his mother ten bracelets. She might be getting jewelry for the next several holidays.

Bev printed out the record of exchange and store credit, and Reid signed on the dotted line. He had almost three thousand dollars of store credit to spend at Three Peaks from now until he was dead. *Great.*

He thanked Bev and headed out. One down, one to go.

He'd promised the Homecoming committee that he'd secure riding lessons and a saddle blanket for raffle prizes, and he didn't want to let them down. Which meant his next task was going to the Lucky Brewer Ranch.

And talking to Margot.

He hadn't spoken to her since she'd returned the ring at Jessie's. He'd texted her last night to ask if he could come by to pick up the saddle blanket, and her response had been a one-word, *OK.* He had stared at that word for a full minute, trying to interpret whether there was emotion behind it, and if so, was she angry? Sad? Eventually he'd just turned his phone off to avoid looking at it. He supposed he'd see her in person soon enough and would know how she was doing.

The drive up to the ranch felt surreal. He drove up the winding paved path, past white-fenced pastures were several sleek show horses grazed. At the T-shaped intersection near the stable, he turned right into the visitor lot and angled into one of the spaces. A few hundred feet beyond the lot was the house that would have been his and Margot's. He wondered what she would do with it now, or if her dad was still gifting it to her.

His stomach churning, Reid walked over to the stable. He found Margot in the large indoor ring, working Pluto through a dressage routine. She sat bolt straight, long blonde hair swishing as she turned Pluto in a tight circle. He followed like a dance partner. Her coach, John, stood at the side of the ring, arms crossed, watching intently.

Reid stopped for a moment to watch her and his chest twinged.

Margot glanced over and nodded at him, then pulled Pluto to a halt. She dismounted and led the horse over to Patrick. They had a whispered, indistinguishable exchange. Patrick left, leading Pluto, and Margot crossed the ring to Reid.

"The blankets are in the office," she said, opening the gate. She pulled off her helmet and smoothed back her damp hair. "I'll take you over."

"Thanks. I know you're busy."

"We were done anyway."

He followed her down the aisle in silence. Funny how you could spend years with a person, sharing a life, and have nothing to say.

The office door was open when they arrived. Manuel López, another stable hand, who'd been a student of Reid's a few years back, was sorting a stack of forms. The young man grinned and leaped to his feet. "Hey. Mr. W., what's up, man?" He still called Reid by the nickname many of the students used, despite being nineteen now and in community college.

Reid high-fived him. "Same old. School's in full swing. I'm on the Homecoming committee again."

"Nice." Manuel grinned. "What's the theme this year, superheroes?"

"I wish."

"Manuel, could you give us a minute?" Margot said.

"Sure." He clapped Reid on the shoulder and scooted out of the office.

Reid shoved his hands in his pockets, fighting a queasy feeling. Did Margot want to have a serious talk?

"Here's the thing," she said, crossing her arms. "I'm happy to donate the blanket." She gestured toward a neat stack of saddle blankets on a nearby shelf. Blue and gold geometric designs were woven into the wool, and each blanket was embroidered with the Lucky Brewer Ranch logo. "But I can't donate the riding lessons anymore."

"What? Why not?"

"Because a package of ten lessons is worth over sixteen hundred dollars. With our plans to expand the business, I can't just give away that kind of money."

He frowned. "I don't understand why this is an issue now. You donated the same package last year, and the kid who won it was thrilled. It's great publicity for the ranch."

"I know, but last year we weren't so close to opening the resort. We have to think about profits a little differently this year."

"But when I asked you a month ago, you were fine with it," he pointed out.

"Things were different a month ago. I was helping out my fiancé."

He looked down, studying the toes of his boots. She was right. Things were different now, and he couldn't expect anything from her beyond a civil relationship. He met her steely blue eyes again and nodded. "I understand. No problem. Thanks for donating the blanket."

"I'll wrap it up for you." Margot took some tissue paper out of a drawer, then reached for one of the blankets. She wrapped the tissue around it and nestled it into a box whose lid was stamped with the Lucky Brewer Ranch logo. As she handed the box over, she said, "You know, these will be a collector's item soon. Pretty soon the logo will change to say Lucky Brewer Resort."

"That's true." Reid thought of the hurt in Jenna's eyes when they'd argued the other day over the resort, and his stomach torqued. He shook away the thought. "Well, take care. I hope the resort is everything you and your family want it to be."

She nodded. "Me too."

He tucked the box under his arm and walked out. He'd brought a change of clothing with him, so he drove straight to the Daly farm.

He took Deschutes out first, meandering past the barn toward Towhee Canal. The sun slid down the sky as he rode, and the air cooled, whispering of fall and winter, of icy nights to come, snow on the ground. A cozy feeling that made him think of wood-burning stoves and hot chocolate.

It occurred to him that this would be the first fall in ten years that he'd been alone. He and Margot had always done either double duty, or once his mom moved to Florida, they had alternated between here and Fort Myers for holidays. This would be his first solo Thanksgiving. He didn't even have the option of seeing his mom; she was going on a cruise with friends.

Maybe a solo Thanksgiving wouldn't be so bad. He could rent a cabin up in the mountains and do some hiking, or if the trails were already slick with the first snows, he could simply hunker down and read. A book, for fun, instead of a student's essay—imagine that. While everyone else was bustling around their kitchens and making small talk with relatives, he could relax. He pictured himself sitting on a small porch, gazing into the forest over a cup of steaming coffee as morning light drifted through the pines.

In his imagination, Jenna stole up beside him. The two of them sat together, wrapped in a thick wool blanket, her head against his shoulder.

He blinked. Where had that come from? He and Jenna were friends. Period. They'd dated, so of course he still found her attractive, but that didn't mean anything. He planned to be single for a long time.

By the time he brushed down Deschutes, his stomach was growling. He should probably just go home for dinner, but he glanced at Jenna's truck in the driveway and then walked up the porch steps.

He knocked on the door and cracked it open. "Hello?"

"In here," called Jenna's voice.

He found her in the kitchen, sitting at the island with her left foot propped on a nearby chair. She was eating a bowl of cereal and wearing sweats. Her hair fell in messy waves and one side of her face bore the telltale crease of someone who'd slept face-down on a pillow.

He wanted to walk over to her, push her hair back from her face, and kiss her. He shook off the thought and pulled up another bar stool. "Did you take a nap?"

"How could you tell?" She yawned.

He smirked a little and pointed to the crease on her face. "I can see the pillow mark."

She rubbed her hand over her cheek, as if trying to scrub it off. "Well, that's attractive."

"No, you look good," he blurted.

Jenna stared at him.

Oops. He pointed to a bowl of pretzels that sat on the island. "Do you mind if I . . .?"

"Help yourself."

He grabbed a small handful and set them on a napkin. "I just came from the Brewer ranch. Margot gave me the saddle blanket for Homecoming, but now that we've broken up, she doesn't feel like she can donate the riding lessons. I guess because they're so expensive."

Jenna frowned. "That seems a bit . . . harsh."

"I suppose. Can't really blame her, though." He sighed. "Do you think your mom would donate any of her pottery?"

"Probably. I'll ask her. She and Dad are in town getting groceries." She dug into her cereal again. "How was the rest of your day?"

Should he tell her? What if it upset her somehow, hearing about Margot? No, that was ridiculous. She was the one who'd listened to him vent right after they broke up. He sighed. "Well, I returned the engagement ring."

"Oh, wow." She frowned into her cereal, as if the pieces of toasted wheat would tell her what to say next. "How do you feel about that?"

He let out a half-laugh. He had no idea how to answer that. His feelings hadn't caught up to the day yet. "I feel like I just failed a big life exam."

"Oh, Reid." She reached over to touch his hand. "You're not a failure."

"I don't know about that. My parents met when they were eighteen, and they got married halfway through college. Mom used to tell me she knew right away Dad was the love of her life. Then there's me. I had . . ." He cleared his throat. His thoughts had started to veer down a path he wasn't ready to explore. "I was with Margot for years, and I can't say I knew. Not like that." He was holding Jenna's hand, he realized. She had left it there and he had wrapped his fingers around it without even thinking. *I didn't know the way I knew with you.*

He squeezed gently and pulled his hand away. The only other thing to do with his hands was eat pretzels. He broke one into miniscule pieces and started eating them one at a time.

"Sometimes things change," said Jenna. "We can't all be your parents. Anyway, Margot wasn't sure either, right?"

"I guess not." He sighed. "I probably shouldn't be talking to you about this. I'm sorry."

"It's okay," she said. "Look, Reid. You both tried for a long time. Ultimately you just weren't right for each other. There's nothing wrong with that. It just means there's someone else for you."

"Maybe," he said. "Or maybe I'm meant to be alone the rest of my life."

"That's absurd. You're going to find someone wonderful."

Reid gazed into her brilliant hazel eyes. Suddenly the thought washed over him: *What if I already did, and it's too late?*

He almost said it. He almost stood up, pulled Jenna into his arms, and kissed her. But he would regret it later, wouldn't he? They both would. Too much had happened, and there were too many years between them.

He stood up and wrapped the remains of his pretzels in the napkin. "Mind if I take these for the road?"

"You can stay for dinner, you know. Mom's making spaghetti."

His stomach growled at the thought of a hot, home-cooked meal. His refrigerator at home held the remains of a package of deli turkey, some mustard, and a piece of bread. It would be easy to stay, to slip back into the past when he was a part of the Daly family. Back when Jenna had offered him her heart.

An offer he had turned down. He'd had his chance, and he'd lost it.

"I have a ton of work to do at home," he said. "Thanks, though. I'll see you at school."

The drive back to his apartment passed in a blur, and he almost rolled through a stop light, slamming on the brakes at the last second. He couldn't stop thinking about the warmth of Jenna's hand in his, or the feeling that he should have stayed.

Jenna limped around the library's computer lab, moving from computer station to computer station, where her students sat doing online research and quietly talking. She peered over the shoulders of Emily and Candice, who were both tapping away on their smartphones, playing a word search game. "Looks like a credible source."

"We were just taking a break, Miss Daly," said Candice, looking up wide-eyed and innocent.

"Uh-huh." Jenna smirked. She waited for the girls to put their phones away, then moved on.

"Miss Daly?"

She turned toward the back of the room. Roberto and Tessa were waving her over, frantic looks on their faces.

She limped over to them as quickly as possible. "Is something wrong?"

"We can't do our story anymore." Tessa looked like she might cry as she shoved a piece of paper into Jenna's hands. "Look at this."

Jenna stared down at a glossy, tri-fold brochure. The front contained a photo of a bright red barn with pristine white trim, surrounded by grassy fields. Across the top, in a scripted font, were the words, *LUCKY BREWER RESORT: Central Oregon's Premiere Luxury Vacation Destination.* The interior was filled with pictures and drawings of the future grand lodge and condos that would lure tourists, along with zippy marketing copy about the luxury features—Granite countertops! Stainless steel appliances! Swimming pools!—that would be offered. The back read, *Opening Next June! Accepting Reservations January 1!*

"This is why the Brewers bought the Morris farm," said Roberto. "And now we can't write about it."

"I don't understand. Why not?"

"Because they beat us to it." Tessa dug through her notebook and produced a sheet of paper. Handing it over, she said, "We found this on Friday night at the library."

It was a printout from the Pine County website, showing that Ed Brewer had applied for a business license for the Lucky Brewer Resort on September first of this year. Its status was listed as *approved.*

Roberto said, "My brother's a stable hand at the ranch, so we called him. He said he knew about the resort, but he couldn't talk about it. He put us through to Margot Brewer."

"You know, she's the one Mr. W. was engaged to," cut in Tessa. "And she said—"

"Well, first she asked us how we found out," interrupted Roberto. "She thought Mr. W. told us."

"We told her about the business license thing," said Tessa. "At first she sounded mad, but then she talked about the resort, for like . . ." She glanced at Roberto.

"Half an hour." He rolled his eyes. "At least."

"Did she confirm they bought the Morris farm for the resort?"

"Yep, and she even said we could quote her." Tessa slumped in her seat. "But now it doesn't matter, Miss Daly. Everyone knows about the resort, so our story isn't interesting anymore."

"Hmm." Jenna nodded. "Okay, so then why don't you write about the long-term impacts it might have on Juniper Creek? Just imagine how this kind of tourism could change our town. It'll be good for the economy, but what if local businesses get pushed out? What if the Brewers buy up other farms? They've been pressuring my parents to sell, for one thing. I'm sure you could interview them."

"Really?" said Roberto.

"Of course. Your story doesn't have to be a big exposé to be interesting. I guarantee you every person in this town will have an opinion about the resort. Some will be in favor; some will think it'll change the town too much. There's plenty to explore there."

"Maybe." Tessa frowned. "When can we talk to your parents?"

"You can come by this evening, if you want," said Jenna. She would text her parents on a break; she knew they'd be willing to help. "Around five? You still need to select one of my mom's pottery pieces for the Homecoming raffle, don't you?" Her mom had agreed right away to donate to the raffle.

Tessa looked at Roberto. "Can you make it tonight?"

"Yep. Thanks, Miss Daly."

"No problem."

She finished her rotation around the room, then went to the teacher station at the front and checked her email. Steph had sent a group email this morning, reminding everyone about the varsity volleyball game this afternoon at 4, and Reid had responded, "Wouldn't miss it!"

The sight of his name and the cheery tone of his email made her stomach skip. For a moment, last night, she'd thought he was going to stay for dinner, and that it would be almost like old times. It was probably a good thing he'd left, though. She didn't need to revisit old times with Reid.

If he was going to the volleyball game, she realized, he probably wouldn't come over to her parents' place tonight. He'd likely head home afterwards, or maybe go out with Steph and the other teachers. Good timing, since Tessa and Roberto were now coming by to interview her parents. Reid didn't need to know how much she'd encouraged their interest in writing about the resort.

Not to mention, she didn't need her students finding out that Reid spent time on her family's farm. It wouldn't matter that he was helping out her parents—that information could explode into rumors about Reid and Jenna dating. Rumors were like matches here. It only took one to start a fire.

***

That evening, Jenna sat in the living room watching Tessa and Roberto interview her parents. Roberto was recording the whole thing on his phone, and Tessa was taking copious notes in her swift, tidy handwriting. "Can you estimate how many hours you spend each week on your second jobs?" she said. "The engine repair and the art classes?"

David and Andrea exchanged glances. "I'd say anywhere from ten to twenty-five hours a week on the repairs," said David. "Depends on the time of year."

"I'm averaging fifteen hours a week for teaching just one class," added Andrea. "That's not counting the time I spend creating my own art pieces, some of which I sell."

"So with your extra jobs plus the farm, you spend . . . about eighty to ninety hours a week each working?" said Tessa, double-checking her notes.

David nodded. "I'd say that's about right."

Jenna winced. Her parents shouldn't have to sacrifice that much just to keep the farm going. They still refused her offer to pay rent, and with her ankle, she couldn't even help with repairs or chores. She'd started volunteering to cook more meals, but it didn't seem like enough.

The conversation continued on as David and Andrea described how water restrictions had impacted their crops. David even brought out a copy of the farm's most recent water bill from the Pine County Irrigation District. "Fifty dollars an acre," he said, stabbing a calloused finger on the bill as he showed it to Tessa and Roberto. "That's up three dollars and fifty cents an acre from last year. If the district keeps hiking rates like this the whole town's gonna run dry, and you can quote me on that."

Tessa and Roberto seemed fascinated by what was, for Jenna's usually reserved father, a tirade. "Can we have a copy of this bill?" asked Tessa.

"You can keep it. I already know what I paid them." David sat back in his seat, frowning. Andrea patted his shoulder.

There was a knock on the door. Jenna excused herself to answer it and was startled to find Reid standing on the front porch.

"Why aren't you at the volleyball game?" she blurted.

"Hello to you too," he said wryly. "I was. I thought it was an away match, but it was home. I already took Deschutes and Buster for a spin."

She glanced over her shoulder in the direction of the living room. "You can come in if you want, but I have students here. They're interviewing my parents for an assignment."

"I better not. They might think we're . . . you know." He took a step backwards, as if his very proximity to the front door might incite a rumor.

"Friends?" she said.

He didn't even crack a smile. "I have to ask you something. Can you come outside for a moment?"

"Sure." She stepped out onto the porch, closing the door behind her. They walked over to the railing and stood side by side looking out over the fields.

After a moment, Reid said, "Margot texted me this weekend to ask if I spilled the beans about the resort. Apparently, a couple of students called to interview her for a journalism project." He raised one eyebrow at her. "Would those be your students?"

He was still talking to Margot? She lifted her chin. "They would."

"And your reason for telling them about the resort after I asked you not to spread it around was . . .?"

"I didn't tell them, per se. Tessa and Roberto wanted to write about the sale of the Morris farm. I just suggested they try to find out why Ed Brewer wanted the land, by searching public records. And by the way, Ed filed for a business license for the resort in September. He put the information out there on the internet. My students just found it."

"So you told them without telling them." Reid frowned. "Margot told me she was going to try to get ahead of the gossip mill. I saw a brochure for the resort in the front office, so I guess she managed it. Your students accelerated the marketing campaign, that's for sure."

His irritation made her skin prickle with heat. "Aren't you taking this a bit personally? The news was going to come out one way or the other. I think the resort is a perfect topic for my students' project."

"Sure." He braced both hands against the railing. "Have them write about the Brewers' big, evil scheme to inject tourism dollars into our town's failing economy."

She crossed her arms. "I don't like that Ed's preying on vulnerable families by pressuring them to sell their land. And the tourism? Sure, that's great, but what happens when everyone wants to go work at the big fancy resort and small businesses like the ice cream shop have to close because they can't hire anyone?"

He spun towards her, eyes flashing. "What about when dozens of new jobs open up and more kids can save money to go to college?"

"What about when this whole place converts to a tourist trap and farms go under?"

He threw up his hands. "We're never going to agree on this."

"Clearly." She stared up at him, the cool air stinging the inside of her nose.

Reid unclenched his jaw and reached down to smooth her hair back from her face. "I had forgotten how stubborn you are."

When he didn't take his hand away, her insides flipped. He stroked her cheek, his touch searing hot in the crisp night air. She held her breath, frozen on the tightrope of the moment.

He bent and pressed his lips to hers as his arms dropped to encircle her waist. She rose up on tiptoe, one hand on his chest. His kiss was warm and sweet, and he tasted of cinnamon gum.

Something thumped behind them. They jumped apart, then both started to laugh when they realized what the sound was: just the front door, which Jenna apparently hadn't closed all the way, banging against the doorframe in the breeze.

"Wow," said Reid, running a hand over his jaw. "We . . . probably shouldn't do that again."

"Definitely not." She suddenly felt overheated in her thick sweater, and the cold air was a welcome balm to her burning skin. This was why she'd liked kissing Reid so much. She'd almost forgotten.

He ran a hand over his lips and shook his head. "I should go. I'll see you at school." He turned and hurried down the porch steps. His key ring jingled as he dug it out of his pocket.

"Wait," she called.

He turned around.

"Was that . . . you know. Was it how you remembered?"

"Kissing you?" He laughed. "No, Pixie. It was better."

"Reid." Her voice cracked. He couldn't leave now, not after those words, not after kissing her like that.

"You're trouble," he said, "big trouble," but he was grinning, and he waved and honked his horn before backing out of the driveway.

As he walked into the Homecoming Committee meeting, Reid realized he had it bad for Jenna.

She was the first person he looked for. The second he spotted the flame of her hair, his mind flew back to the kiss on her porch last night. *A mistake,* he'd been telling himself all day. *Yes, but the best kind of mistake,* he kept thinking.

A mistake he wanted to make again.

Logic dictated he should pull up a seat next to some of the students and avoid any further proximity to the woman who was already driving him out of his mind, but there was an empty chair next to her. And anyway, he wanted to ask for a copy of her essay grading rubric. Yep, that was it, he needed to discuss work.

He plopped into the metal folding chair, wondering why the seats always felt ice-cold no matter what temperature the rest of the building was. "How's it going?"

She jumped. "Sorry, I didn't hear you sneak up on me."

"Long day?" Or was her mind just somewhere else, lingering, like his, on that moment?

"Kind of."

She went silent, looking down at her notepad and doodling on it. The frown on her face didn't belong to someone who was reminiscing about a romantic kiss. Reid didn't want the students to hear their conversation, but . . . He leaned over. "Are you okay?"

She glanced around. "I can't talk about it here."

"Understood. Maybe later." Reid's stomach lurched. He'd never liked waiting to hear bad news. He still remembered that phone call the summer after he graduated high school, his mom stammering, *Something's happened to your father,* him yelling, *What, Mom, what, just tell me.* The way he'd ended things with Jenna, abrupt, sudden, a clean break. Get it over with.

"Hey, people!" Ryan hopped up onto a chair and clapped. "Let's get started. We have a huge list to get through today." He pointed to the easel containing the giant notepad, the front page crammed with tasks in four colors of Sharpie. "Mr. W. and Miss Daly? Did you both call your list of chaperones?"

"I have a few left." Reid made a mental note to contact them tonight. The school guaranteed a specific student-adult ratio at all school functions, and although some teachers would chaperone too, the school relied heavily on a network of parent volunteers.

"Me too," said Jenna. "I'll call them this week."

Ryan scrawled "in progress" next to that item, then pointed his Sharpie at a girl with curly black hair. "Erin. What's the 4-1-1 on our balloon order?"

The students launched into a discussion of the remaining items on the list, chattering about which tasks were done and what was left to take care of before the dance. Since the committee was self-sufficient at this point, Reid listened with half an ear. He kept glancing at Jenna, trying to gauge by her expression what she was thinking. Finally, he reached over, slipped the pen from her hand, and wrote, *When can we talk?*

She glanced down and held out her hand for the pen. When he gave it back, she wrote, *Right after this?*

He gave her a thumbs up, his chest tightening. *Come on, Reid,* he thought, *grow a spine.* He couldn't just keep replaying the kiss in his memory for the next decade; at some point, they had to talk about it. He braced himself, trying to predict what she would tell him: that the kiss had been a mistake, that he had no business kissing anyone after coming out of such a long relationship, that she didn't have feelings for him.

By the time the meeting ended, Reid was nauseated. The teachers' lounge was occupied by a math department meeting, so he and Jenna went back to his classroom and shut the door. He made her take the more comfortable chair at his desk, while he folded his long frame into one of the students' desks, which all had chairs attached. His knees knocked against the underside of the desk, and he winced as he shifted in the chair. Best to get it over with. He launched in. "About Monday night . . ."

"I know, I know." She clapped a hand to her forehead. "I got caught up in the moment, and I know you just broke up with Margot, and I'm sorry. I just . . . I'm sorry."

His heart sparked with hope. *I'm sorry* was different than *It should never have happened.* She hadn't said it was a mistake, or that she never wanted to see him again. "You don't have to apologize, Pixie," he said. Her nickname fell from his lips easily. "I can't say I regret that kiss."

"You don't?" She lifted her head.

"No." Reid blew out a breath, not sure he remembered how to do this. It had been ten years since he'd asked anyone out. "What are you doing tonight? Can I take you out to dinner?"

"Like a . . . like a date?"

"Exactly." He smiled. "Like a date. We could go into Redmond, maybe. When's the last time you went to The Sawmill?" The restaurant had been around since high school and had been a favorite destination after football games.

"Not in ages. That sounds good." She pulled herself up, bracing against the desk, and reached for her crutches. "I have to do some grading. Do you want me to meet you there later?"

"Nah." He checked the clock. "I need to stick around and get some work done too, so I'll drive us. I can drop you off here on the way home."

She frowned. "What about the students?"

"Most of them won't be here by the time we leave." He shrugged.

"Some of them might be."

He winked. "Then I guess they'll have something to gossip about."

***

Reid sat back in the red and white striped booth and set down his menu, already imagining the huge cheeseburger he was about to order. He hadn't been to The Sawmill in months—it specialized in burgers and milkshakes, not Margot's favorite fare. The restaurant was built to resemble a large cabin, with a slanted wood-paneled ceiling and heavy dark wooden beams throughout.

He glanced over at Jenna. Her hair glowed under the warm soft lighting. Her freckled cheeks plumped as she smiled at him, but she'd been quiet in the car, and something lingered in her eyes. Could she be nervous? He certainly felt like an awkward teenager again, not sure how to impress the girl who'd agreed to go out with him. This is Jenna, he reminded himself. They'd known each other since middle school. "Remember when we'd come here after football games?"

"Of course I do. We would all get those jumbo milkshakes." She dipped her head to study the menu. "They still serve them, you know. Maybe we should order one."

"Might have to split it." He patted his stomach. "I don't quite have my high school metabolism."

She snorted. "Please, you're . . ." Her face went red, and her voice trailed off.

"I'm what?" He tugged on her menu. "Come on, Pixie, what were you going to say?"

"Nope. I'm deciding what to order." She bent her head even lower and sank down in her seat.

"Okay." He grinned. She had clearly been about to compliment him. Feeling reckless, or maybe just courageous, he said, "Well, you look beautiful, but you always do."

She glanced up. "Oh," she said softly, her lips parting.

He almost scooted over right there and kissed her, but their server interrupted to take their order. As soon as the server left, Reid slid closer to Jenna and took her hand. He was ready to talk some more about how pretty she looked, to see if he could bring the flush back to her cheeks.

Then he noticed the way she was sitting. Brow furrowed, shoulders tensed, gnawing on her bottom lip. "Pixie, what's bothering you?"

"I need to talk to you about something."

"Something besides Monday night?" His pulse sped up. "What happened? Are you okay?"

"I'm fine." She glanced around the restaurant, as if she expected someone to be listening to them. "It's about the Lucky Brewer Resort. I don't want to upset you, but I *have* to tell someone."

The bottom dropped out of his stomach. They hadn't spoken about the resort since Monday, but he'd thought they were dropping the topic. Jenna felt differently about it, and that was it. "Do we have to talk about that now?"

Her grip on his hand tightened. "Just listen before you jump to conclusions. Okay, you know Roberto and Tessa interviewed my parents for the journalism project. Because . . . well, you know because you came over." She cleared her throat.

"I definitely remember." He winked.

She smiled, but it faded quickly. "My dad had been telling them how high the water rates are this year, and he gave them a copy of his bill from the irrigation district. Well, Roberto's older brother works for the Brewers."

"I know Roberto," said Reid. "He was a student of mine. He's a stable hand at the ranch. I ran into him a fair amount when I kept Deschutes over there."

She nodded. "Roberto told me this morning that he talked to his brother last night, and he pulled one of the ranch's irrigation bills for comparison. My dad paid fifty dollars an acre this year for water. Guess how much the Brewers paid? *Thirty-five* dollars an acre. Fifteen dollars per acre cheaper."

"What?" This didn't sound right. Rates were set yearly by the Pine County Irrigation District, and as far as Reid knew, everyone paid the same rate. If you owned more acreage, your bill was higher. The math was pretty simple. "Did the district overcharge your parents?"

"No. I checked the Pine County Irrigation District's website. They publish their rates every year. This year's rate is fifty an acre."

Fifty an acre, when the Brewers had only paid thirty-five. Reid tried to make sense of this. There must be an explanation. "Do they give a discount for large acreage?"

"That's what I thought too, because the Brewer Ranch is the only farm over five hundred acres in all of Juniper Creek. I called the irrigation district during my prep, and they don't give discounts. The rate is standard across the whole county." She took a sip of her water. "And here's the other thing Tessa, Roberto, and I found today during class. There's now a registration on the Oregon Secretary of State website for the Lucky Brewer Resort."

Reid frowned. Wasn't registering your business a normal part of starting one? But then Jenna went on, "The registered agent, you know, the person who can receive service of process, is someone named Allen Eames."

"Eames," he murmured. "Should I know who that is?"

"I had to look him up. He's an accountant with an office in Crystalvale," she said, naming the small town east of Juniper Creek. "But he also sits on the board of the Pine County Irrigation District. Which votes on water delivery schedules and, more importantly, water rates." She punched a finger on the table with the finality of a lawyer who'd just given a successful closing argument.

Reid dropped her hand. The temperature seemed to have dipped in the restaurant, or maybe his blood was running cold. "You're not suggesting . . ."

She nodded. "I'm *absolutely* suggesting that the irrigation district is giving Ed Brewer a discount under the table. Allen Eames is connected to the resort somehow, so he must be getting something out of this. No wonder Ed wants to buy up other farms. It's much cheaper for him to irrigate that land than it would be for the original owners."

"Are you sure about this? You're taking Manuel's word about the rates." He couldn't imagine it. He'd spent hours with Ed over the years, and the man had always struck him as a savvy businessman, but an honest one. Would he really take a cut rate on his water when so many other farmers were struggling?

Jenna's eyes flashed. "I don't have a smoking invoice, but Manuel has no reason to lie about it. Roberto didn't even tell him why he wanted to know, other than for a school assignment."

Reid leaned his head against the back of the booth. What if Jenna was right? And worse, what if Margot knew? No, surely, she wouldn't condone something unethical. "Well, Margot and her sister wouldn't have anything to do with this."

"I hope not. But regardless, the difference in rates is putting small farms in jeopardy. It's not right. Something has to be done."

"What kind of something?" He eyed her warily.

She glanced down and played with the edge of her napkin. "I was hoping we could talk to Margot."

"We?" Oh, good. His ex-girlfriend and his ex-fiancée. It sounded like a party. "What would *we* ask her?"

"I wouldn't accuse her of anything. I just want her to confirm the rate difference. She might be totally unaware of what's going on. Or maybe Manuel was mistaken and pulled an old bill. Either way, we'll know for sure."

"Then what?"

"I haven't gotten any farther than that," she said. "But we can't just let this go." She turned a pleading gaze on him. "If we don't talk to Margot first, my students are going to call and try to interview her again. I asked them to hold off for a few days, but I can't tell them not to write their story. They think they have something here, and I agree with them."

Reid heaved a sigh. The last thing he wanted to do was upset Margot further. But Jenna did have a point. It was one thing to purchase additional land as part of a planned, legal business. It was another matter to benefit from unauthorized water rates. If the Brewer ranch really was getting a price cut, Margot would want to know that and address it with her father. After all, as she herself had told Reid, someday she would be responsible for the entire Brewer enterprise.

"All right," he said. "I'll help you talk to her."

"Thank you so much." She grabbed his hand again. "Can we call her tonight?"

He had to laugh. "Is that my cue to ask for a couple of to-go boxes?"

Jenna gave him a sheepish grin.

"I'll get the check."

***

An hour later, Reid and Jenna sat down across from Margot at Sunrise Cafe, which despite its moniker was open until midnight every night except Sundays. Students often used it for late-night study sessions, but right now it wasn't too busy. The three of them had ordered various kinds of tea, and the three white mugs sat like chess pieces on the table between them.

Margot perched on the edge of her chair, her purse still slung over her shoulder, looking like a deer about to bolt. She touched the handle of her mug, watching the steam curl up from the surface. "Well? What did you need to talk to me about?"

"Thanks for meeting us," said Reid. He realized he was drumming his fingers on the table and folded them together. "I think you're aware that Jenna's students are doing research for a class project."

"About the Lucky Brewer Resort, apparently." Margot gave Jenna a dry look. "Your students sped up our advertising campaign. My sister and I spent all day Sunday finalizing our marketing materials."

"I heard." Jenna nodded. "Initially, my students were writing about your dad buying the Morris farm. I gave them some ideas on getting started, but they found the information about the resort. It was out there if you knew where to look." She wasn't going to apologize, Reid realized, and he felt a small spark of pride. Not many people stood up to Margot.

"Things have changed, though. My students found some conflicting information." Jenna was fiddling with her napkin, clenching it into a tight ball, letting go, then clenching again. Her tea sat untouched on the table. "They're now trying to confirm whether everyone is subject to the same water usage rates. Pine County Irrigation District charges fifty dollars an acre, but do you know if your family actually pays that much?"

The arch in Margot's eyebrows became more severe. "Why wouldn't we pay what we owe? What are you getting at? Be straight with me."

"Well . . ." began Reid.

"We think your dad negotiated a cheaper water rate under the table," said Jenna.

There it was. Reid had to admire her bluntness. The accusation sat there, sharp-edged and glinting like a knife blade.

Margot blinked a few times, then shook her head. "Where would you get that idea?"

"A confidential source." Under the table, Jenna nudged his foot. On the way over she'd worried that if they told Margot about Manuel's involvement, she might fire him. "We're hoping you can pull one of the ranch's water bills so we can fact-check."

"Fact-check?" Margot snorted. "You're making this sound like a *New York Times* investigation. I assure you my family pays the same water rates as everyone else in this town."

Reid's lungs seemed to loosen, and he could take full breaths again. None of this was true. Jenna's students had gotten the wrong information somehow, that was all.

"You personally handle the ranch's finances, then," said Jenna.

"We have an accountant, like most businesses do." She tossed her hair. "That doesn't mean our water rate is different."

"Fair enough," Jenna said. "Why is Allen Eames the registered agent for the future Lucky Brewer resort?"

"He's our accountant. Nothing exciting there. Sorry to disappoint you and your students."

"But he sits on the board of the Pine County Irrigation District." Jenna leaned forward. "They set water rates. You don't think he might have negotiated a special deal for your dad?"

"Hang on."

"One that's making it easy for him to push out local farmers and buy up their land."

Margot, eyes flashing, pushed her chair back from the table. "These are some serious accusations. I'd like to know what you think, Reid, since you've been so quiet. Do you think my dad's capable of something like this? You must, since you're the one who called me."

Reid wanted to shrink to the size of a marshmallow and melt away. He and Margot hadn't parted on the best terms, maybe, but it wasn't as if one of them had done something unforgivable to the other. Didn't he owe her father, the man who was once going to be his father-in-law, the benefit of the doubt? Yet he couldn't shake the sickening feeling that Jenna and her students were onto something. She was staring at him now, her amber eyes pleading. He looked from her to Margot. "I think this is pretty easily solved by you pulling one of the ranch's water bills. It's probably nothing, but I know how much you care about the future of the business. If something is going on, don't you want to know about it?"

Her shoulders slumped and she took a long drink. "I'll look into it."

"Thank you," said Jenna. "Really, Margot, we so appreciate it."

She glanced at Reid. "Could I talk to you for a second? In private?"

"Uh . . ." Reid frowned, but Jenna was nodding at him. "Sure. Outside?"

He followed Margot out into the cool night. Golden light spilled over from the cafe onto the sidewalk. "What's up?"

Margot fiddled with the ends of her long hair. "Is something going on with you and Jenna?"

"What do you mean?"

She rolled her eyes. "Come on. I'm not blind. You just came from somewhere together, and the way she looks at you . . ."

"What way?"

"Like you invented starlight. Don't tell me you haven't noticed."

He rubbed a hand across his forehead. "I feel strange having this conversation with you."

"Just tell me," she said softly. "I don't want to find out from someone else."

"Honestly, I don't know. We went out to dinner tonight. The thing is, we went out before, and I hurt her before, so . . ." He shrugged. Across the street, a couple walked down the sidewalk with their arms around each other, heads tilted together. "I should really be single right now."

"Maybe," she said. "But love doesn't listen to rules."

"I didn't say love. Slow down the train there." He forced a laugh. It sounded like he was choking on something.

Margot stepped toward him, as if she was going to hug him, then caught herself and lightly touched his arm instead. "If I find anything, I'll let you know. Take care of yourself." She turned and strode down the sidewalk. It reminded him of watching her walk away at The Angry Pigeon, a moment that seemed to have happened years ago. And yet his heart didn't hurt the way it had that night. It twinged a little, maybe, but it didn't ache.

He looked through the window at Jenna. She had slumped down in her chair, her bad leg stretched out in front of her, and she was reading a book. It looked like it might be the Agatha Christie he'd read to her the night she sprained her ankle. She turned a page, her eyes wide at whatever was happening in the story.

Love doesn't listen to rules, Margot had said. Maybe love wasn't the wrong word to describe what was going on between him and Jenna. Maybe it was exactly right.

Jenna's heart skipped a beat as a sleek silver Jetta pulled into the guest spot in front of Reid's apartment. "Is that her?"

Reid joined her at the window. For a moment he leaned so close that she smelled the cinnamon of his aftershave. "Yep. I'll get the door."

Jenna watched as Margot got out of the car with her purse and a manila envelope in hand. After last night, Jenna had guessed there was a fifty percent chance that they would hear from Margot again—at best. At lunch today, though, Reid had pulled her aside to say that Margot had texted him and wanted to meet in private.

"Did she find something?" Jenna had asked.

Reid had shrugged. "I assume so, but that's all she would say."

Jenna turned away from the window. Should she hug Margot? Shake her hand? She opted for hovering awkwardly behind Reid as he opened the door.

Margot stepped inside and she and Reid did an awkward greeting dance—leaning away from each other, then air-hugging without really closing the distance between them. A hug was out, Jenna decided. She smiled instead and offered to take Margot's purse.

The three of them sat down, Reid and Jenna on the couch and Margot in the reclining chair nearby. Reid scooted down so he was wedged against the far end of the couch, as close to Margot—and as far away from Jenna—as possible. She felt a little twinge. Was he embarrassed to sit close to her in front of his ex?

Silence fell between the three of them. Reid broke it first. "Anyone want any tea or coffee?"

"No thanks. Here." Margot handed the manila envelope across, her hands shaking.

"Looks like . . . you found a lot of invoices," said Reid.

"Open it."

Jenna scooted closer to look over Reid's shoulder, and this time he didn't move away. He opened the envelope flap and withdrew a stack of documents.

As he paged through them, Margot said, "Those are samples from the last three years of irrigation bills. I never look at these because, like I said, Allen does our accounts. Our rate, for the last three years, has held steady at thirty-five dollars an acre."

"For the last three years?" Jenna's stomach clenched. As Reid paged through the bills, yellow highlighted numbers flashed past where Margot had marked the rate. 35, 35, 35 . . .

"And what's this?" Reid held up a stapled stack of what looked like printouts from an accounting program. More highlights filled the first page with neon yellow warning signs.

"Those are records from our business accounts. I found all these unusual transactions. Cash withdrawals. Payments to another account I didn't even know we had. Checks made out to Allen Eames, supposedly for professional services, but sometimes there are multiple checks in a month. What accountant charges you four times a month? And the payments to Allen are more than it would have cost us to pay the normal water rate, so I don't know what's going on. I think my dad might be in some kind of trouble." Tears filled her eyes.

"Okay. It'll be okay," said Reid, his voice low and steady. "I'm sure there's an explanation."

Margot groaned and dabbed at her eyes with the sleeve of her chunky sweater. "This is my fault. I've always left the financial side of the business to my dad. Bailey and I handle all the marketing and the customer-facing aspects of the business. I was planning to transition to managing more of the money when we opened the resort, but I should have done it sooner." Her eyes closed, and more tears slid down her cheeks.

Jenna hopped up and ran to the kitchen. Reid didn't have tissues or even real napkins, just paper towels, so she tore off a few and brought them to Margot. "Here." She sat down on the floor next to the chair and squeezed Margot's hand. "This isn't your fault. You had no reason not to trust your own father."

"Thanks." Margot paused to blow her nose. "I need to hire a CPA to audit all of our books. For all I know, we don't even have the money to build the resort, much less operate it." She heaved a sigh.

"What can we do to help?" asked Reid. "Have you talked to your lawyer?"

She gave a very un-Margot-like snort. "The man who's worked for my dad for twenty years and would do anything for him? No. I haven't even told Bailey. She'll be crushed. She worships our dad."

"You could report him to the irrigation district," said Jenna. "Or at least report Allen. If he's the one tampering with invoices, wouldn't the board do something?"

"I've thought about that." Margot clutched the wad of paper towels like it was a stress ball. "But every scenario I think of ends badly for my father. The district could try to press charges against him for water theft, even. I can't put my dad in that position. But I can't sit here and do nothing."

Jenna and Reid exchanged glances. There had to be something they could do. Jenna's mind raced through other possibilities. Could they involve city council somehow? Should they confront Allen themselves?

"What do you know about Allen?" she said. "Has he been your accountant long?"

"For about five years," said Margot. "I've met him once. I don't know that much about him, I guess. Why?"

"We need more information." Jenna smiled. "And I think I know someone who might help us."

***

Jenna held the manila envelope tight against her chest as she hurried down the sidewalk downtown. She couldn't jog yet, but she could finally speed-walk without her crutches, thank goodness. She turned off Main Street onto First Street and made her way two blocks down to a two-story home painted pale green. She took a set of uneven wooden steps onto the narrow porch. A sign on the front door read *The Juniper Creek Gazette.*

Matt hadn't said whether she'd need to call when she arrived, but when she tried the door, it was unlocked. She stepped inside. The small front reception area, which must have once been a living room, contained a boxy mid-century style couch, a small coffee table, and an antique desk crammed with a laptop, printer, phone, and three potted succulents.

A young woman in glasses sat behind the desk. She wore a flannel shirt and jeans, and her hair was thrown into a careless bun. "Hi," she said, pushing her chair back. "Are you Jenna?"

Jenna nodded. "I have a three p.m. appointment with Matt O'Reilly. I know I'm a little early."

"No problem. I'm Eva." The young woman shook Jenna's hand. "I'll take you back."

Jenna followed Eva down a narrow hall, past a couple of half-open doors. The whirring of a copy machine and low conversation drifted into the hall. Eva stopped at the last door on the left and knocked. "Matt? I have Jenna Daly for you."

"Send her in," said the deep, pleasant voice that she recognized from their phone conversations.

Eva held the door open. As Jenna stepped inside the office, a man rose from a large scuffed wooden desk covered with stacks of paper. He edged around the desk and shook her hand. "Sorry, tight quarters in here. I'm Matt. Nice to finally meet you."

Eva waved at them and left, shutting the door behind her. Jenna took a sagging armchair that was crammed between Matt's desk and a battered file cabinet.

Instead of going back to sit down, Matt perched on the edge of his desk to face Jenna. He was younger than she'd expected, probably in his early thirties. He had closely cropped brown hair, broad muscular shoulders, and glasses—like a real-life Clark Kent, she thought.

Matt grabbed a notepad off his desk and fished a pen out of a nearby holder. He flipped through a few pages, narrowing his eyes at whatever was written there, before turning to a fresh page. Pen poised to write, he said, "You told me a little bit on the phone, but talk me through this thing with Ed Brewer again."

She shifted in her chair. "Where should I start?"

"Anywhere you like."

"Okay, well, you know my students are working on a journalism project." She explained about Tessa and Roberto's original topic—Ed Brewer purchasing the Morris farm - and how they'd learned of his plans to build a luxury resort.

Matt scribbled across his notepad at what appeared to be light speed. "And the land is for the resort?"

"We assume so. But he can afford to buy more property, in part, because he's getting a discount on his irrigation water." Jenna opened the envelope and pulled out the documents Margot had brought over yesterday. She'd added printouts of the Lucky Brewer Resort's business registration and the irrigation fee schedule from the Pine County district's website. "He's paying fifteen dollars per acre less than he's supposed to."

Matt whistled as he shuffled through the pages. "Where did you get these invoices?"

"From his daughter, Margot. She wasn't aware of this until recently. And Allen Eames, this guy who's listed as the registered agent for the resort? He's both the Brewers' accountant, and a member of the irrigation board."

"Which votes to set the water usage rates," murmured Matt. "Interesting."

"Exactly. Isn't that a conflict of interest?"

He scratched his head. "Well, since the board has set the same water usage rates for everyone, as shown by your own research"—he held up the printout she'd provided from the website—"in theory it's not a conflict for him to merely sit on the board. But since, allegedly, Eames has either convinced the board to set a separate rate for Brewer, or is doing this on his own, then yes. *That's* a conflict of interest. And contrary to board policy, I'm sure." He slid the pages behind his notepad and fiddled with his pen, tapping it against his chin. "Have you or anyone approached the irrigation district about this?"

"Not yet," said Jenna. "Margot is afraid the district will come after her dad."

"For thousands of dollars in unpaid fees?" His eyebrows went up. "I could see that. How many acres is the Brewer ranch, do you know?"

"About fifteen hundred."

He scribbled some figures on his notepad. "Let's assume, say, twelve hundred of those are irrigable. Because he's not irrigating every square inch of his property. Right? That's twelve hundred . . . times three years . . . and the rates may not have been constant, but let's say he was supposed to be paying fifty an acre all three years. . ." He fell silent, his pen scratching across the page. His eyes widened. "He could owe well over fifty thousand dollars. But he's running a pretty lucrative business, right? Breeding and boarding show horses? Riding lessons at 160 an hour, according to their website, which I've looked at. Fifty thousand dollars is a chunk of change, but it's not millions. It shouldn't make or break his business."

"It shouldn't, but Margot looked at the ranch's accounts, and she thinks they're in trouble. Look at the last batch of pages there. Her dad's funneling a bunch of money to Allen Eames, but she doesn't know why."

"Really," said Matt, drawing the word out so much that he lent it several extra syllables. "Well, that *is* interesting. I have to ask, how come Margot isn't here? This involves her family."

"She's too upset." Margot had agreed to let Jenna approach Matt on one condition—that she didn't have to come along.

Matt nodded. He flipped to the final page of the documents and his lips quirked upward as he held up the letter Margot had written, attesting to the accuracy of the documents. "Backing up your sources, I see. Nice. You said on the phone that you thought I could help. Where do you see this going? An exposé on the secret financial ruin of Ed Brewer?" He winked. "I can't imagine Margot wants that."

"Not quite," she said. "We were hoping that you could look into Allen Eames. He's the one piece of the puzzle we don't have. He doesn't live in town, and even Margot doesn't know much about him. If we can find out more about his business dealings, we might be able to convince Ed to cut ties with Eames."

"Interesting tactic." Matt wedged the pen behind his right ear. "You're asking me to use my journalistic resources to do investigative reporting for a story I'm not writing and can't run. Correct?"

"I—I guess . . ." Jenna's heart sank. Maybe this had been a mistake. "We're trying to respect Margot's wishes for how to handle this. It's her family."

"You keep saying 'we.' You have another partner in crime?"

"No, I mean, yes. My friend Reid. Well, also Margot's ex. It's complicated," she said. Matt's eyebrows went up again, and Jenna wanted to disappear into the armchair cushions. "Uh, we're all, sort of, friends. Reid's another teacher, and the journalism project was kind of his idea, so anyway, he's helping." *Stop talking, Jenna*, she thought. "We're not after a story unless there's no other option. I hope you understand. But we are willing to pay you for your time." Jenna had known they couldn't ask the owner of a small-town paper to do random investigative work just for fun. With her parents stubbornly refusing to let her pay rent, she had savings. She'd foot the bill if it meant Ed would finally stop trying to buy up land, including her own family's farm.

"Nah." Matt waved his hand. "That's not necessary. I come from a farm family, you know. My dad's parents ran a little horse ranch outside Terrebonne for years. If this stops small farms from suffering, well, that's what journalism is about. Exposing the truth. Helping the little guy."

"Thank you," said Jenna. "By the way, I'd still like to bring you in to speak with my students."

"Sure thing. Eva manages my calendar, so just call her anytime to set something up." He hopped down from the desk, and she stood up as well. He grinned. "I'm not trying to kick you out of my office. But I assume that's all you needed, unless you're looking for my review of Dan Rather's *What Unites Us*. Spoiler alert: it's very good."

Jenna laughed. "That was everything. Thanks again."

"No trouble at all. I'll walk you out."

He held the door for her and they walked down the hall. As they stepped out onto the porch, he said, "I'll be in touch once I find something on Eames. If you're interested, maybe we can discuss it in person. Have dinner or something. Or not. You can think about it." He grinned. "Don't get into too much trouble, now, Nancy Drew."

Before Jenna could formulate a response, he winked and spun around, heading back inside. She stared at the door as it clicked shut. Had Matt just sort of asked her out? *Dinner or something?* Was dinner a date?

She shook her head and headed down the street. The funny thing was, if she'd never left San Francisco, say, and had met Matt under other circumstances, she probably would have been interested. He seemed smart, funny, maybe a little overconfident, but an intelligent guy. But even his Clark Kent vibe didn't do it for her. All she wanted, Jenna, realized, was the tall lean man with shaggy blonde hair, whose smile could reduce her to a puddle.

All she wanted was Reid.

"Well, great!" she blurted. "I'm in love with my ex!"

"Good for you, honey!" said a creaky female voice. An elderly woman was walking down the opposite side of the street. She carried a cloth grocery bag in one hand and a sheaf of lettuce in the other. She waved the lettuce at Jenna and yelled, "Go get him!"

"Thanks." Jenna's whole body burst into flames of embarrassment. Good one. She could admit her feelings to an empty street—well, and one stranger—but not to Reid.

Back at her car, she lingered in park, her phone in hand. Should she call him? Should she just let out her feelings? But what if he didn't feel the same? He'd asked her out on a date, yes, but that didn't mean he loved her. Maybe he just had nostalgia-attraction. That was a thing, wasn't it?

She tossed her phone in the back seat so she couldn't reach it and started up the car. Reid had asked her out to dinner before. If he had real feelings for her, he'd make another gesture. Or he'd say something. She just had to be patient.

Right, patience. Her number one quality. Her fingers itched to reach for her phone already, to call him and tell him everything. No, she thought, I'm not putting myself out there again. It's up to him.

She just hoped he would come through.

Reid centered a poster-board star shape on a sheet of silver paper. "How many of these do we have to make again?"

Jenna looked up at him. For some reason she had chosen to sit on his classroom floor—not a desk, not even his desk, which he'd offered, but the dirtiest possible place to sit. All of the probable bacteria on the tiles didn't seem to bother her, though. Surrounded by pieces of silver paper, she sprawled comfortably against his small bookcase. "About a hundred," she said. Her scissors made little snicking noises as she cut into the silver paper.

"Right." He shook his head and began sketching around the stencil. "This is why I became a teacher, you know. I desperately wanted to make dozens of paper stars." The Homecoming Committee had decided that the dance theme of "Forever and Always" was best represented by celestial decor, which meant Reid and Jenna were now cutting out star shapes by hand. If they'd been at a larger school with a larger budget, they probably could have just ordered decorations, but they didn't have the money to blow five hundred dollars at a party store, so here they were. Really, though, Reid didn't mind. Tracing stars onto paper was a relaxing change from correcting students' writing and photocopying assignments. And he was here with Jenna, which made it all the more fun.

When they'd first joined the committee, he'd dreaded chaperoning with her. Now he couldn't wait.

Chaperoning . . .

"Shoot." He groaned. "I still have a couple parents to call about chaperoning."

Her eyes widened. "Oh my gosh, me too. I've been so distracted with everything else."

"We still have time." He frowned at the large calendar on her desk. "But we should probably call them today or tomorrow."

"Thanks for the reminder." Jenna pointed to the half-moon stencil that leaned against the bookcase. "Don't forget we also have to make moons. We'll be here awhile."

"We might have to order pizza."

"Not if you work faster." She grinned. "Are you trying to recreate *Starry Night* over there?"

"I'm being accurate," he said. "Precise. You know, all the things I teach my students to be in their writing."

"Uh-huh." She waved her completed star at him. "Ninety-nine to go."

"Haste makes waste, Miss Daly."

She stuck her tongue out at him, then gently set the star aside. "Do you think our teachers did this? Spend hours making decorations to hang in the gym?"

"Don't know. We never made it to our Homecoming to find out." He smiled, recalling that moment they had stood on top of Pilot Butte, waiting for his dad to give them a tow, when he'd finally gathered the courage to pull Jenna close and kiss her. They had been dating for a few weeks by that point, but every time he had thought about kissing her, he'd been too shy to go through with it. He had forgotten a lot of details about high school, but that moment was crystallized: the sun in her hair, the freckles on her shoulders, the surprise and joy on her face when he leaned down.

Jenna smiled back and started tracing around her second star. He could see the top of her head, the neat line where her hair parted. It tumbled long and loose past her shoulders, and he thought about that night at karaoke when she'd worn it that way, and the way her hair had smelled like flowers.

If he asked her out again, maybe he could find out.

She glanced up. "What?"

"Nothing." He removed the stencil, frowned at the outline, and decided it was good enough to cut out. "You know, I felt so guilty that we didn't make it to Homecoming our senior year."

"Guilty? Why?"

"Because you got all dressed up and did your hair and stuff. You wore that blue dress. The one with the little strap, uh, things, in the back?" He sketched lines in the air with one finger, hoping she knew what he meant. He didn't really know how to describe dresses. "You know, crisscrossed."

"Spaghetti straps." She laughed. "You remember what my dress looked like?"

"It was blue, wasn't it?"

"It was bright blue." She pursed her lips. "I still have that dress, you know. I found it in my closet the other day. Wonder if it still fits." She shrugged.

They fell silent, the only sounds were the snipping of scissors and the faint hum of the fluorescent lights. Reid cut his star out inch by inch, trying to find the words to start. *I care about you. I think we should have dinner again. I want to be with you.* His classroom door was open, though, and students occasionally passed by on their way to sports practice, or other activities. He couldn't confess his feelings to her at work. It had to be somewhere better, more romantic. "Are you going to stay with your parents much longer?" He had continued working on the Dalys' farm three mornings a week, and Jenna was always up at an early hour too, doing chores. He worried a bit about whether she was running herself into the ground. There were shadows under her eyes that he hadn't noticed in August.

"I think so," she said. "I feel like my parents need the help. Until I can be sure the farm's okay, and that they're okay, I don't want to move out."

He nodded. "No more offers from Ed Brewer, I take it?"

"Not that I know of. Oh!" Jenna set down her scissors. "I wonder if Matt emailed me." She dug into her purse. "He called yesterday and said he was close to finishing his report on Allen Eames. He thought he'd have it by today, but I haven't seen . . ." Her voice faded as she grabbed her phone and tapped the screen. "Oh my gosh, he did it. Come see this."

Reid scrambled out of his seat and dropped onto the floor next to her. Looking over her shoulder, he read the email from Matt.

The attached report outlines everything I was able to glean on Allen Eames. In summary: the man is shady.

As you already knew, he's an accountant, but looks like he also develops commercial real estate. Or he did when he lived in Texas. Several years ago, his investors sued him for fraud and misappropriation of funds. It seems that he forgot to tell them about his astronomical gambling debts. He ended up with a pretty generous plea deal in exchange for his cooperation with prosecutors, so he didn't do any time. This all wrapped up five years ago. Guess when he moved to Oregon? Five years ago.

He's renting a little apartment in Crystalvale, so he isn't flush with cash. My guess is that he sees the Lucky Brewer Resort as his chance to turn his finances around and make a buck. I'd report him to the irrigation district board as soon as you can, and steer Ed Brewer far away from any further association with this guy.

It's a shame we're not writing the story. It would make a good one.

"Holy mackerel," breathed Jenna. She skimmed through the attached writeup he'd sent, then forwarded the email. "I just sent it on to Margot. So, now we do it."

Reid took a deep breath. "It" was the plan he, Jenna, and Margot had developed, and it was risky. It involved gathering all of the farm owners together—or as many as they could, anyway—and having Ed publicly admit to and apologize for his irrigation scheme. He would also offer to make it right by setting up a trust fund to benefit local farm families.

Ed didn't know about any of this yet. Margot planned to confront her father with the truth, but Reid had no idea how the man would react. Would he confess? Explain himself? Lie? And if he did agree to the public apology, how would the town react? What if they wanted blood?

"I need to loop everyone else in," said Jenna. "I can talk to my parents tonight and we'll start making calls."

"I'll check in with Margot one more time," he said. "She has to be one hundred percent on board. This is her dad, after all."

"I know. I can't imagine how she feels." Jenna shook her head. She put her phone back in her purse. "Thank you, by the way."

"For what?"

"For caring about what happens to our town. For . . . for being on my side."

"I'm always on your side, Pixie." He touched her chin, and her hair brushed against the side of his hand.

She smiled, but then glanced over her shoulder at the open door.

Reid got back up and moved toward his desk. His mind started humming with the beginnings of a plan, a way to tell Jenna how he felt about her—the right way. "What are you doing tomorrow night?"

"I might be making decorations if we don't finish these." She picked up her scissors again. Her cheeks were pink.

"What about that dinner we didn't get to finish? We could go back to The Sawmill. Maybe order a jumbo milkshake this time."

A smile spread across her face. "That would be fun. Great."

"Great," he said.

They both started laughing. "We're just as awkward as we were in high school," said Reid.

"Hey, speak for yourself." She picked up the discarded portion of paper, which she'd crumpled into a ball, and tossed it at him. Reid caught it, thinking how easy it was to be with her, as easy as catching the outline of a star.

***

Reid tapped one shoe on the floor, rapid rhythm, as he waited for Margot at the Sunrise Cafe later that night. She was coming from dressage practice and had texted him she would be a few minutes late. He'd already scarfed down a scone, and now he flipped through news headlines on his phone.

A milk frother hissed as one of the baristas made a latte, a jarring accompaniment to the acoustic guitar music coming from the speakers. A couple students from his second-period class sat nearby, reading *The Scarlet Letter*. He was pleased to see them actually doing homework. A few weeks ago, he might have worried about his students spotting him talking to his ex-fiancée, and the rumors that might swirl as a result. Now, though, who cared? He was going to live his life. He grinned.

The little bell on the front door chimed against the glass. Margot walked in, brushing something from her riding pants. She waved at him, then went to place her order.

A minute later, she sat down across from him, holding a mug that was frothy with milk. The barista had drawn a delicate leaf pattern in the foam. She took a sip and sighed. "How are you?"

"How are *you*? You read Matt's report?"

She nodded. "About ten times. I can't believe my dad would even hire someone like that. This guy has been doing our accounts for three years, Reid." She grimaced. "We're going to hire a CPA to audit our books. I just hope we can get through to Dad."

"When's the big discussion?"

"Tomorrow morning. Wish me luck. Bailey and I own shares in the business, but Dad still owns the majority. We don't have a lot of leverage."

"You've got the truth."

"Sometimes that's not enough." She lifted the mug and swirled the foam around, as if it might tell her the future. "Bailey and I agreed, though. Even if Dad denies everything, I'm going to be there on Saturday."

"Really?"

She met his gaze. "Yes." Her expression was iron, the way it had been the night they broke up, when she made it clear the business came first. "Bailey's pretty torn up, and I wouldn't put her through that anyway, but I'll be there." She set down the mug without taking a sip. "I guess that's our leverage with Dad. We're telling the town what happened whether or not he agrees."

"That's what a good business owner does. The right thing. You're gonna make one heck of a CEO. Margot Brewer, head of the Lucky Brewer empire."

She sighed. "Thanks, but I don't know about empire. Let's start with getting our books back in the black."

"Fair." He nodded and glanced around the shop. He could stall her with small talk about dressage practice, but he had a second reason for meeting her in person, and he needed to get it over with. "There's something else I need to talk to you about."

Margot drained the last of her latte. "Uh-oh, sounds ominous."

"No, no." He paused for breath. "I just need to let you know that I, uh, Jenna and I have gotten pretty close the last few weeks, and, well, I have feelings for her."

She blinked. "You're. Kidding. I'm shocked," she said, totally deadpan.

Reid snorted. "Okay, then, I guess you already knew."

"Well, let's see, she was your first love, she's a total sweetheart, and every time you're around her, you act all jumpy and awkward. You get downright *nervous*. I've never seen you that way." She shook her head. "I was kind of waiting for this to happen, to be honest."

Her words stung. He'd thought he was being respectful, fighting his feelings for Jenna in the wake of his breakup with Margot. When the three of them had met up recently, he'd tried not to treat Jenna any differently, not wanting Margot to feel awkward. But no, apparently, he'd worn his heart on both sleeves with a neon sign that even his ex could see. "I'm sorry."

"Why? It's a little weird to talk about, but . . ." She shrugged. "You guys seem like you'd be really good together. Are you going to tell her how you feel?"

He couldn't believe she was acting so calm. "I'm, uh, I'm going to recreate the way I asked her out to our senior year homecoming. Roses, a note, a teddy bear. Kind of silly, I guess."

"No, that's sweet," she murmured. "You always have been good at those romantic gestures."

"I just wanted to tell you in person. I didn't want you to hear it from someone else."

"I appreciate that."

He hesitated, then reached for her hand. "Thank you. For taking this so well, and for being such an important part of my life for so long. I know the last few months haven't been great, but you got me through the worst time in my life after my dad died. You pretty much saved me. I owed you a lot better than I gave you, but you're an incredible woman."

"We did all right together, didn't we? We had a lot of good times." She squeezed his hand. "For what it's worth, you have my blessing with Jenna. Not that you need it."

Warmth filled Reid's heart as a weight lifted from him. He had everything: a great job, in one of the most beautiful places in the state. Peace with his ex. And Jenna, a woman who made him feel like he belonged in a way he never had with anyone. He was one lucky man.

Tomorrow, he would tell Jenna how lucky he was. He would say the words that had been threatening to spill over all day today: *I love you.*

And if his luck held, she'd say them back.

Jenna whistled as she walked toward Sunrise Cafe. After she and Reid had finally finished cutting out the paper stars, she'd run home for dinner and taken care of a few chores around the farm. Now she planned to spend the rest of the evening grading. Her backpack was stuffed full of second drafts of her students' news articles, although she'd also crammed in *Peril at End House* for reading on breaks. She could always judge her workload by how quickly or slowly she was making it through a book. Right now, she was only halfway through the novel. It had been a busy month.

Pausing outside the cafe, she checked her phone. She'd texted Reid earlier to ask if he'd talked to Margot, but he hadn't answered yet. She hoped Margot was still on board, because otherwise a whole bunch of people were cramming into her parents' house on Saturday for no reason.

She smiled, thinking about tomorrow's date with Reid. She was trying not to get too excited—she definitely wasn't ready to tell him she loved him for fear of scaring him off—but she was already imagining sitting down with him, lingering over dinner, holding hands across the table. A real date.

She pocketed her phone and reached for the door handle, but a familiar face inside caught her eye. She froze and stared through the cafe window.

Reid and Margot sat at a small table near the back of the cafe. They leaned towards each other, holding hands. Reid smiled in a way that looked tender and caring.

Jenna gasped and backed away from the door. She was certain her heart had stopped beating. Reid was supposed to be calling Margot on the phone, not taking her out for a coffee date. What. The. Heck?

Tears burned her eyes. Had she misread all the signals? Reid had been acting interested, and he'd just asked her out for dinner today. She was sure he'd almost kissed her today at school. Why was he holding Margot's hand?

Oh, Lord in Heaven. She wiped her eyes with her jacket sleeve. Part of her thought there was a reasonable explanation for the scene in the cafe. Reid hadn't explicitly said he would call Margot, he'd said he would check in with her. But then why wouldn't he tell Jenna he was taking her out to coffee? And what about the handholding? That hadn't looked like two exes on good terms. It had looked like a date.

She should probably try to call him, but he was still in there. With Margot. And she had no appetite to walk in and confront him in public. She turned and strode down the sidewalk. A bright blue OPEN sign shone in the window of Creekside Gift Shop. She wandered in and coughed, her nose assailed with the competing smells of a dozen kinds of candles.

"Can I help you?" said a teenage girl behind the counter. She had blue and purple hair woven into braids, and she was staring at her phone.

"I'm good," said Jenna. The girl didn't even seem to hear her, which was fine. Jenna was not in the mood for small talk. She ducked in between two shelves and stared at the mugs, picture frames, and other trinkets. Her backpack tugged at her shoulders, and she hefted it into a more comfortable position.

She stood eye to eye with a row of ceramic angel figurines. They all had large childlike eyes and they held ceramic hearts that said things like *Be Mine* and *True Love.* Valentine's overstock, no doubt, but they seemed to be mocking her. The image of Reid and Margot holding hands was seared into her brain.

She needed an angel that said *Super Confused.*

Her eyeballs were leaking again. She dried them on her sleeve and took a determined sniff to suck back any further tears. She wasn't going to fall apart in front of a bunch of cheesy decorations. She would go home and think things over and come up with a plan.

"Thanks," she said to the girl behind the counter, as she headed for the door.

The girl was still engrossed in her phone. "Let me know if you need anything."

"Mind-reading abilities," muttered Jenna. She swung open the door and stepped out into the cold.

***

Back home, Jenna managed to greet her parents without them catching on that anything was wrong. She hurried upstairs and tossed her backpack to the floor. Abandon all grading, ye who enter here. Plopping onto her bed, she took out her cell phone and stared at the lock screen, a photo she'd taken looking out from the front porch, with the Three Sisters in the hazy distance.

The adult thing to do, probably, was to call Reid. Give him a chance to explain and ask him to clarify how he felt. But Jenna had already put her heart on the line once for him and look how that had turned out.

She set down her phone and played with the edges of her duvet cover. Reid had been her only long-term relationship, and the only person she'd ever loved. In college she'd dated here and there, but not seriously, and she'd never connected with anyone romantically in San Francisco. It had been months since she'd been on a date. She wondered if she knew how to fall for anyone . . . anyone besides Reid.

She reached for her phone dialed. With every ring, she felt more nauseated. At the sound of his cheery voicemail greeting, she hung up without leaving a message.

Groaning, she threw herself back against her pillows. She was a coward. She couldn't say goodbye to Reid, even when there was nothing to say goodbye to. She might have fallen for him—again—but he was sending mixed signals. If he did still have feelings for Margot, then she needed to open herself to other possibilities. She couldn't just sit at home, pining for Reid Walsh for another decade.

She stared up at the ceiling, visually tracing abstract outlines in the plaster texture. As a child she used to try and find shapes in them. Dogs and faces and elephants. She used to search for them every night before she turned the lights out, like constellations. Now they just looked like what they really were: nothing.

Rolling over, she picked up her phone again and texted Reid.

I'm sorry, I can't make dinner tomorrow night. I need some time and I think you do too, to really think about what's best for each of us long-term. I'm sorry.

***

Jenna checked her phone—again, probably for the thousandth time that day—before she walked into La Rosa Blanca to pick up the takeout she'd ordered for dinner. Her parents were out on a date night, so she was on her own, which suited her mood just fine.

Once again, she read Reid's text. He'd called her last night, but she hadn't picked up and he hadn't left a voicemail. The text had popped up this morning: *I feel like I've done something wrong and I don't know what it is. I understand you need some space, but I hope you'll talk to me when you're ready.*

She'd avoided Reid all day at school, even though their classrooms were adjacent, by eating lunch in her classroom and taking her prep period in the library. And he had left school right after the bell rang, walking past her classroom without a glance in her direction.

Guilt had nagged her all day, aching like a wound, but she'd gritted her teeth against it. She knew she should talk to him. He was probably hurt, but then again, *why had he taken Margot out to coffee last night?*

She could just ask him the question, like an adult. But why hadn't he told her upfront? That would have been an adult thing to do, too.

Ugh.

She slipped her phone into her purse and walked into the restaurant. La Blanca Rosa exuded warmth and coziness. The yeasty scent of flour tortillas permeated the air, making her stomach growl. Red, yellow, and turquoise tiles decorated the walls. Strung from the ceiling were paper garlands in every color of the rainbow. The lights cast a warm gold wash over the yellow chairs and red upholstered booth seats.

She had just paid for her meal when someone called, "Jenna! Hey!"

Matt O'Reilly sat at one of the smaller booths near the back. She hadn't even noticed him, even though the restaurant was fairly empty. He grinned and waved her over.

She hesitated, but the sight of a friendly face warmed her. She wandered over and slid into the seat across from him. "Hey. What are you doing here?"

He closed his laptop. "Just switching it up while I work, but I could use a distraction. You want to stay and have a bite? Whatever you ordered smells good."

"Chicken enchiladas." She set the takeout box to the side. "Sure. If you don't mind me crashing." The thought of a quiet night in an empty house didn't sound so appealing, and all the food smells were making her stomach rumble.

"You're not crashing. I can work on this story later. Salsa?" He slid a miniature cast iron pot toward her. It was loaded with fresh house-made salsa. A basket of warm tortilla chips sat next to it.

She dipped a chip in and lifted it up, flinging salsa across the table. A blob landed on Matt's white t-shirt. "Oh my gosh. I'm sorry."

He smiled and dipped his napkin into his water glass. "No problem," he said, dabbing at his shirt. The salsa smeared, leaving a pinkish stain.

"I'm really klutzy. You know, throwing salsa on people, falling off a horse."

"It's fine," he said. "We all have our flaws. I can barely follow a recipe. When did you fall off a horse?"

"A few weeks ago. He spooked at a snake, and just bolted. Sprained my ankle." She smiled wryly, but her heart wrenched, remembering Reid taking her to the doctor, sitting on the couch, reading to her . . .

"See," he said, "this is why I never ride horses."

She stared at him. "You live in Juniper Creek and you've never ridden a horse? I thought your grandparents had a horse farm."

"They did. I rode when I was a kid. Horses just scare me. I prefer riding golf carts."

"You're missing out." She crammed the chip into her mouth and reached for another one, this time dipping it more cautiously.

He smiled at her, and her stomach fluttered. This felt like an accidental date. Matt couldn't have known what happened between her and Reid, but he did have great timing. This felt nothing like her night at The Sawmill with Reid, a night laced with hope and possibility. But it did feel . . . well, fun, at least. In a different way.

Maybe she ought to be more open to new possibilities.

"So," said Matt. "What were you planning before I interrupted your evening?"

Moping in my room. "Just grading and reading." She shrugged. "Nothing too exciting." Oh no, did she sound boring? She'd forgotten how to communicate with adult males. She really was hung up on Reid.

"What does an English teacher read for fun?"

Books. Familiar ground. She could talk about books for hours. "Well, I love mysteries. Tana French. Megan Abbott. Agatha Christie."

He nodded. "Miss Marple or Hercule Poirot?"

"Poirot, hands down."

They launched into a discussion of their favorite authors, only pausing for Matt to order. When his food arrived, she was surprised how quickly the time had gone. She and Reid could always talk about books, too, but it was nice to know that there were other well-read guys out there. Maybe there was hope for her dating life after all.

"Hey," said a familiar voice.

She looked up. Margot was walking toward her. Oh, great. The woman who might or might not be back together with Reid. Resisting the urge to throw a napkin over her face and hide under the table, Jenna plastered on a side smile. "Margot. What are you, uh, doing here?"

The other woman gave her a weird look. "Grabbing takeout. I thought you were having dinner with Reid tonight."

Matt frowned. "What?"

"There was a change of plans." Jenna grabbed her water and sucked down half the glass. Maybe it was the spiciness of the chicken, but she suddenly felt hot and the booth seemed cramped. "Long story."

"You're Margot Brewer, aren't you?" Matt's eyes lit up, and he extended a hand to her. "I'm Matt O'Reilly. I've been helping you with your little research project."

"Nice to meet you." Margot shook his hand, but her gaze swung back to Jenna. "Can we talk outside for a minute? In private?"

"Um, sure." Jenna's heart raced. Was Margot going to tell her that she and Reid were back together? To Matt, she said, "I'll be right back."

"Great." Margot spun on her heel and stalked toward the door.

Jenna followed, barely keeping up. Margot seemed angry, but why? Her imagination ran amok, quickly constructing a fight between Reid and Margot over him asking Jenna out. In the thirty feet it took to get outside, she decided they must be back together, and Margot was here to tell Jenna to back off.

The second they got outside, Margot turned, her blue eyes flashing darkly. "You're having dinner with that guy? What's wrong with you?"

"What?" Jenna felt like she was in a play and had forgotten her lines. She was having dinner with Not Reid, so why did Margot care?

Margot glared. "Reid and I had coffee last night, and he told me he was taking you out to dinner tonight, and he was so excited about it. Now you're standing him up for someone else?"

"No!" Her heart sank, and the suspicion crept over her that she'd made one too many assumptions here. "I did tell Reid I couldn't make dinner tonight, because I . . . I thought he wasn't sure how he felt about me. I ran into Matt by accident and he asked me to sit down with him, that's all. I thought you and Reid were . . ." Her voice trailed off at the incredulous tilt of Margot's brows. "I saw you two at Sunrise Cafe last night, holding hands, so I figured you were back on."

"We weren't *holding hands*," said Margot. "He grabbed my hand when he was thanking *me* for being so understanding that he wanted to be with *you*."

Hope and cold panic spread through Jenna's body. "Are you sure?"

"No, I completely misunderstood when he said he had feelings for you." Margot rolled her eyes. "The two of you are so obtuse when it comes to each other. Honestly, I think Reid fell back in love with you the night of the back-to-school barbecue, and you clearly feel the same. The way you look at each other, there's just something . . . well, special." Her expression softened. "I hate to admit that Reid and I never had that. Not in the same way."

Jenna felt her face going hot. "I do love him. I've tried not to. I would never—I mean, if you two were still together, I would never even suggest . . ."

"I know that." Margot smiled. "Don't worry, I'm not going to crumple into a heap when you two ride off into the sunset. I miss being in a relationship and having a partner, but I think Reid and I are pretty different. He loves being a small-town teacher and there's nothing wrong with that. You're one too. But I have a business to run—if we survive this scandal, anyway—and I need someone who wants to share that with me in every way. You know?"

"I do. You deserve that." Jenna wanted to hug her, but she wasn't sure Margot was the impulsive hugging type, so she touched the woman's shoulder. "Thank you for handling this so graciously. You're amazing."

Margot smirked. "Yeah, I kind of am."

The two of them burst into laughter.

"I should probably get back inside," said Jenna. "And tell poor Matt what's going on, although I don't know how I'm going to explain everything. So . . . you don't think I totally blew my chances with Reid? It's not too late?"

Margot grabbed her arm and steered her towards the restaurant. "Jenna, finish your dinner and then just *talk* to Reid, for crying out loud. Use your words. Why doesn't anyone communicate?"

It was tough love, Margot-style. This time, Jenna did give her a quick hug. "I'll see you tomorrow."

"Can't wait," said Margot dryly.

Jenna hurried back to the booth. "Sorry," she said, sliding into her seat. "I didn't mean to ditch you."

"No problem. Everything okay?"

"Yeah. Um . . ." Her hair was falling into her eyes. She shoved it back. "I think I owe you an apology. I'm glad we ran into each other, and I'm enjoying dinner, but I just found out that . . . uh, well, Reid and

I were kind of starting to date, and I thought it might be over, but it looks like it's not."

"I see." He wrinkled his brow. "I think, anyway. You were supposed to go out with Reid tonight, but you stood him up?"

"No!" Why did everyone have to use that phrase? "I told him we should wait. I thought he still had feelings for Margot, but according to her, he does not."

"Interesting." Matt glanced toward the front of the restaurant, where Margot was signing a receipt next to a takeout box, then blinked at turned back to Jenna. "Well, it sounds like you and Reid have a lot to talk about."

"I'm sorry. I didn't mean to give off the impression that this was . . ."

"A date?" He smiled. "Nope, this is just two friends having dinner. You see, unfortunately for you, we're friends now. I'm hoping that will continue."

She smiled back. "Absolutely."

"Good. Then get out of here and call Reid, or whatever you need to do. I'll see you tomorrow."

"Yes. Seven p.m." She grabbed her purse and checked to make sure her keys and phone were still there, then slid out of the booth.

"Margot's definitely coming tomorrow, then?" he said.

Hmm. Jenna pursed her lips, holding back a smile. "Yep, she'll be there. Have a great night, Matt. It was really good to see you."

The second she got outside the restaurant, she dialed Reid. Please pick up. Once, twice . . . three times . . .

"Hi, you've reached Reid Walsh. I'm not available right now . . ."

"Reid," she said. "I hope you're home. I'm coming over."

***

Jenna's heart drummed wildly as she knocked on Reid's door. Should she have waited until tomorrow? Waited until he at least answered his phone? What if he wasn't home? Also, if he was home, what if he didn't want to talk to her?

Plus, she'd popped a mint on the way over, but what if her breath still smelled like chicken enchiladas?

She heard footsteps from inside. A moment later, the handle twisted, and the door cracked open. Reid peered out, eyes slightly puffy, hair sticking up in several directions. "Hi."

"Hi. I don't know if you got my voicemail. I tried to call. Can I come in?" Her voice sounded wobbly. Darn nerves.

"Oh, sorry. I was taking a nap. Come on in." He stepped back and opened the door wide.

Jenna had to hide her surprise when she stepped inside. A greasy pizza box sat on the coffee table next to crumpled paper towels and a glass full of melting ice. A rumpled blanket draped over the couch, and a book sprawled on the floor next to a roll of more paper towels. The last time she'd been here, the living room had been spotless. She'd never seen anything out of place in Reid's life before.

He sat down on the couch and gave her a hesitant smile as he patted the spot next to him. He was wearing sweats and a t-shirt, and he looked soft and vulnerable, and her heart cracked open.

Sitting down next to him, she said, "I need to explain some stuff."

"Okay," he said. "You didn't explain much last night."

"I know. I'm sorry." She reached for his hand, and to her relief, he squeezed and held on. "I walked by the Sunrise Cafe last night and saw you holding Margot's hand. I panicked . . ."

Reid's eyes slid shut, and he sighed. "You thought I still had feelings for her. Pixie, no." He met her gaze again and took her other hand. "I met up with her so I could tell her in person how I feel about you. I didn't want her to hear it from the rumor mill. She was great about it, and I was thanking her, and I took her hand, but it wasn't like that. I swear, I—"

"I know." She touched a finger to his lips. "Margot told me."

He did a double take. "What?"

"I saw her tonight." She explained how she'd run into Matt at La Rosa Blanca, then Margot. "She explained your whole conversation at the cafe. Also, she told me the two of us were, quote, 'obtuse' when it came to each other."

He smiled. "Sounds like something she'd say. So . . ."

"So." She angled towards him so she could look him directly in the eye. She didn't want to say it first, ask it first, be the one to put it all out there. She wanted him to take that risk. When he just looked at her, as if contemplating a piece of art, a dam broke. Tears burst out of her with ferocity, fueled by old deep wounds.

"Whoa, whoa, what's wrong?" He pulled her close and she sobbed on his chest. This wasn't how she'd pictured this conversation, but now that she'd started crying, she couldn't seem to stop.

"Here." He leaned down and swiped the roll of paper towels off the floor. Tearing off several, he handed her a wad. As she blotted her eyes and nose, he said, "Please tell me why you're crying."

"Because I'm scared." She tried to laugh, but it came out like a wet snuffle. "We've already been through one breakup, and you're the one who walked away. I understand why you did, but I just—I never once questioned how I felt about you. Now we're back here, and you've been trying to figure out your life while I've just been trying to figure out how not to be in love with you. I feel like I'm the one that's always been sure about us."

"Pixie." He cradled her chin with one hand, keeping a tight grasp on her other hand. "That might have been true in high school, when I was a kid, but it's not true now. I'm so sorry I hurt you then, and I'm sorry it took me awhile to get my head on the right way, but I have never been surer about anything than I am about you." He leaned close, touching his nose to hers. "I hope you'll give me a chance to prove that."

"Oh," she said. "I mean, yes."

He pulled her close and kissed her, and she fell into the warmth of him, and he felt like home.

Eventually they settled back against the couch. Wrapping his arm around her shoulders, he said, "Just to clarify: I love you."

"I love you, too." She smiled, brushing a crumb off his cheek. "You had a little pizza there."

"I was living the bachelor life tonight, as you can see. Real exciting." He kissed her cheek. "I was planning to watch *The Office.* Do you want to stay for awhile?"

"I'd love to." *Grading, schmading.*

Reid flipped on the TV, and they curled up together. Hazy with peace, Jenna thought she didn't want to stay for awhile. She wanted to stay forever.

Jenna set the last tray of crackers and cheese on the kitchen island and surveyed the plates of sliced veggies and deli meats, the small bowls of olives, the containers of pasta salad and the pans of bean dip. It looked more like the Dalys were hosting a Superbowl party rather than an unofficial town hall. "Mom, you need anything else?"

"Nope. All set." Her mom smoothed out the front row of soda cans in the fridge. "We just need people to show up."

"With pitchforks." A wry look crossed Margot's face, but there was real fear in her eyes, and she hugged her arms close as if she was freezing.

"I don't think so, honey." Andrea came to stand next to her and put a gentle hand on her shoulder. "All you can do is tell the truth and take responsibility. People will listen."

Margot nodded a few times, as if to convince herself. "I hope so, but I'm not sure we have a lot of credibility. In the equestrian community we're pretty respected. We treat our horses like royalty, we provide quality riding instruction, and we have top of the line facilities. But a lot of our customers aren't from Juniper Creek, so people in town don't know us that well. A lot of them just think we're a family of snobs."

Jenna tried to muster a look of surprise, but Margot just snorted. "I know you know what I'm talking about. Even in high school my family had that reputation. Some of the girls—not you—were so mean to me. Outside of riding, I didn't really have any friends."

"I'm sorry," said Jenna. "I had no idea."

The other woman shrugged and tossed her glossy blonde braid over her shoulder. "It was fine once I went to college. My point is, we've isolated ourselves in this community for quite awhile. Longer than we should have. I hope everyone gives us a chance to talk, that's all." She craned her neck toward the back door. "They're still out there." When she and her dad had arrived half an hour ago, Ed and David had gone out back to chat. Margot had said her dad was nervous, and Jenna figured her dad, in his quiet way, was probably giving Ed a pep talk.

"Dad's good at calming people down." Jenna glanced at the clock. "I thought Reid would have been here by now."

"He's always just on time." Margot shook her head. "Did Matt say when he was coming? He seems like the type to be early." She glanced down and picked at some fluff on the sleeve of her sweater.

Interesting. "He should be here any . . ."

The doorbell rang.

"Okay." Jenna locked her gaze on Margot's, reassured when she saw the steel return to the other woman's eyes, shutting out the fear. "Let's do this."

The two of them went to the front door and Jenna pulled it open. Matt stood there, bundled into a puffy black jacket and a wool cap. His breath steamed out in small clouds. "Hey." His eyes lit up, gaze sliding straight to Margot. "The woman of the hour. How do you feel?"

"Let's put it this way," she said. "I'd rather be having a root canal."

Jenna invited him in, and he kicked off his shoes in the entry way. "Thanks for having me," he said, giving her a quick hug before turning back to Margot. He gave her a much longer hug, which she returned.

"There's food in the kitchen if you're hungry," said Margot.

"Always." Matt patted his belly and offered Margot his arm. The two of them walked toward the kitchen, with Jenna trailing behind. Matt leaned in to say something, and Margot tipped her head back and giggled.

Jenna's eyes grew wide. She'd never actually heard a sound that high-pitched come out of Margot before.

Since she'd left the front door unlocked, she went back into the kitchen and grabbed a soda from the fridge. Her stomach was hopping too much for food.

More neighbors arrived in short order, along with Tessa and Roberto. Jenna figured they deserved to be here, since in some way they'd started this whole thing. Pam Rustigan and her husband Joe showed up, and Steph and Elisa came for moral support. Most people knew each other already, and the chatter in the kitchen swelled as people caught up and loaded plates with snacks.

Jenna and her parents hadn't told everyone exactly what was going on; they'd only said the Brewer family had something important to discuss with the community. A few people shot Margot curious looks, but she was locked in a conversation with Matt, her eyes alight.

Jenna checked the clock and her stomach clenched into a tight ball. Where was Reid? It was almost seven.

The next moment, he walked into the room, and everything felt calm and right again. She hurried over to him and he pulled her into a hug.

"I'm so glad you're here," she murmured.

"Wouldn't miss it." He leaned down and kissed the top of her head. "It's all going to go just fine."

Jenna's mom went to get David and Ed, and the three of them walked back into the kitchen. As soon as Ed entered the small crowd, the mood shifted. The laughter faded and several people shot curious glances at him.

Jenna's parents gave her a nod, and she raised her hand. "Everyone, can I have your attention?" When the group had turned her way, she said, "Thank you for coming, especially on such short notice. We're here to talk about the Brewer ranch and some things we've learned that impact all of us. You all know Margot Brewer and her father, Ed. They would like to speak."

Margot left Matt's side and came to stand by her father. She reached for his hand and looked up at him.

"Folks." Ed cleared his throat a few times. Like Margot, he was tall and lean. The deep lines around his mouth and eyes deepened as he surveyed the waiting crowd. "I'm here to ask your forgiveness. I . . ." He coughed and dug a rumpled handkerchief out of his pocket. Dabbing at his eyes, he whispered something to Margot. She nodded.

"Please excuse us both. This is a bit emotional." Margot let go of her dad's hand and squared her shoulders. "As you know by now, our family has been planning to convert a large portion of our ranch into a luxury resort, which was supposed to open next summer. When my father bought the Morris ranch, we were excited because it would give us even more land to build the facilities on. My sister and I have been under the impression that our finances were in good order and that this project would make us even more profitable." She glanced down. "Unfortunately, Bailey and I recently learned that one of the reasons we've had additional cash flow, is that we're getting an unauthorized discount on our irrigation water. All of you are paying fifty dollars an acre, which is the official rate. We're only paying thirty-five."

Murmurs swept through the room, and several people began talking. Pam Rustigan, who could never really stop being a principal, said, "Quiet, quiet. Let's hear what they have to say."

Ed wrung his gnarled, rough hands together. "My accountant, Allen Eames, is on the irrigation board. Allen said he could cut me a deal on our water rates, and well, I didn't ask questions. A resort is a huge operation, and any extra cash helps. That's what made it so easy to buy the Morris farm. I . . . I knew I could add it to the ranch's property and irrigate it for less than anyone else would pay."

"So you decided to cheat us on our irrigation water?" sputtered Hank, one of the neighbors, whose family owned a farm a few miles down the road from the Dalys.

"I didn't think of it as cheating at the time," said Ed. "I thought of it as smart business."

Hank crossed his arms and glared. "I'm disappointed in you, Ed. I would have thought you had more integrity."

"Um, there's more," said Margot. "Dad?"

Ed heaved a shaky breath. "I've been funneling a lot of money to Allen this year, supposedly for the resort. He told me he had found us investors, and they needed capital up front. Turns out he was probably lying about that."

"Matt?" Margot glanced over her shoulder at him. "Can you explain this part?"

As Matt came forward, Jenna noticed how close he stood to Margot—shoulder to shoulder. He adjusted his glasses and said, "I was asked to investigate Allen's business dealings. The man has a history of gambling and cheating investors." He summarized everything he had learned about Allen through his investigation. "This is not the first time Allen has cheated a business partner out of thousands of dollars on a real estate project. I'd say he's up to his old tricks."

The small crowd erupted in conversation and advice, some of it shouted. "That's thousands of dollars you owe the irrigation board," snapped Hank. "I don't care what your accountant told you. This isn't right."

Jenna's dad raised both hands. "Folks, stop. Just stop," he said. The group grew silent, meek looks on their faces. "I think it's clear that this Allen Eames character needs to be stopped. We can report him to the irrigation board. But Ed, you said you were also here to ask our forgiveness and our help. Why don't you tell us what you have in mind?"

"A little mercy, for starters," said Ed. "I know you could all rightly sue me, and Allen. And I'd understand if you did. But I'm asking you to give me a chance to make everything right. I'll self-report to the irrigation district and get my rate adjusted immediately. I'll pay back what I owe the board. And I'd like to offer more than that."

"We're proposing the creation of a grant for local farms," said Margot. "We'll contribute fifty thousand dollars and appoint some of you as the trustees. Any struggling farm can apply for grant money and get assistance to make it through hard times."

Silence greeted her proposal, but several people nodded, eyebrows raised. Hank uncrossed his arms.

"I'll be severing all ties with Allen," added Ed. "As to the resort . . ." He glanced down at Margot. "We're going to put those plans on hold. The Lucky Brewer Ranch will continue, although we may be selling off some of the land to get our finances back in order. But if we ever do decide to open a resort, we'll be talking to our neighbors about it, openly."

Jenna nudged Reid and whispered, "Did you know they were stopping work on the resort?"

"No, but I'm not surprised."

Pam came forward and slid her arm around Margot's shoulders. "I think you were very brave to tell us all this," she said. "Both of you." She turned to address the room at large. "One of the best things about Juniper Creek is the compassion we show each other. It's one of the values I teach my students, and it's a core value of this community. I think the plan Margot and Ed have proposed sounds like a good idea, and I'd volunteer to be a trustee of this new grant. I think we can all agree to put a little faith in the Brewers while they make this right." She narrowed her eyes at Hank.

"Absolutely," David said. "And let's report Allen to the irrigation board immediately. He doesn't belong there."

Everyone burst into conversation, chiming in their agreement to this plan. Several people surrounded Margot and Ed, and a few even hugged them. Both Ed and Margot appeared to be holding back tears.

Jenna hugged Reid. "We did it. Well, Margot did."

"You started it, I think." He kissed her cheek. "You're stubborn, Pixie, you know that? Don't ever change."

She grinned. Looking around the kitchen, her heart filled with peace. Hank was talking to Ed, Margot was nodding at something Pam was saying, and Matt stood close by chatting with Tessa and Roberto. Her mom and a couple other neighbors were talking about what to call the trust.

Jenna glanced up at Reid. "You know what Shakespeare would say. 'Love all, trust a few, do wrong to none.'"

He chuckled. "Do you have every sonnet and play memorized?"

"No, just a few of them." She smirked. "That's from *All's Well That Ends Well*, by the way."

"I knew that. Um, definitely knew that." He pulled her into his arms. "You don't mind if everyone sees us together, do you?"

"Nope."

His eyes sparkled with some secret amusement. "Do you remember how I asked you to be my girlfriend in high school?"

"Roses and a teddy bear." She would never forget him handing her the bouquet and the bear in math class, or the handwritten note reading, Jenna Daly, will you go out with me? She'd dried the roses and saved them, along with the note—until he broke up with her, at which point they went in the trash. The bear, though, was still stuffed in a box in the garage.

"Well, good. All I have to say is . . . be alert."

"Be alert." She grinned. "What, you're going to ask me out again? When is this happening exactly?"

"Soon." He kissed her forehead. "And I'm going to do it right."

Jenna stared at the list of Homecoming chaperones with a sinking feeling. She counted again. Twelve, thirteen, fourteen including Reid and herself. They needed sixteen. Pam was a stickler for the ratios, and she would be upset if they didn't have the requisite number of adults present. Plus, they would need the extra hands to work on cleanup after the dance.

This was her fault. She had forgotten to call those last two parents on her list. She dug through her bottom right drawer and found the file folder where she'd placed her list of parent names and phone numbers. The only ones she hadn't called were John and Lynn Stevenson—two people, the exact number they needed.

Okay, no need to panic. She could call them right now. The school was on a modified schedule today to accommodate Homecoming assembly, and right now everyone was on a short free period, so she had . . . yikes, two minutes before the assembly started to get ahold of John and Lynn. She punched in their home phone number and listened to it ring. After four rings, it clicked to voicemail.

She hung up and tried the cell phone number listed for Lynn. Please pick up, please pick up . . .

"This is Lynn."

"Oh, Lynn." Jenna let out a breath. "Hi, this is Jenna Daly, from Juniper Creek High School. I know this is super last minute, but could you and John possibly chaperone the Homecoming dance?"

"Isn't that tomorrow? We'd love to, but we'll be out of town. We're leaving for Tahoe tomorrow morning. John and I always go this time of year. Have you been? We rent this fabulous cabin . . ."

The bell rang, and Jenna winced at the noise. "I'm sorry, I have to go. Thanks anyway!"

She hung up and sprang to her feet. Okay, well, Reid had also had a few people left on his list, and they only needed two. If he'd called the parents on his list, then they should be fine. It was fine.

She darted into the hallway, joining a stream of students coming from the library. There was no sign of Reid's tall lean form, but he was emceeing the assembly, so he was probably already in the gym. She jogged down the hall, weaving around and dodging clusters of students. One of them laughingly yelled after her about running in the hall. She waved and doubled her speed.

She slipped into the gym and spotted Reid near the sound system, testing his microphone. She raced over to him and slid to a stop, her sneakers squeaking on the floor. "You got all your parent chaperones, right?" she gasped.

"Check, check, check." He flipped the microphone off and frowned. "Uh, oh." His eyes widened. "No. I never called the last two on my list. Shoot! Are we short?"

"By two. I forgot to call mine, too, until just now. They're in Tahoe."

He grimaced. "Okay. Well, we'll have to figure it out after the assembly. Don't worry, Pixie, it'll be fine." He patted her shoulder absently as he scanned the crowds of students flowing into the gym.

We had one job, Jenna thought, still fighting panic as she took a seat on the bottom bleachers next to Steph and Elisa. Well, two jobs if you counted picking up cupcakes. At least she knew she wouldn't screw that up. Still, what if they couldn't get two more chaperones? Where would she even find time to locate chaperones? She had to teach all day and decorate for the dance after school.

Reid stepped forward, microphone in hand. As his gaze swept across the gym, he met Jenna's eyes, and she was sure she saw him wink. She smiled and tried to relax into her seat on the rock-hard wooden bench.

***

"Hello, Juniper Creek!" Reid boomed into the microphone. "Are you awake? Good morning!"

The crowd tossed back a weak and scattered "good morning."

"Let's try that again. Who's excited for Homecoming tonight?"

"We are!" yelled the students.

"I couldn't hear you. Who's excited?"

"We are!"

He did the shtick a few more times, bringing their responses up to a roar. "All right everyone, let's get it started! Our cheerleaders are here to get you all fired up!" He stepped aside, and gestured to Roberto, who opened the gym door. The cheerleaders, who were waiting just outside in the hall, funneled in, screaming and waving black and gold pom-poms. Ryan Brandon, who was running sound, punched a button and rock music blasted through the gym, ricocheting off the walls. The team dashed into formation and began a dance-y cheer routine.

Reid got out of their way, so as not to get beaned by a flying cheerleader, and consulted his notes. The marching band was next, followed by the introduction of the football team. Then the Homecoming Court would parade in, and . . .

"Hey, Mr. W." Roberto pulled on his sleeve. "After the cheerleaders, say you have a special announcement, okay?"

"A special announcement?" he repeated. "Um . . . okay?"

"Don't worry." Roberto grinned. "It's all good. Just say it."

"You've got it, man." Reid shrugged. Roberto was a good kid, so he wasn't worried about this mysterious announcement, but he was curious. Maybe there had been a recount in the Homecoming court votes. He remembered that happening his own junior year. It had been quite the scandal.

The cheerleading routine ended, and the students clapped and whooped. The cheerleaders jogged toward a section of the front bleachers that had been reserved for them and sat down.

"Okay, everyone, that was our talented Juniper Creek varsity cheerleading team!" Reid walked forward. "And now we have a very special announcement!"

He looked around. Roberto had disappeared. Reid tried again. "A very special . . ."

Ryan jumped and fiddled with the sound system. A popular country love song blasted over the speakers.

The auditorium door reopened, and in stepped two football players, carrying Roberto on their shoulders. Laughter swept through the room. Roberto wore a tux jacket over his soccer uniform, and he held a huge bouquet of wildflowers.

Ah, of course. Reid should have known this had something to do with asking a girl to the Homecoming dance.

The football players hefted Roberto to the ground and the three of them huddled together. One of the players pointed towards the bottom center of the bleachers. Kids began looking at each other, trying to figure out who they were gesturing to.

Roberto nodded and the football players clapped him on the back. He swept the microphone out of Reid's hand and strolled over to the bleachers, where Tessa Morgan sat. Her face turned beet red and she buried her head in her hands, but when she looked up again, she was grinning.

Roberto dropped to one knee. Just at that moment, Ryan dropped the volume on the music so everyone could hear. "Tessa Morgan," he intoned. "I think you are the most beautiful girl I've ever known. Will you go to Homecoming with me?"

Awwwww, intoned the students.

"Oh my gosh, yes," gasped Tessa.

Roberto handed her the flowers and pulled her into a hug. The entire auditorium went wild with applause.

Roberto stood up and ran the microphone back over to Reid. "Thank you, everyone. Back to your regularly scheduled Homecoming assembly!" he hollered. He gave Reid a friendly punch on the arm as he jogged off.

Reid grinned. You had to admire the kid's panache.

He glanced over at Jenna to see how she was reacting. Although she didn't even see him—she was saying something to Pam—he smiled at the pure joy on her face.

Reid had been like Roberto, once, a long time ago, when he handed Jenna Daly a bouquet of roses and asked her out. Unafraid and unapologetic. Now, thanks to Jenna, he'd found that piece of himself again.

He couldn't wait to show her.

***

Jenna tugged one of the bungee cords she'd hooked to her truck. It seemed to be holding tight. The cords crisscrossed over a tarp, which was protecting the boxes of Homecoming decorations inside the truck bed. She felt a cold raindrop plop on her forehead and glanced up at the sky. A storm front was moving in, and heavy rainfall was predicted all weekend. Just what she needed when she had to haul bunches of decorations to City Hall.

She tried texting Reid one more time: *I'm taking the decorations over. Are you coming?* They'd both had to go back to their classes right after the Homecoming assembly, and when she'd gone next door to look for him after school, he had already disappeared. She'd tried calling him, with no answer. He was supposed to be her co-chair. What was going on?

"That looks fun," said Steph, behind her. "Is that for the dance?"

Jenna turned around. "Hey. Yeah, I have to go set up at City Hall. Reid is supposed to help me, but I can't find him."

"I saw him leaving right after school." Steph shrugged.

Leaving? Where would he go? Unless he'd left something at home . . .

"I'm not busy. You want some help?" offered Steph.

"That would be great," said Jenna. "You'd think he could have told me where he was going, but . . ." She shrugged and unlocked the passenger side door for Steph.

"Is your truck supposed to make that noise?" asked Steph warily, as they rolled out of the parking lot. The vehicle emitted an odd grinding sound as Jenna turned onto the road.

"I'm sure it's fine." Jenna patted Lucy's dashboard. "I'll have my dad look at her this weekend."

"So how's it going with your boyfriend?" Steph nudged her. After the night of Ed Brewer's confession, when Jenna and Reid had celebrated with some pretty obvious PDA, Steph and Elisa had bombarded Jenna with questions.

"He isn't my boyfriend." She rolled her eyes and tried to hide her smile. "I mean, not officially, I don't know what we are."

"Please," said Steph dryly. "You better make me a bridesmaid at your wedding."

"You're getting a little far ahead, aren't you?" Jenna's heart skipped a beat at the thought of a wedding. The funny thing was, she could picture herself marrying Reid. She could picture it far too easily. *No, don't get carried away*, she told herself. She had allowed herself to fall head over heels for Reid in high school and she'd only gotten hurt. She needed to enjoy where things were at with him. Take it slow.

Right.

She and Steph chatted about their classes, but her mind was half on the conversation, half occupied with wondering where Reid was.

As she neared City Hall, traffic slowed to a crawl. A van marked *Juniper Creek Water Bureau* sat in front of the sidewalk, blinkers flashing, and several men and women in neon vests and hard hats were walking in and out of the building. Bright yellow caution tape marked off the public entrance to City Hall, and more tape was strung across several storefronts. The sidewalks looked wet.

As it hadn't rained yet, wet sidewalks were bad.

"That looks . . . um . . ." said Steph.

"Yeah, it does." Jenna parked on the opposite curb and hopped out. Steph came with her, and they jogged across the street to the steps that led up to City Hall.

Jenna flagged down a woman in a hard hat and a neon yellow jacket. "Excuse me, hi. What happened here?"

"Pipes burst," said the woman, gruffly. "We're working as fast as we can."

"Is there flooding inside City Hall?" asked Steph.

"Honey, there's flooding up and down this whole block." The woman gestured in either direction. "Whatever you came here for, you'll have to come back." The walkie-talkie on her hip buzzed, and she stepped over the caution tape in front of the steps.

Jenna and Steph stood staring at the mess of tape and water and blocked-off entrances. "I'm guessing it won't be dry by tomorrow," said Steph.

Jenna swallowed back tears. The students had worked so hard to prepare for the dance. Everyone had their dinner plans and their outfits, and the students were all expecting to walk into a starry wonderland in an elegant ballroom.

As she glanced down the street, she realized one of the closed-up shops was Evergreen Bakery. "Hang on, I'll be right back." She strode down the sidewalk and peered past a web of caution tape across the open bakery door. Susan was inside, wearing fishing waders and rubber boots, mopping up the floor. All of the lights were off.

"Susan?"

The woman wiped sweat from her forehead with the back of her glove. "Yep?" Her expression softened when she saw Jenna. "Oh, sweetheart. Please tell me you're not here about the cupcakes for the dance."

Well, that answered that question. There would be no cupcakes. "I just thought I'd check." Jenna surveyed the inside of the shop. In the dim light, it was hard to tell the extent of the damage, but there appeared to be a huge pool of water in one corner, and moisture was seeping up the walls. "I'm so sorry. Can I do something?"

"No, Rob's on his way over." Her husband. "There's three inches of water in some places. This is going to take hours to clean up, not to mention dealing with insurance."

"That's awful."

Susan sighed. "I've seen worse, but it's not good."

"You don't have any cakes in the back, or anything, that I could take to the dance?"

Susan shook her head and swirled the mop across the floor. "I'm just a one-person operation. That isn't how I work. Your best bet is to go into Redmond and see if you can get a sheet cake from a bakery there. Or even a Fred Meyer. Unless you want to make the cupcakes yourself."

Jenna gaped at her. "You'd give me the recipe?"

"Only if you swear on your life that you won't tell anyone I gave it to you." Susan winked. "It's a trade secret. There are some people in town who would be very, very upset if they learned I gave out this recipe."

"I promise."

"Hang on, then." Susan disappeared into the back and returned a couple minutes later with a slightly wrinkled sheet of paper containing handwritten recipe. As she handed it over to Jenna, she warned, "These are pretty labor-intensive. Do you have a cooking torch?"

Jenna gulped. "Uh, no."

"Well, then you better buy one." Susan winked. "Good luck, honey."

"Thank you so much," gasped Jenna. She dashed across the street to her truck, clutching the recipe like it was gold.

Steph had climbed back into the passenger side already to avoid the rain that had started falling. "What's that?" she asked as Jenna clambered into the car.

"The recipe for the S'mores cupcakes. The bakery's flooded." Jenna handed her the page and started up the truck. "Guard that with your life. And do you know where I can get a cooking torch?"

"Good heavens," sighed Steph. "Okay, tell you what. Let's go back to school and you find out what's going on with the dance. I'll go find a flamethrower."

"A cooking torch."

"Like for crème brûlée. I know. I'll find one." Steph squeezed her shoulder. "Take a few breaths."

They drove back to the high school. By now it was nearly three-thirty, and the rain had started really coming down. Even with the tarp over her truck bed, Jenna was worried about water seeping in and ruining the decorations. She found a parking spot as close to the high school as possible and even backed her truck in so she would be able to more easily unload it.

"That sound cannot be good," muttered Steph, as she jumped out of the truck.

Jenna patted Lucy dismissively. "She's just old, that's all."

Steph shook her head. "I'll text you later when I have the fire-making thing. Do you want me to just pick up all the ingredients for the cupcakes as long as I'm out?"

"Actually, that would be amazing."

"Can we use your kitchen to make the cupcakes, at least? Mine is tiny."

"Yes." Jenna impulsively ran over and gave her a hug. "You're such a good friend."

"And boss. Don't forget I'm your boss." Steph patted her on the back. "Okay, go find out what's happening with Homecoming."

Reid stared at the email on his phone. It was an announcement from Pam Rustigan to all staff, students, and parents, notifying them that Homecoming would now take place in the gym, due to flooding at City Hall.

He groaned. While not exactly a disaster, this meant extra work for him and Jenna, as well as their parent chaperones. City Hall actually had a small ballroom with beautiful old windows, which were intended to be a focal point of the decorations. There were three chandeliers they'd planned to hang streamers from. It would take a lot more work to make the gym look . . . well . . . celestial.

Oh, and he still had to dig up two more chaperones.

Jenna had texted him in all capital letters, betraying her panic. *HOMECOMING IS AT THE GYM B/C CITY HALL FLOODED. ALSO WE HAVE TO MAKE TWELVE DOZEN CUPCAKES. WHERE ARE YOU?*

On my way, he texted back.

Cupcakes? he thought. The bakery must have flooded too. He hoped Jenna knew how to bake, because unless the students wanted a bunch of hot dogs and burgers, Reid would be no help in that department. His past baking experiments had been, to say the least, interesting.

He glanced into the back seat and checked the bouquet of roses again. They still looked good, their petals just starting to fully open. The card was tucked in among the buds. He'd tied the bouquet to the teddy bear's paws so it looked like the bear was holding the flowers. He nodded. He was going to do this.

He peeled out of his driveway and headed for the school.

About twenty minutes later, he reached the gym. Holding the bear and flowers behind his back, he sidled through the doors.

The gym was a storm of activity. Rock music blasted through the space. All of the students from the Homecoming committee were running around, carrying and setting down various decorations. Pam

Rustigan was using a helium pump to blow up silver and white balloons. Other staff and students carried folding tables in from the cafeteria. Blue crepe paper streamed from both basketball hoops in elegant swirls, and students were looping more crepe paper over the doorways. The drama department had even somehow gotten involved; Reid spotted the drama coach dragging an enormous arched window on wheels into the gym.

He spotted Jenna and Elisa corralling a massive piece of black butcher paper which was partially taped to the center of one wall. With Elisa as her spotter, Jenna stood near the top of a stepladder, precariously leaning over as she smashed the paper against the wall. It peeled free, curled over and began rolling up.

Reid walked over to them. "Can I help you with that, Miss Daly?" He pulled the bear and flowers from behind his back and held them out to her.

Jenna looked down at him and shrieked. The ladder wobbled. Elisa's eyes widened as she grabbed and steadied it.

Okay, he hadn't meant to startle her quite that much. *Note to self, don't ask a woman out when she's standing on a ladder.*

"What are you doing here?" gasped Jenna, scrambling down the ladder. "What's all this?"

"I'm here to ask you to be my girlfriend." He grinned.

"It's exactly the same as in high school." She lifted the note attached to the bear, and her lips formed a surprised rosebud. "Oh, Reid. This is so sweet." She glanced to her left, and her face went pink. "We have a bit of an audience."

He followed her gaze. Almost all of the students, parent volunteers, and teachers had paused to stare. Some of the students were whispering to each other. Shrugging, he pulled her into his arms, which was quite a feat with a teddy bear and a bouquet of flowers in hand. "Are you going to say yes?"

She stood up on tiptoe and wrapped her arms around him. "Yes," she whispered.

A burst of applause and cheers filled the gym. Jenna jumped back, a sheepish expression on her face, and took the bear and flowers from Reid. He dropped a kiss on her forehead, which elicited a few snickers from some of the students.

"Nothing to see here, folks." He waved. "Just asking her to Homecoming."

"You guyyyyys." Elisa drew out the word into several syllables as she leaned in to examine the bear. "This is so cute."

Jenna grinned up at Reid. "It's perfect."

Wait until tomorrow, Reid thought. The words almost burst out of him, but he held them back. He had waited for Jenna for years. He could wait twenty-four more hours.

"Oh my gosh," she groaned. "What are we going to do about the chaperones? And I have to meet Steph at my place in like, twenty minutes to make the cupcakes. Did you see my text?"

"I saw. That stinks about the bakery." He crossed his arms and looked around the gym. The drama coach was locking down the casters on the bottom of the window set piece, while two students waited with streamers in their hands. Every adult in the gym was already chaperoning. Maybe Jenna's parents could help? "Would your mom and dad chaperone?"

"Actually . . ." Jenna pursed her lips. "I have an idea, but I don't know if you'll like it. Do you think Margot would chaperone? Maybe that's too weird, but . . . I kind of feel like we've been through a battle together. I think we're even friends."

He thought for a moment. He knew just what she meant. "I don't know if chaperoning is her thing, but sure. Let's ask her."

"I'll call her right now." Jenna handed him the roses and stuffed bear to hold onto and grabbed her phone. Reid listened as she had a quick conversation with Margot, her eyes lighting up.

"Thank you so much. I'll send you the volunteer form in a few minutes." She hung up and announced, "She'll do it. And she's found our last chaperone."

Reid's eyebrows went up. "Bailey's coming too?"

"No, it's Matt." Her smile faded. "Oh, gosh, is that okay? Will you feel too weird?"

"I won't feel weird at all." Reid pulled her in for another hug. "I'll be with the only girl I want in the world."

***

The bells on the door jingled as Reid stepped into Three Peaks Jewelry.

The Homecoming dance started in less than ten hours. He recognized that his plan was a little . . . bold. But now he knew, without a doubt, that he and Jenna loved each other. Sometimes, in love, you couldn't play it safe. Sometimes you had to be bold.

And that time was now.

As he'd hoped, no one else was inside, except for Bev. She stood at the counter, staring at a ledger and muttering to herself.

She looked up as he got closer. "Oh, Reid. I didn't think I'd see you back here so soon. Doing some early Christmas shopping?"

"Not exactly," he said. "I'm hoping you can help me find something on short notice."

***

At seven p.m. that evening, Jenna stood in front of her closet. She'd managed to bake 200 cupcakes and find chaperones, but not to figure out what to wear to the dance. She rifled through the dresses in her closet, most of which she'd shipped home from California. A basic black shift dress. A black blouse. A gray skirt. Her old wardrobe had certainly not been an adventure in fabric hues. All of them were perfectly appropriate to chaperone a dance, but she wanted something more . . . special. After all, the last twenty-four hours had been quite special. She smiled at the bouquet of roses and the stuffed bear from Reid, which now sat on her dresser.

At the back of her closet, she spotted a splash of blue fabric. She tugged on the garment to free it from between two pairs of pants and eyed her high school Homecoming dress. The French blue bodice was covered in lace. Several small straps, linked together, came up the shoulders before crisscrossing in the back. The A-line skirt was full but not puffy and came to her knees. Spaghetti straps weren't exactly dress code for school, but if she paired it with a sweater . . . She pulled a white cardigan off a hanger and draped it over the dress. Perfect.

Or it would be if it still fit.

She stepped into the dress and zipped up the side. It felt snug, but not tight. She checked out her reflection in the full-length mirror and twirled back and forth, pleased. With the addition of the cardigan, it was just right. The only trouble was shoes. She had a few pairs of heels in her closet, but her ankle still felt a bit weak, and she didn't want to risk tripping and re-injuring herself.

Her cowboy boots sat on her shoe rack, one leaning against the other. Why not? There were no rules that said you couldn't wear boots to a dance. She pulled them on and smiled at her reflection. Somehow, the boots were perfect.

A glance at the clock told her there was no time to do her hair, so she left it long and loose. She dashed on mascara and picked up her purse. She was due at the school by seven-fifteen. She and Reid had originally planned to carpool, but he'd texted her this morning to say something had come up, and he would meet her at the dance instead.

"Oh, sweetheart, you look beautiful," said her mother, as Jenna walked into the kitchen. Andrea and David sat at the kitchen island, drinking tea.

Her dad got up and put his arm around her shoulders. "Good choice on the boots."

Jenna laughed. "Can you guys help me get the cupcakes into my truck?" She and Steph had stayed up half the night baking the famous S'mores cupcakes. The first batch had been underbaked, and Jenna had burned the frosting on five cupcakes while she got the hang of the cooking torch. But crammed into her parents' fridge were twelve dozen S'mores cupcakes, just as the students had ordered.

It was raining steadily, so Jenna's dad escorted her out to her truck with an umbrella. They stacked the Tupperware containers behind the seats as well as in the passenger seat. They'd run out of containers, so the final dozen cupcakes sat on a cookie sheet, which Jenna cautiously balanced on top of the Tupperware.

"Be good now," said her dad with a wink. "Curfew's at midnight."

"Uh-huh." She hugged him one more time, and then drove off.

As she pulled onto the highway, the rain showers turned into a downpour. *Finally.* She hoped this was a good sign for the coming winter, and for the promise of snow. They needed it.

She turned on her windshield wipers and cranked the radio, singing along to Carrie Underwood. The miles went quickly, and she turned onto the exit that would take her along a back road half a mile to the school.

A clicking noise and a small light drew her attention to the dashboard. The check engine light was on. Okay, nothing to panic about. Didn't a check engine light just mean something with the electronics? No other lights were on. It was probably not an emergency. She took a deep breath and, just to be safe, slowed to a few miles under the speed limit.

Lucy sputtered and coughed. Under Jenna's foot, the gas pedal vibrated. She felt the power steering go out, the wheel locking in her grip. She gritted her teeth and pressed on the brakes, but they, too, had little give. She yanked on the emergency brake, and with one final sputter, the truck jerked to a stop in the middle of the road. The cookie sheet with the cupcakes unseated itself, sliding to the floor with a squish.

"Crud!" Jenna flipped on her emergency blinker. Nothing happened. Lucy was well and truly dead. At least Jenna was off the highway, but she was also still half a mile from school. *Okay, don't panic.*

She leaned down to check the cupcakes. The cookie sheet had tilted over, and most of its contents had landed frosting-side-down on the floor of her truck. She plucked one off the floor, wiped all the frosting off on the tray, and then took a bite. The sugary maple and dark chocolate flavors blended together in a perfectly moist cake. No wonder Susan guarded this recipe closely. It was amazing.

Stuffing the rest of the cupcake into her mouth, she reached for her cell phone.

It was dead.

"Oh, no, no, no," she muttered. Panic bubbled up. How could she have forgotten to charge her phone? Granted, she had been distracted with the need to bake dozens of cupcakes. And the change of venue to the gym. And the fact that Reid had said he loved her. Okay, she had legitimate excuses. But none of those told her what to do now.

She cracked open the driver's side door and winced as icy rain blew into her face. Leaning over, she popped open the glove box and pulled out the flashlight. "Sorry, cupcakes," she said, patting the Tupperware. "You can't come with me."

She watched the road cautiously, but no car lights approached. She was alone. She climbed out of the truck, draped her jacket over her head, and started walking.

***

Reid frowned as he checked the time. Where was Jenna? She had been due with the cupcakes at seven-fifteen, according to Tessa, and it was now past seven-thirty. He had tried her cell, but it had gone straight to voicemail.

"I can't get ahold of her," he said to Tessa and Roberto, who stood with him at the dessert table. "I might need to come up with a new plan if—"

"There she is!" gasped Tessa, pointing.

Reid turned around.

Jenna walked into the gym. She gave him a small, sheepish wave and held up her hands. Her hair was plastered to her face and she was dripping water.

He ran towards her and pulled her close. "What happened? Are you okay?"

"I'm f-f-fine." She was shivering. "Truck broke down. My phone died. I need to call a tow truck . . ."

"You *walked* here?" Reid pushed her hair back from her face. "How far?"

"Like half a mile?" She shrugged. "Had to get here somehow. I had to leave the cupcakes behind . . ."

"Don't worry about the cupcakes," he said. "I'm just glad you're okay. Let's get you changed."

She laughed. "Into what? Sweats from the lost and found?"

"Actually, I have another idea."

***

Twenty minutes later, a much drier Jenna took Reid's arm and walked back towards the gym. He had apparently helped out with the school play last year, so he had known where all the costumes were kept. They'd dug out a bright yellow princess dress with puffy sleeves, which fit Jenna surprisingly well. Her cowboy boots poked out from beneath the long skirt. She'd managed to half-dry her hair and pull the frizzy waves into a ponytail. It wasn't exactly the look she'd imagined for Homecoming, but it was certainly better than resembling a nutria in a pond.

Jenna had used Reid's cell to call her parents, who had assured her they would call a tow truck and told her to enjoy herself. She wasn't sure if Lucy could be fixed, but right now, she didn't care.

Now that her body temperature had returned to normal, she could fully admire the transformed gym. Even having seen the completed decorations last night, she was stunned at how magical the room looked now. A large window, which had been part of the set for a play, stood in front of black butcher paper covered with silver stars. Students waited in line to get their picture taken in front of it.

Cafeteria tables lined the perimeter of the room. They were covered in white tablecloths and tea lights were scattered across them. Silver balloons attached to mason jars danced from each table. The dessert table, while short twelve dozen S'mores cupcakes, still boasted an impressive array of cookies. The lights were low, and a disco ball spun above the dance floor.

Jenna waved to Margot and Matt, who stood across the room, arm in arm as they observed the students. Margot wore a black dress that showed off her tan and her blonde hair, and Matt wore a suit. He leaned over to whisper something in Margot's ear that made her laugh.

"They look happy together," commented Reid. "I'm glad for her."

"Me too." Jenna looked up at him. "Do I look completely ridiculous in this outfit?"

"Not at all," said Reid. "You look beautiful. Wait here for a second, okay?"

Bemused, Jenna watched as he strode over to the deejay booth, which was being run by none other than Saul. The man wore a suit that belied his long beard and ponytail. His two Chihuahuas were with him, wearing sparkly silver sweaters.

Reid said something to Saul and the man nodded. The upbeat pop tune faded, and a romantic country song came on in its place. Around the room, teenage couples moved close together and swayed back and forth.

Reid motioned to someone; Jenna couldn't see who. The next thing she knew, ten students, including Tessa and Roberto, were coming to stand by Reid. Each of them held a bouquet of white roses.

Reid held his hand out to Jenna.

She walked toward him, her heart pounding. Something special was happening. She didn't dare to hope. But the look in his eyes told her everything.

Reid dropped to one knee.

"We've been apart for ten years." He gestured to the students who stood behind him in a semicircle. "There's one bouquet for every year we've been apart. Those years were all worth it, because they led me back to you. You said that true love never changes, and you were right. My love for you will never change." He pulled a small black box from his pocket, snapped it open, and held it up. "Jenna Daly, will you marry me?"

Jenna gasped as she stared into the box. Nestled into the velvet was a rose gold filigree band set with tiny diamonds.

She leaned down and cupped Reid's cheek with one hand. "Love 'is an ever-fixed mark / That looks on tempests and is never shaken.'" She smiled. "That's a yes."

Reid grinned as tears slid down his cheeks. He pulled the band free and slid it onto her finger.

Jenna grabbed his hands and pulled him to his feet. As the students around them cheered and clapped, she stood up on tiptoe to loop her arms around his neck.

He leaned down, pulling her close, their noses touching.

"Chaperones aren't supposed to kiss, are they?" she said.

He shrugged. "Too late," he said, and drew her tight for a tender kiss. His lips felt like home.

"Congratulations, Mr. Walsh and Ms. Daly!" boomed Saul over the microphone.

The crowd applauded. The students who'd helped with the proposal rushed over to Jenna and Reid, hugging them and examining the ring. Other teachers, and even Matt and Margot, came over to congratulate them.

Finally, the small crowd dispersed. Saul put on another slow song, and Reid and Jenna put their arms around each other and swayed to the music.

"I think this is the dance we were supposed to have back in high school," he said, his blue eyes full of promise.

"No." She smiled up at him. "This is the dance we're supposed to have now."

She leaned against his chest and let the softly strummed notes of a guitar carry them both home.

THE END

About the Author

Amy Kristen Marshall believes in happily-ever-afters, and all of her stories include them. She loves writing romance because it gives her a chance to explore real-life relationship issues with a dose of optimism.

Amy and her husband, Brad, have been together ever since a super-fun blind date and a very long, and even more fun, second date. They live and write together in the beautiful, but slightly damp, Pacific Northwest. When they aren't drinking coffee or puzzling over their next books, they're walking their cats on leashes. Yes, really. It can be done.

Follow Amy on Instagram, @amykristenmarshall, for announcements about her next project.

Made in the USA
Middletown, DE
19 January 2021